Jasper's MOUNTAIN

JOHN INMAN

Dreamspinner Press

Published by
Dreamspinner Press
5032 Capital Circle SW
Ste 2, PMB# 279
Tallahassee, FL 32305-7886
USA
http://www.dreamspinnerpress.com/

This is a work of fiction. Names, characters, places, and incidents either are the product of the author's imagination or are used fictitiously, and any resemblance to actual persons, living or dead, business establishments, events, or locales is entirely coincidental.

Jasper's Mountain
Copyright © 2013 by John Inman

Cover Art by Reese Dante
http://www.reesedante.com

Cover content is being used for illustrative purposes only
and any person depicted on the cover is a model.

All rights reserved. No part of this book may be reproduced or transmitted in any form or by any means, electronic or mechanical, including photocopying, recording, or by any information storage and retrieval system without the written permission of the Publisher, except where permitted by law. To request permission and all other inquiries, contact Dreamspinner Press, 5032 Capital Circle SW, Ste 2, PMB# 279, Tallahassee, FL 32305-7886, USA.
http://www.dreamspinnerpress.com/

ISBN: 978-1-62798-072-2
Digital ISBN: 978-1-62798-073-9

Printed in the United States of America
First Edition
August 2013

*Entrenched in darkness
He fled into strong arms for
A safe, loving home.*

—Agnes Cousino

Chapter ONE

JASPER STONE'S ninety-acre ranch was comprised, for the most part, of scree, scrubland, and a spattering of sandstone boulders strewn up the side of the Juniper Mountains, a short drive east of San Diego, California. There was also a thirty-acre pine forest on the bottom end of the property where the land flattened out, which Jasper jokingly called his own private Endor. Sometimes when the wind was just right, one could smell the grand Pacific Ocean, which lay just to the west, mixed in among the scent of pine.

Smack in the middle of Endor was where Jasper had his home—a rustic four-room cabin with all the amenities of a Motel 8, which Jasper figured were all the amenities anybody really needed. The cabin had never seen a coat of paint, but it did boast an Internet connection, a phone, a decent furnace for winter months, a good roof, and running water. It was clean, bright, and cheerful, if a little short on frills. Oh, and it also had a front porch with log railings. The porch stretched from one end of the cabin to the other. There, Jasper would sit in the evening with his long legs propped up, feet on the rail, nursing a drink. Pondering. His sundry collection of dogs and cats would lie sprawled on the plank floor around him, ever mindful of the rockers on Jasper's rocking chair. None of them wanted to get their tails under *there*.

While the sun dropped behind the mountain, they would watch in companionable silence as the darkness deepened and gathering shadows slowly gobbled up the surrounding forest. With only the squeak of the rocking chair to anchor them in the darkening glade, Jasper and his four-legged buddies would sit and listen as the day sounds dwindled down and the night sounds ratcheted up, enjoying every peaceful, solitary minute of it. It was all music to Jasper's ears. The owls and pigeons hooting and cooing in the treetops. The crickets chirruping in the scrub. The occasional pinecone rattling down the roof and landing with a tiny thud in the dirt after falling from the tall sugar pine that stood at the side of the cabin.

But when the light was gone completely and the stars were bright overhead, the mosquitoes would come out, thirsty for blood. Only then would Jasper shuffle everyone inside and latch the door behind him, shutting out the darkness and the bugs and firmly closing the book on another day.

The interior of the cabin was a little lax on ambience, unless you liked things simple, which Jasper did. One end of the living room was dominated by a huge flagstone fireplace. The fireplace was so large that in the warmer winters, with a properly tended fire, Jasper sometimes did not need to light the furnace at all.

The cabin boasted a living room, kitchen, library, and a cozy little bathroom with a shower stall. Jasper's furniture was solid and unassuming. All of it pine, and all of it old.

In a loft at the top of a skinny flight of stairs sat Jasper's bedroom. The window at the head of the bed overlooked the roof of the front porch. The bed was comfortable and big and usually strewn with animals from one end to the other. Unlike in a Motel 8, no Magic Fingers machine—where you insert a quarter and get the bejesus shaken out of you—was attached to the bed. Being single, if Jasper wanted magic fingers, he used his own. And if he wanted a good shaking up, he simply went jogging.

If he wasn't eating or sleeping or tending the fire in the fireplace, Jasper could usually be found in the library. It was his favorite room. There, where every wall was a bookcase from floor to ceiling and every bookcase was packed to the gills with Jasper's favorite books, Jasper would spend his time, sitting at his desk, writing. While published, with six books to his name scattered among the shelves around him, Jasper's writing had never really taken off. It earned him a little money—not much. But since Jasper wasn't in it for the money, that didn't matter. Writing was his greatest love. It had been since childhood. In truth, he was thrilled to have his fiction published at all. He expected no Pulitzers. He simply wanted to tell his stories. And so he did. Every night. Every morning. Every time he wasn't doing something else, Jasper was writing. His love of writing filled his heart and made him whole. He was content to have it there inside him.

Jasper's ranch wasn't really a *working* ranch because nothing much grew there aside from Jasper's stories, except taxes and alligator lizards. Jasper had alligator lizards up the ying yang. Not literally, thank God. But they were pretty much everywhere else. And the taxes, well, *everybody* had those, so he couldn't really complain about that.

The cabin was comfortably tucked away inside Endor, Jasper's jungle of pinyon pines and Joshua trees and the lush California junipers that gave Juniper Mountain its name. The beautiful, pine-scented forest was home to all the indigenous small mammals one would expect to find in this little corner of the Southwest, from bats to raccoons and everything in between. Aside from the alligator lizards, which could be spotted poking their heads up every time you turned around, Jasper had periodic visits from possums, skunks, rattlers, hawks, squirrels, chipmunks, foxes, and rabbits. On occasion one could even spot a coyote or, a little more unnervingly, a mountain lion, lurking among the trees or boulders on the mountainside. So far the coyotes and mountain lions had simply been passing through, not lingering long enough to cause any trouble, and for that Jasper was truly grateful. Still, Jasper took no chances. That's why he herded his dogs and cats through the cabin door every night, locking them safely inside.

Besides, he liked their company.

The surrounding foothills of the Juniper Mountains were only beginning to be threatened by the encroachment of urban sprawl. More dangerous than the four-footed predators, the mountain had begun to attract fast-talking contractors and eager real-estate speculators with big, phony smiles and bottomless checkbooks. They were there to cash in on the surging need for new housing in the Southwest. Jasper had fielded a few offers already—offers aimed at incorporating his ninety acres into the feeding frenzy for undeveloped land—but he had firmly repelled each and every one of them. And usually, he repelled them with a minimum of courtesy. Jasper's ranch was his home. Every square foot of it. Rocks, trees, lizards—the whole shebang. He wasn't about to chop it up into parcels and see the animals run off to have his side of the mountain buried beneath a quilt of strip malls and cookie-cutter housing developments and eight-lane highways. Not to mention the people who would come stampeding in right behind the builders.

Jasper wasn't particularly fond of people. On the whole, Jasper thought people *sucked*. And not in a good way.

He was, however, crazy about animals. Aside from the wild ones, the slew of tame ones that shared his property were welcome guests, each and every one. He had three dogs of indeterminate breed that had strayed onto the property at various times and decided to stay. The dogs were named Bobber, Jumper, and Lola. He had also adopted two stray cats, Fiji and Guatemala, both male, thank God, or he would be up to his ass in cats. Not that he minded cats. He just didn't want too many of them running around and threatening the small wildlife that also shared his forest home. Although he didn't mind that Fiji had acquired a taste for alligator lizards. God knows Jasper could spare a few of those.

Jasper was thirty-two years old. Once married. Once divorced. Now batching it and happy to be doing so. He was a good-looking guy. Six two. Strong. Broad shoulders. Fuzzy chest and legs. His hair was brown and curly and almost always in need of a cut, which he sometimes did himself with questionable results. He could shave at dawn and, by noon, his five o'clock shadow was already beginning to peek through. He was quick to smile, had a dimple in one cheek when he did, and his eyes were as blue as a summer sky, or so his ex-wife once told him—before she blacked them both with an electric skillet and damn near killed him.

Jasper couldn't much blame her. He hadn't fucked her in two years when she came at him that day with the skillet. And he hadn't fucked her because he had simply lost interest. Not with sex. Just with her. And with women in general.

The day she bonked him with the skillet was the day he admitted to himself he was probably gay. He didn't admit it to *her*, mind you, or she might have set the skillet aside, hauled out the shotgun, and blown his ass to smithereens. After all, the fact that your husband is gay is a tidbit of information most women would prefer to receive *before* the wedding invitations go out, not three years after. Women don't seem to have much of a sense of humor when it comes to stuff like that.

Anyway, after the episode with the skillet, Jasper's wife packed up her clothes in a huff, cleaned out the one bank account they shared, hired a couple of goons to come back two days later with a truck to haul off every stick of furniture they owned (this was before his move to the mountain), and pretty much left Jasper standing in an empty apartment. As happy as a clam.

Jasper often suspected if his ex-wife knew how happy she had made him by leaving, she never would have left. That's the kind of woman she was.

Perhaps not so strangely, her leaving also coincided with Jasper learning of the demise of his million-dollar inheritance, which he suspected his wife had been awaiting with eager anticipation, even willing to hang around fuckless for two years until she got her hands on it.

Jasper's father had amassed a sizable fortune with a chain of gun shops scattered across California. Toward the end of his life, before the man was diagnosed with the Alzheimer's that would soon turn his brains to oatmeal, his father liquidated the gun shops, selling them off one at a time. Then he turned right around and donated the money, along with everything he had in the bank, to charity. Every goddamn penny. He left nothing in his portfolio but ninety acres of worthless scrubland that meandered up the side of Juniper Mountain and a rundown cabin that sat in the middle of it, which had not been lived in for years.

Jasper suspected he had only left that because he had forgotten about it. Or perhaps he couldn't find a buyer. Either way, upon his father's death, Jasper learned his million-dollar inheritance had been reduced to a few tons of sand, a shitload of boulders, a bazillion fucking alligator lizards, and a rundown cabin stuck in the middle of a bunch of juniper and Joshua trees.

Strangely enough, Jasper didn't really mind.

His wife, however, did. Jasper had not seen the woman since the day the will was read. (She bravely returned for the reading, speaking gentle words of reconciliation with Jasper, even going so far as to apologize for bashing him in the head with the electric skillet. She played nice right up until the moment she learned his inheritance had been reduced to some rocks on the shank of a butt-ugly mountain, and just like that, she was off again in another huff. Didn't even say good-bye. And there was not a day in Jasper's ensuing life he did not appreciate the fact she was gone.)

Happily, she had never learned of Jasper's secret bank account containing the hundred grand his father gave him on his twenty-first birthday. That was before his father took it into his diseased head to give everything else to a bunch of strangers. Jasper supposed he had always known things would not end well with the little woman. That's why he'd never let her get a whiff of his secret nest egg. Good thing too. That hundred grand, invested well, was now, eleven years later, almost double what it had been originally. And Jasper, with his simple life, supplemented by the meager income from his writing, was able to live quite handily on the interest. Only occasionally did he need to siphon off a bit of principal for emergencies.

So with a little help from his father's twenty-first birthday present, and with the labor of his own two hands, for the most part, Jasper renovated the cabin he'd inherited and made it livable. One sunny Sunday morning, he drove a rented U-Haul into the foothills of Juniper Mountain with everything he owned stuffed in the back and tied to the top. He threw open the windows of the cabin to let the pine-scented air inside, arranged his belongings the way he wanted them, and told himself he was home.

He had not regretted turning his back on the city for one single moment since. He loved his quiet life on the mountain. It would have been nice to have someone to share it with—someone other than his ex, of course—but being alone was not a deal breaker. He managed to live life on his own quite happily.

And he wasn't living a thousand miles from civilization, after all. He could still hop in his Jeep and roar down the mountain into the city any time he chose.

In fact, during the first year or two of his self-imposed seclusion, he did exactly that, driving into the city and coming to terms with what it really meant to be a gay man. He hit the gay bars, made a few hookups, learned what it was like to sleep (and have sex) with other men, and for the most part enjoyed it all. But he didn't enjoy it enough to bring anyone back up the mountain with him. He didn't enjoy it enough to feel an overwhelming desire to share his life. If there was a man out there Jasper would want to wake up to each and every morning of his life, he had somehow missed him in his nocturnal ramblings. He understood lust perfectly well, but love, true love, had eluded him. And after a while, Jasper stopped looking for it. Now the trips into town were few and far between. And what trips there were, were mostly shopping jaunts. He rarely went to the bars any more. After a while, the bars had become depressing to Jasper. The desperation of the people drinking inside them.

The frenzied, sticky sexual encounters in strange rooms, strange beds. The hastily scribbled phone numbers on the backs of napkins, and the promises to call no one ever followed up on. It all took a toll on Jasper's psyche. And once he realized that fact, he stopped putting himself through it. Just like that.

So in the final tally, the gay bars in town were a lot like his ex-wife. Unmissed. Unlamented.

And now here he was. Single, not too unhappy about it, enjoying his reclusive life on the side of his little mountain.

ALL these thoughts finally stopped rambling through Jasper's head on this fine August afternoon as he laid the hammer at his feet and gave his back a good stretch. It's not easy sinking fence posts and stringing fence wire by yourself. It's a two-man job at best.

He spat a mouthful of staples into a gloved hand, poured them into his trouser pocket so he wouldn't lose them, and gave Jumper's upturned face a good chin rub. The big black dog gave his tail a lively shake by way of thanks, so Jasper scratched his chin again.

"What do you think, boy? Will it hold a couple of pigs?"

Jasper and Jumper studied the stretch of wire fencing he had just strung around a half acre of ground behind the back shed. Jasper had decided it might be fun to acquire a pair of hogs. A male and a female. Set them up in their own little love shack and see what transpired. Who knows? He might even get some free bacon out of it someday, if they managed to reproduce and if the mountain lions didn't take them.

Jasper's ranch was far enough from the city he didn't have to worry about zoning laws and all that crap. Hell, he could raise a herd of rhinos if he wanted. But for now, hogs would do fine.

Later, he'd think about a calf. But not for a while. He'd see how it went with the hogs first.

And later, for the first time in a *long* time, he would also think about running into the city. He could tell by the recurring bulge in the crotch of his blue jeans that Jasper Junior was aching for a little action. It had been two months or more since his last trip down the mountain for anything other than groceries. Jasper loved his reclusive life—he truly did—but he also loved the feel of a man's skin against his own every now and then. The feel of hands other than his own exploring his body and his own hands exploring the body of another. Groins straining as juices erupted. The taste of come. The heat of it.

Jasper chuckled, shaking his head and rubbing his gloved hand over the aching hardness at his crotch. Well, Jesus, *that* thought had most certainly done it. Now he was definitely going to town. And here he thought he had sworn off the bars forever. Well, resolutions were made to be broken. At least his were.

A quick shower, a bite to eat, and he'd be off.

He scooped up his hammer and hoisted the remaining roll of fencing wire onto his shoulder to lug it up to the lean-to behind the cabin, where he stored everything he couldn't find room for anywhere else. It was time to seek out a little sexual companionship. Yes indeedy.

It was time for a little fun.

AND that's exactly what Jasper had. A *little* fun.

At 3:00 a.m. he was steering the Jeep along the interstate, approaching his exit, eager to get back home. He had succeeded in doing what he set out to do. Namely, performing the sex act with someone other than himself for a change. But it was, as usual, a disappointment. Cold. Anonymous. Emotionally unconnected. Sometimes Jasper didn't know why he bothered. His dick would have to explain it. He certainly couldn't.

He had solved the problem of being horny, for the time being at any rate. He also had a pleasant buzz on from all the beer he had drunk while perched on a barstool at the Eagle Saloon, making himself available. Yet mixed in among the beer buzz and the relief of being sexually satisfied, at least for the moment, was a wee smidgeon of shame. Somehow Jasper couldn't shake the feeling he was simply getting too old to be cruising bars and snagging tricks wherever he could find them. Maybe it really was time to settle down. What if he could find a guy who liked his little mountain as much as Jasper did, and who didn't mind a herd of dogs and cats and wildlife hounding his every footstep? What if the guy was someone willing to commit himself completely to Jasper, as Jasper was sure he would be willing to commit himself to this unknown man he was forever daydreaming about? If Jasper could put all those disparate what-ifs together, then mold them into a good-looking hunk of manhood who was as attractive to Jasper as Jasper was to him, then perhaps they could both be happy.

The most important ingredient of this whole what-if scenario, of course, was love. That had to come first. And frankly, Jasper never let anyone hang around long enough for *either* of them to be thinking about love. The most he and his tricks ever got around to considering was the most enjoyable way to get their rocks off, after which they would toddle off home in their own separate directions, guilt-free, commitment-free, and hopefully disease-free as well.

His trick tonight had been a looker, no question. But already Jasper had forgotten the man's name. He remembered his body fairly well, the responsiveness of it, the eager release of passion, the total lack of conversation. But that's about it. Even the man's apartment, where the tryst took place, was forgettable, although Jasper did recall a pretty impressive saltwater aquarium shimmering in the background as their two bodies, naked and eager, merged in the aura of blue light it cast across the bed.

The trick seemed to have enjoyed Jasper's body well enough, gurgling compliments even while Jasper coated the guy's throat with a torrent of come. Jasper smiled at that thought.

But still, the shame was there. Alive and well behind Jasper's smile.

After what seemed an eternity, Jasper spotted his turnoff. The Jeep bounced over the horrendous washboard of ruts and potholes that heralded the beginning of the mile-long lane leading up to his property. Jasper's headlights, jarred up and down and sidewise by the bumpy path, stabbed strobelike beams of light through the surrounding trees of Endor. And when Jasper steered around a sharp turn in the lane that circumnavigated a boulder the size of a house, his headlights illuminated a coyote standing in the middle of the path with a rabbit dangling from its mouth. Jasper thought he saw the coyote's upper lip pull back in a snarl at being interrupted, and in the next second, the animal, still holding its limp prey in its teeth, was simply gone. Vanished into the shadows like a fleeting thought. Here one second, gone the next. Jasper actually blinked. Wondering if he had seen the coyote at all.

With motor roaring and tires spitting gravel behind him, Jasper climbed the last steep incline up to his cabin, where he bounced to a stop in a cloud of dust with his headlights aimed directly at the front door.

And then Jasper blinked again. Any residual beer buzz disappeared in a flash of clarity. *Nervous* clarity.

The front door, the door he had securely locked before he left for town, was standing open. Wide open. And there was a light burning inside the cabin.

A light Jasper had not left on.

Jasper eased himself from the Jeep, opening and closing the squeaky door as quietly as he could. He stood there, as tense as a tree, while the cloud of dust his tires had churned up settled around him. An owl hooted somewhere off in the junipers. The moonlit trees around him were blurred by mountain mist, a precursor to dawn. It was in these quiet final hours of night that the scent of pine was always strongest. Even in his uncertainty, Jasper took a second to inhale the sweetness of it. And it was at that moment Bobber, Jumper, and Lola came bounding through the open front door to greet him. Heads high, tails flapping back and forth, they circled him with grins on their faces, pushing their snouts into the palms of his hands, stepping on his feet, brushing themselves against his pant legs.

Jasper absentmindedly stroked the three dogs, but his eyes never left the front door. He could see no movement of beast or shadow inside the cabin. There was no sound of fleeing footsteps or windows being flung wide to aid escape. There was no banging of the back door as an intruder scuttled off into the shadows of the trees. The cabin was dead silent. Jasper could see now the light that burned was toward the back, in the kitchen.

While Jasper's father had made his fortune in the gun trade, Jasper himself did not like firearms. He did own a rifle and a small pistol, both gifts from his father back before Alzheimer's addled the man's brain, but Jasper rarely touched them. And thanks to numerous hours spent at firing ranges, also a gift from his father back in Jasper's high school years, Jasper knew how to handle the guns he owned. They were, in fact, resting in one of the closets at this very moment. Loaded and ready for bear, as his father used to say. For what good is a gun if it isn't loaded? His father used to say that too. But the guns were there in case of *natural* predators. Rattlers. Mountain lions. Wild dogs. It never occurred to Jasper there might come a day on his little mountain when he would need to arm himself against a *human* invader.

And now that the time may have actually come, Jasper found himself in the awkward position of quite possibly having the human invader situated *between* himself and his guns.

Well, shit.

"Heel," Jasper said softly, and with fists clenched, his dogs obediently at his side, he stepped nervously toward the porch.

After the initial shock of finding his front door wide open and a light burning inside the cabin, it finally dawned on Jasper that whoever the intruder was, he must now be gone. Otherwise the three dogs would not be so unconcerned. He knew they were better watchdogs than that. Had heard them, in fact, carry on like lunatics at coyotes a quarter mile away. Certainly, if a stranger was parked in his kitchen eating Jasper's food and drinking Jasper's beer, one of the dogs would have mentioned it by now.

Still, Jasper craned his head around the jamb of the front door like he was expecting it to be removed by a machete or something. When his head remained attached, Jasper gazed down at the three dogs, who were at that moment gazing up at him as if wondering what the hell his problem was. They seemed to be saying, "Are we going in or not?"

So Jasper said, "Okay, okay," and stepped inside.

The cabin was dead silent. The only sound Jasper heard was the faint ticking of the alarm clock in the loft upstairs. That clock always was a noisy fucker.

He stepped farther into the cabin, peering around, moving from room to room as quiet as a mouse. He peeked around the kitchen door. Everything was where it should be. Nothing out of place. The refrigerator closed. Dishes still stacked neatly in the drainer by the sink where he had left them. No new dishes lying dirty in the sink. Or on the table. Or anywhere. The ceiling light burned gaily—the ceiling light Jasper was sure he had flicked off before he left for town.

The back door was closed and locked. But then, the back door locked itself when it closed, so the intruder could have left that way and Jasper wouldn't know it.

He opened the door and flicked on the outside light, which was just a bare bulb stuck to the backside of the cabin beside the kitchen window.

What small amount of ground the light illuminated showed Jasper nothing. No burglars. No bears. No Sasquatches. Nothing.

He shut the back door and continued to search the cabin.

His first stop was the closet in the living room where he kept the guns. He found them right where he had left them, months ago. In fact, he could feel dust on the rifle when he picked it up. He didn't bother making sure it was loaded because he knew it was. He merely rested the .22 on his shoulder, safely aimed at the ceiling, with his finger well away from the trigger, and set off to continue his search. He knew he'd never use the gun on anyone. Not as a gun, anyway, although he might use it as a club. Still, it was a comfort having it close.

Looking around, poking his nose everywhere he could think to poke it, Jasper quickly realized all the rooms and all the closets were the way they were supposed to be. Empty of all humanity but himself.

With the ground floor secured, Jasper climbed the rickety staircase to the loft above. There he found everything in order as well. His two cats, Fiji and Guatemala, were sound asleep on the bed and only stirred when Bobber stuck his nose in one of their butts. That elicited a threatening hiss, and Bobber immediately backed off. The big red dog, part setter and part God-knows-what, had learned a long time ago that Fiji and Guatemala were notoriously cranky and their teeth and claws were as sharp as carpet tacks. And they were in no way averse to using every weapon at their disposal on presumptuous dogs. With alacrity, it might well be added.

Jasper bit back a smile at the thought that Bobber, fifteen times larger than the cat, could be cowed so easily. Then he forgot about the dog and stomped back down the stairs to the ground floor. He stepped through the front door with a flashlight he had grabbed in the bedroom and took a stroll around the cabin.

North, south, east, and west, he found absolutely nothing out of place. No footprints on the ground. No sign of a break-in at the windows or doors. Still, Jasper was certain someone had been in his cabin, but he could only suppose who they were, how they got in, and the purpose for their being there, would be three more unexplained mysteries he would take to his grave. Everybody has a few of those, after all.

In that supposition, Jasper would soon be proven wrong. He would meet his intruder before another night darkened his mountain.

And that intruder would change his life.

The next morning, Jasper woke up sneezing. He squinted against the sun, which was streaming through the window of the loft like a laser beam intent on searing a path of destruction directly into his brain. Guatemala was snuggled up against the side of his head, hogging most of Jasper's pillow. He had one foot tucked comfortably in Jasper's ear and his tail twitched as he slept, tickling Jasper's nose. Thus the sneeze.

Jasper's legs were numb because Lola, the beagle mix, was sprawled across one of them, sound asleep, and Bobber lay sprawled atop the other. They were both snoring like lumberjacks. Bobber was so out of it, he was drooling on Jasper's thigh. Yuck.

Jasper gazed down the length of his body and long legs, across the backs of both Lola and Bobber, to see Jumper sitting at the foot of the bed, eyeing him with a hopeful expression. He gave the dog a little finger waggle of greeting and was answered by the sound of Jumper's tail whapping the floor behind him.

The only creature missing was the other cat, Fiji. The orange tabby was probably out catching alligator lizards for his breakfast. Fiji could be spotted stalking the little fuckers at all hours of the day and night. Once in a while, he would generously present one to Jasper, all bloodied and mangled, to show his devotion. But more times than not, thank God, Fiji simply ate the damn thing and was done with it.

Jasper's first thought, after assuring himself that his animals were present or accounted for, was of last night's strange occurrence. Now, with a few hours to let it all sink in, he had pretty much come to the conclusion that he, and no one else, had left the front door open and the kitchen light burning when he left for town. He had found nothing missing. Seen no signs of forced entry. He *must* have been the culprit. God knows he had been eager enough to get down off his mountain and act like a slut. Thinking with his little head alone, small wonder Jasper didn't notice leaving the front door open and the light burning brightly behind him.

But since no harm was done, he decided to put it out of his mind completely.

Jasper eased his numb legs out from under Lola and Bobber and swung them over the side of the bed. As soon as the blood started moving again, and the pins and needles abated, he stood up and yawned, flinging his arms wide and giving his back a good stretch. Naked, with his morning woody pointing due north and bobbing around in front of him, already eager for a little more action, Jasper stepped to the window to look outside.

It was going to be a beautiful day. From where he stood, he could see the pile of lumber he had dumped near the fence he'd constructed the day before. One more task to accomplish, and his pigpen would be ready for the two young shoats he had already paid for.

But first, breakfast.

He threw on a pair of boxer shorts, dashing Jasper Junior's hopes of at least a hand job to brighten the morning, and thumped down the stairs into the kitchen. The sound of his clomping footsteps brought all the animals thundering along behind him, toenails tapping, jostling for position, as ready for breakfast as Jasper. The sound heralded each and every morning of Jasper's life these days, and the happy racket of that clamoring herd of creatures following him down the staircase never ceased to start his day with a smile. It was good to have companionship, even when it was only a pack of animals doing the companioning.

Now firmly convinced the night's adventure was of his own making, Jasper waded into breakfast with his usual enthusiasm. To get the animals out from under his feet, he poured dog and cat food into their individual bowls, which they attacked with gusto. Even Fiji ambled in through the tiny cat door embedded in the kitchen window to join the throng. Only when all of his charges were contentedly chowing down did Jasper go about feeding himself. He guzzled black coffee while whipping up eggs, ham, toast, and hot cereal. And all the while he sat in the kitchen demolishing breakfast, he jotted down notes for the novel he was currently writing, which was never out of his thoughts completely. Between notes for the book, he considered exactly how to go about tackling his project for the day, which was to build a hog house for his new pen out back.

Jasper wasn't much of a carpenter. He readily admitted it. Still, how hard could it be to construct four short walls and stick a roof on it? The pigs wouldn't need a spiral staircase leading down to a basement billiard room, or a parlor in which to partake of high tea when they were tired of wallowing in the mud. All they required was one simple room and a roof. No parquet floors, no cathedral windows, no apses. Just a fucking hog house. Basically, a matter of connecting a few boards and topping it off with a few sheets of tin. What could possibly go wrong?

That thought made Jasper chuckle. Since moving to his private mountain domain, Jasper had run head on into his own ineptitude several times. The fence surrounding the new hog pen was a prime example. It had taken him over a month to construct, and that was only after he tore it down and started from scratch—twice. Even now, as he inhaled his oatmeal, he wasn't sure he wouldn't walk outside and see it topple over in front of his eyes.

Jasper could parse a sentence 'til the cows came home, but stick a hammer in his hand, or any other tool for that matter, and it was always an iffy proposition. After all, he was a city boy. Born and bred. Although he was big and burly and looked butcher than hell lugging a hammer around, his skill with the damn thing was more a matter of luck than anything. Looks could be deceiving. Yes indeedy. And after the fence fiasco, he had two or three hammer-crushed fingernails to prove it.

Breakfast finished to everyone's satisfaction, Jasper dressed for the day in his usual jeans and T-shirt. He carried his work boots out to the porch and plopped his ass down in a rocking chair to tug them on and lace them up. While he did that, he breathed in the pine-scented air. Heaven. Tucking in his shirt, he stepped off the porch and headed out back.

Since Jasper Stone was basically a happy guy, this day began the way most of his days did. With music. He whistled a soft melody, mindlessly it seemed, as he puttered around behind the cabin, and soon the whistling became humming. Then a few slightly off-key lyrics crept in. Before he knew what was happening, Jasper was belting out a tune from *Big River*, one of his favorite Broadway musicals. What he lacked in vocal skills, which was a lot, he more than made up for in enthusiasm. He was all the way up to the big finale when Lola, the little beagle mix, erupted into a mournful howl of rebuke.

"Everybody's a critic," Jasper mumbled with a grin, and he went back to humming. Lola lay down in the dirt and closed her eyes, obviously relieved.

With the sun an hour higher in the sky and the day heating up right along with it, Jasper worked with the post-hole digger to sink the corner beams for his new hog house. Once the beams were buried and in place, he set about nailing plank walls to the framework. That took him most of the morning. By the time he started getting hungry and was nearly ready to break for lunch, he had removed his shirt and hung it over one of the corner posts.

Jasper might not have been overtly aware of the fact, but he was pretty damn nice to look at, slaving away in the sun with sweat running down his naked back and soaking the seat of his blue jeans. Sawdust flecked Jasper's hairy chest and flat tummy, and his jeans hung low enough on his strong hips to show the faintest hint of pubic hair peeking over the belt buckle. His arms were nicely muscled, and his biceps rolled around while he worked. Flexing. Unflexing.

The sun felt good on his back, even if it was getting hotter than hell. He stopped for a moment to wipe the sweat from his face with a yellow bandana he'd pulled from his back pocket. He saw a squirrel watching him from the cabin roof. And behind the squirrel, he saw Fiji stalking the poor thing. Jasper picked up a pinecone and flung it onto the roof, scaring away the squirrel. Fiji flung Jasper a disgusted look and started licking his rear end, which Jasper figured was his way of saying "fuck you" for scaring away lunch.

Jasper laughed. Cats. Always grumpy.

He tossed his hammer to the ground and tugged off his work gloves as he strode to the cabin. Inside, he pulled a jug of cold water from the fridge, downed half of it, then made himself a sandwich. He swallowed it in four bites. When he was done, he headed back outside. He figured if he stuck to it, he could finish the hog house before dark. It wouldn't be pretty, but it would be standing. That was good enough for him, and Jasper was pretty sure it would be good enough for the pigs when they arrived. As far as he was aware, pigs weren't too snooty about where they laid their heads at night.

It was while Jasper was fighting with an eight-foot length of tin roofing that he spotted the footprint. He found it in front of the lean-to at the back of the cabin. Jasper didn't know why he hadn't seen it before.

It so astounded him, Jasper dropped the corrugated tin at his feet with a clatter, kicking up a cloud of dust in the process, and stared at that footprint for a minute. He laid his booted foot alongside it and compared the two. The footprint was a good two inches shorter than his own size twelve. Also, the tread etched in the dirt looked like it came from a sneaker. Jasper wore sneakers when he jogged, of course, but he sure wouldn't be able to run in a sneaker *that* size. Not unless he chopped his toes off first. It was so small it almost looked like a girl's shoe. Or a kid's.

Jasper stood with his hands on his hips and did a 360-degree turn, checking out the surrounding countryside: the hog pen, the back of the cabin, the glade where the cabin sat, and the rutted lane leading out to the gravel road, more than a mile distant, that eventually led to the freeway and the world beyond.

He sure didn't see any girls. No kids either. No nobody.

He looked back at the footprint, squatted down on his haunches, and gave the print a little flick with his fingertip, as if trying to coax a few secrets out of it. But if that was what he was doing, it didn't work.

Finally, Bobber came and sniffed at the print. If Jasper expected the black mongrel to go hightailing it into the trees hot on the trail of whoever left the mysterious footprint, he was sorely disappointed. Bobber fell over onto his back and asked for a belly rub instead. Some tracker he was. Some watchdog too.

While Jasper idly rubbed Bobber's belly, making the big dog grin like a fool, he thought things over and finally admitted someone *had* been in his cabin last night. He couldn't remember the last time he'd had visitors on the place. Be they invited or uninvited. And since the footprint certainly wasn't his own, what else was he supposed to deduce?

The big question was, what the hell was he supposed to do about it?

He looked around for a mate to that one footprint. He ducked into the lean-to and examined the dirt floor of the six-by-twelve-foot shed in the meager light that spilled through the doorway. He saw nothing out of place and no sneaker treads anywhere. He stepped outside and walked back and forth across the grounds surrounding the cabin until he had covered every square inch. He found nothing. He sauntered off into the trees, thinking he might see something there that would lead him to understand who had left a footprint at the back of his cabin, or what their purpose had been in being there. Again he found nothing.

Finally, facing the fact that he could do nothing at all about the damn footprint, Jasper set an upside-down bucket over it to keep it pristine, although he wasn't quite sure what purpose that would serve. Then he gathered up his sheets of tin roofing and went back to work.

Two hours later, he had a hog house. It wasn't pretty, and stepping back to take his first good look at it, Jasper realized it was a little cattywampus. But still, it was good enough for a couple of pigs. At any rate, it didn't appear to be on the verge of falling over anytime soon.

Jasper dragged his tools and extra sheets of roofing tin back to the lean-to and stored everything where it belonged. Then he returned to the damn footprint and lifted up the bucket. He moved the bucket over a couple of feet, sat his ass down on it, and just stared at the footprint like a man who is trying to work out a problem in his head. He didn't realize it, but with his elbow on his knee and his chin in the palm of his upturned hand, wearing nothing but blue jeans and work boots, he looked remarkably like Rodin's Thinker from the waist up. The only difference was, Jasper wasn't quite as naked from the waist down.

And the young man watching him from behind a boulder, tucked in among a copse of seedling pines about three hundred yards away, was more than a little disappointed by that fact.

Chapter TWO

IT WAS a strange road that had led twenty-year-old Timmy Harwell into that clump of seedling pines. It was even stranger that, with his life on the line and the hounds of hell nipping at his ass, he should take a break from his own troubles long enough to appreciate the beauty of the half-naked man sitting on the bucket in front of him.

He had been watching the man for hours. Good lord, he had been sitting out here in the bushes for two full days! At first, Timmy had no idea what had suddenly grabbed the guy's interest and made him stare at the ground with such rapt attention. Then, with a sudden quickening of his heart, Timmy thought maybe he *did* know. Timmy had walked past that very spot the night before. *Run* past it, actually, after fleeing silently through the back door of the cabin at the first sound of the rattletrap Jeep clawing its way up the hill.

By now, the guy *must* be wondering why he'd returned home the night before to find his front door open and the cabin lights on. Timmy figured he was probably lucky the dude hadn't armed himself like a SEAL and started beating the bushes looking for the intruder who broke into his house. Even if the intruder *hadn't* stolen anything. Timmy didn't have the energy to run anymore. He wanted to rest. To lie low. If it meant hiding in a clump of fucking brambly pine trees until he figured out what to do next, then so be it.

The dogs' barking hadn't bothered Timmy much the night before when he first stepped onto the man's porch and began picking the lock on the front door. They were inside. He was outside. Besides, they were just saying hello. Hell, Timmy and the dogs were old friends by now. They had already checked him out several times as he hid in the woods for hours on end that first day. Was it only yesterday he'd lain among the stickers and the pinecones watching the man build his crookedass fence? It felt like a month ago. After that first long hot day had crawled to an end, Timmy was still forced to stay hidden while the man spiffed himself up like he had a date or something. When the guy finally hopped in the Jeep, looking freshly scrubbed and sexy as hell, Timmy breathed a sigh of relief. And when the Jeep was at last headed down the hill and the taillights had disappeared in the distance, Timmy knew he was finally alone. He rose on creaking joints and approached the still cabin.

Timmy was more than ready to break into the joint by then—don't think he wasn't. He was hot, thirsty, hungry, and sore from about a bazillion insect bites. And that was after the *first* day of cowering among the saplings on a bed of scratchy pine needles.

Timmy didn't know it, but he was even more of a city boy than Jasper. He wasn't used to squatting in the bushes with nine million fucking bugs gnawing away at him like maggots on a carcass. Didn't like it one bit. But he couldn't go any farther. He couldn't. He was exhausted, and he needed to figure out what to do, formulate a plan. If he had to hide in a bunch of bushes out in the middle of nowhere to do it, then that's what he would do.

Of course, even Timmy knew he only had himself to blame for the trouble he was in. Still, that didn't make it any easier.

And to be honest, even after a horrible long day sitting in the fucking weeds—or baby trees or whatever the hell they were—Timmy had no real intention of actually *burglarizing* the man's house. He just needed to snatch something to eat and drink. He was starving to death, and he was so goddamned thirsty he thought maybe he was teetering on the tippy-tip verge of a heat stroke. At least he imagined he was.

Timmy was a little prone to exaggeration. He was well aware of it too.

So he stuck his penknife into the lock on the front door, carefully, so as not to leave any scratches, and started working his magic. It took exactly thirteen seconds for the front door to pop open. Timmy was good at picking locks. House locks. Ignition locks. You name it. Of course, he usually had the proper tools with him when he did it. But in a pinch, a penknife would do as well.

The moment the door opened, the dogs shot through it to greet him, prancing around and wagging their tails. Timmy bent and petted each one in turn. He liked dogs. And these were nicer than some. Lousy guard dogs, of course, but he wasn't about to fault them for that.

The first thing Timmy did after gaining access to the cabin was head straight for the kitchen sink, cup his hand under the faucet, and chug down about a gallon of water. Damn, he was thirsty! He almost felt like he was getting sick. Wouldn't that be the icing on the cake. Come down with the flu in the middle of running for your life. Great.

While he slurped up the water like a gazelle at a watering hole, he spotted an envelope propped on the kitchen windowsill directly above the sink. It was addressed to Jasper Stone. So that was the hunky guy's name. It suited him, Timmy thought. Jasper. A sexy name for a sexy guy. Very nice.

When his tummy was starting to slosh from all the water he had slurped down, Timmy turned and cast a critical eye around the kitchen. Happily, it looked like good old Jasper was well stocked with groceries.

Since he didn't want his presence known, he scavenged around and only ate a little bit of this and a little bit of that. A slice of ham, a couple of slices of bread, a few spoonfuls of potato salad sitting in a big tub in the fridge, one banana. Things that wouldn't be missed, hopefully. It was hard holding back his hunger and not pigging out on everything he could find. Took some will power, that. His hands were actually shaking with the effort. Or were they shaking because he was coming down with something? He was afraid he knew the answer to that question all too well.

Finally, with his hunger reasonably satisfied, Timmy moved to the living room and collapsed on the sofa to rest for a minute. He stretched out his long legs with a groan, propping his feet on the coffee table. After being so cramped up and unable to stand for an entire day while he hid his sorry ass in those damn bushes, it was bliss to finally relax the leg muscles and straighten his knees and sit his ass down on an honest-to-God piece of upholstered furniture. The three dogs gathered around him as he laid his head back and closed his eyes. He absently scratched and patted each of them in turn while his body unwound. Before he knew what he was doing, he was fast asleep.

He only woke up when headlights flashed across the walls of the cabin. He blinked his eyes and listened with horror to the guy's beat-up old Jeep rattling and clawing its way back up the hill outside the cabin. My God, he'd slept for *hours!* He had no idea what time it was, but it smelled late. Really late. In fact it smelled so late, Timmy figured it might actually be *early.* The wee hours of the morning.

He lurched to his feet and almost fell over. His head swam, and his legs felt like rubber. He felt a chill run through him and knew beyond all doubt he was indeed getting sick. Well, shit. He'd have to muddle through anyway. What other choice did he have?

Expecting another long wait in the bushes outside, he managed to snag a few apples from a basket by the back door on his way out. And before the hunky owner could walk through his front door, Timmy had snuck back out into the night like a thief, which he supposed he really was. *Okay, let's be honest,* he told himself. *You are a thief. No supposing about it.*

That's what got you into this mess to begin with. Never forget that for a minute.

That was last night. Now, twelve hours later, after another long day of hiding, Timmy Harwell sat among the saplings munching on his fourth and final apple. He was as sick as a dog, now. Had thrown up twice. His poor body was being battered by both chills and fever. They sort of came in spurts. He was dying for another drink of water, but he knew he had to stay hidden until he figured out what to do.

He stared intently at the guy sitting on the bucket a few hundred yards away. Timmy couldn't stop himself from staring. And he wasn't staring because he was afraid of being discovered either. Not by this guy. This guy didn't frighten him. Not really. No, he was staring because the man with the tight jeans and no shirt was so damn nice to look at. Jasper Stone was a hottie, no two ways around that. And while Timmy sat and stared at the gorgeous man in front of him, his mind began to drift. Pretty soon he was reliving the revolting chain of events that had brought him to this place.

It all started with the Caddy. The beautiful black Caddy SUV. It was an Escalade Hybrid. God, it was cherry. The very latest model too. Absolutely stunning hunk of metal and rubber and chrome. Spotlessly clean. As black as midnight. Fully loaded, the price tag must have bumped heads with ninety grand easy. Yep. One damn fine automobile. And oddly enough, Timmy knew the Caddy was trouble the first time he laid eyes on it.

Did that stop him? Nope. Timmy readily admitted he was kind of stupid that way.

It was funny, but all Timmy's troubles seemed to start with automobiles. That's what happens when you love something too much. Brings you nothing but heartache. Every. Single. Time.

Timmy loved sucking dicks too. Loved the feel of a man's skin trembling beneath his hands. Loved the feel of a man's hands and lips on his young body. But even those sensations couldn't compare to sliding his ass around on the leather seat of a finely tuned Caddy. Well, maybe sometimes it could. He grinned.

But back to the SUV.

This particular Caddy was going to be the death of him. Timmy was already convinced of that, and he didn't even *have* the damn thing anymore. Not really. He had gotten rid of it the minute he understood what sort of mess he'd landed himself in. But still, it was too close to where he now lay hidden. He should have run farther when he had a chance, but now it was too late. He was too damn sick to go anywhere.

Christ! He sat hunkered under the saplings, sweating bullets in the heat, getting sicker by the minute, rolling the last apple core over and over in his hand while he thought it all out. All his poor choices. All his asshole decisions. The beauty of the half-naked man in front of him. Too many disparate thoughts for his poor pea brain to process all at once. But it was kind of funny the way, even in the middle of running for your life, and coming down with the flu on top of *that*, the sexy thoughts could still float to the top like cream in a crock of farm-fresh milk.

Timmy Harwell made a concerted effort to ignore the aching erection in his pants as he tried to pinpoint the exact moment in his young life when he'd turned so goddamned stupid. And after a minute or two, he thought he had it figured out. Before long his hard-on was forgotten completely. The ache had moved from his dick to his heart. The memories overwhelmed him.

Lord, he really was stupid.

Why else would he be running for his life from the meanest man in TJ?

Timmy was a good person at heart. At least he thought he was. He was from a good family, too, or so everyone always used to tell him. He supposed he had made a few wrong turns during the course of his life, but hell, who hadn't?

Timmy figured his one big fault was he had always hated being poor. Hated it as a kid. Hated it as an adult. *Still* hated it, even after all that had happened to lead him to this stupid mountain, hiding behind this stupid boulder and this stupid bunch of baby trees, watching a gorgeous man with no shirt sit on a fucking bucket and stare at a stupid footprint. *Timmy's* footprint.

Again, the memories flooded in. He thought of his childhood. His miserable fucking childhood.

Timmy grew up in foster homes because his parents died in a car crash when he was three. He did not remember them at all. He had photographs that had followed him around from one foster home to another, but to him they were the photographs of strangers. He could not count the times he had stared at those black-and-white photos, willing a memory to pop into his head of the man and the woman in them, had pleaded with God to please allow him one little flash of memory so he would know they were truly his parents. But if God heard his pleas, He didn't respond.

And in Timmy's young mind, that was the end of God. He had never asked for anything again. One day he had simply dropped the photographs in the trash. They meant nothing to him. They could be pictures of anybody. *Anybody.*

Timmy suddenly shuddered, and somewhere in the back of his mind, he knew something was seriously wrong. This wasn't the flu he was feeling. This was something worse. His joints felt like they were on fire. As if someone had flicked a switch, his energy evaporated and his memories vanished. Just like that. He rolled over onto his side and curled up in a ball atop the crunching pine needles. A sudden stomach cramp made him let out a shuddering groan. The sound of it surprised him. Through a curtain of tears, he watched a ladybug crawl across the ground in front of his eyes. He tried to smile when she spread her pretty porcelain wings and prepared to fly away, but he couldn't quite seem to manage it.

Before the ladybug left the ground, Timmy was unconscious. His waking mind had simply shut down. The fever and chills thundered through him, and in that torturous darkness, his inner reflections faded as well. Timmy knew nothing more.

He did not wake when Lola poked her head through the saplings. It was the smell of sickness that drew her there. She moved silently forward and sniffed the reeking puddle of vomit on the ground. Then she stepped closer to smell the sleeping man's breath. She watched him shiver with cold even as she felt the unnatural heat radiate off his body in waves. Understanding his helplessness, she curled up beside him to give him solace. To keep him safe. Lola had a good heart too.

Soon, with her chin on Timmy's shoulder, she fell asleep. Periodically, the young man would cry out, and when he did, Lola would open her eyes and whimper.

But the man heard nothing.

Even Lola understood he was somewhere else.

THROUGH a haze of sickness, Timmy's second night in the scrub drew to a close without his awareness. It would be morning soon. He could sense that much. Even now a smear of red lit the sky to the east. His illness had intensified during the night. He saw only inward now, as truly sick people often do. He was frightened. Frightened for himself. Frightened by the pain thundering through him. His head throbbed. Every joint, every digit, ached. He had never been this sick in his life. Every organ seemed to cry out in misery.

God, he was pitiful.

In some dim recess of his mind, he was aware the brown-and-white dog was gone. She was no longer lying next to him, warming him, giving him comfort. He missed her company, but he missed her heat even more. He felt so alone, so *unwanted*, lying out in the elements like this without one single human being worrying about him, tending to him. No family. No friends. No one.

If he had been well, those self-pitying thoughts would have made him chuckle at himself. But not now. So weak he could barely lift his head off the ground, he couldn't find the energy or the will to chuckle. Even if he had wanted to. The possibility of dying actually began sneaking into his thoughts. And if he did die, he wondered if anyone would find him. Or would he lie here for the rest of eternity in these goddamn bushes until his bones were scattered to hell and back by the weather and the wildlife, until no vestige of humanity was left to him at all? Like roadkill, rotting in the heat. Would the reek of his decomposing body bring the handsome rancher, Jasper, clambering into the undergrowth with his nose under his shirt to locate the source of whatever it was stinking up his front yard?

A great shudder ran through Timmy as he lay with his cheek to the ground, his arms wrapped around himself, fighting off the chill stuttering through his body with what little strength he had left. He wasn't too sick to know he was in bad shape, and if he didn't get inside pretty soon, he would be even worse off. If this was the flu, it was the worst case he had ever suffered. He was beginning to think it was pneumonia instead. Wouldn't that be the icing on the cake.

Being hunted like a rabbit wasn't bad enough. Now he had to be damn near bedridden on top of it.

Except he didn't even *have* a bed.

The first drop of water that splattered cold against his cheek made him start. He opened his eyes to see what it was. Rain. Great. Just what he needed.

He fought back the urge to cry out: that's how fucking miserable he felt at that very moment. If he hadn't been too sick to analyze it, he would have realized this was perhaps the lowest moment of his life. And the sound of other raindrops plunking the pine needles around his head assured him it wasn't about to get any better either.

He almost wept when he struggled into a sitting position to look around. God, *everything* hurt. His head throbbed. His lungs felt like they were on fire. The cold air he sucked in seemed to stoke the flames of pain with every breath.

The rain was falling faster now. Faster and colder. Timmy's shirt was plastered to his back in no time. It felt like a coating of ice against his skin. He was shuddering so ferociously he could hear his teeth chatter. It couldn't be that cold, for Christ's sake. This was Southern California. It was because he was sick. That was all. He wasn't going into hypothermia or anything. He was simply ill and had to get in out of the rain.

The only shelter he could think of in his pain-addled mind was the hog house he had watched the man build that day. It wasn't far away.

Maybe three or four hundred yards. It wouldn't be warm in there, but it would be dry. It would be out of the rain.

Timmy clattered to his feet like a bucket of bolts. Jesus. His bones felt like they were coming unhinged from each other, all his connections deteriorating, the sinews in his arms and legs snapping apart one after another, twanging like broken guitar strings.

He stumbled through the darkness, holding his chest, ducking his head against the ever-increasing rain, hoping he was going in the right direction. When he walked smack into Jasper Stone's brand new fence, Timmy knew he was. He headed toward the rickety gate he'd watched the guy build two days ago and stepped into the pen. Somehow, he had the common sense to close the gate behind him.

Hide your footprints too, he told himself. But he was too sick to even consider it. If he got down on his hands and knees to wipe out his footprints, he might never get back up again.

The rain was quickly becoming a torrent: icy cold and coming down so hard the drops actually hurt when they hit his skin. Or maybe that was because he was sick, too, as all his nerve endings were jangling like a bunch of fucking Christmas bells. At least, if he was lucky, the rain would wash away his footprints. He could hope, anyway.

When he ducked his head through the opening in the hog house, he could smell the freshly cut wood. He couldn't see a thing inside, it was so dark, but he thought he could feel sawdust beneath his feet. And it was dry. Blessedly dry.

He stumbled into the corner as far away from the door as he could get and dropped down to sit with his back against the wall. His head fell wearily forward, and again his body gave a shudder as the sickness rattled through him.

With trembling fingers, Timmy unbuttoned his soaked shirt and peeled it off his back as one peels a blister from a burn. He was cold without the shirt, but he was colder with it. He wadded it up in a damp ball and used it for a pillow as he slid sidewise to the ground. Hugging himself against the chill, he curled up in a fetal position, moaning and shivering and wishing to God he had never laid eyes on that goddamn Cadillac Escalade. Satan on wheels. That's what it was.

Timmy closed his eyes and let illness overtake him once again. At least he was out of the rain.

If only he could get himself out of trouble so easily.

One lonely tear leaked from his eye as his misery carried him into sleep. *I'm sorry*, he muttered into the darkness, directing the words to no one in particular. Or maybe he was directing them at himself. He wasn't sure. And it didn't much matter.

Once again, Timmy let despair overwhelm him. This time he didn't stir until hours later, when a bristly, cold snout, which sure as hell wasn't human, sniffed and slobbered at his neck, startling him so he jerked awake with a hoarse cry. Then another face, and this one *was* human, hovered into view. Timmy squinted to get a better look, but he couldn't seem to focus. Human fingers brushed the hair away from his eyes, and a warm palm was laid across his forehead.

The hand felt good. Timmy tried to smile, but the moment he did, a lightning bolt of pain shot through his skull. His mind darkened and he knew no more.

And outside, the rain let loose with its fiercest downpour yet, peppering the hog house's new tin roof and making a horrendous racket.

Timmy didn't hear or feel a thing. Even when he was scooped up in strong, gentle arms and carried away.

Chapter THREE

THE rain finally stopped. Jasper turned off the windshield wipers of his old Jeep and made himself comfortable for the long ride home. Every once in a while, he looked down at the passenger seat beside him and grinned. Sitting there in a cardboard box, and staring back at him with ferocious concentration, were two tiny piglets. A male and a female.

They were freshly weaned and only weighed about twenty pounds apiece. But boy were they rambunctious.

Rambunctious and noisy.

They were Yorkshires, with white, bristly coats. The pink of their skin showed through at their snouts and ears. Their little curly tails were so cute that every now and then Jasper reached over and pulled one taut just to watch it spring back into a spiral. He could swear the little pigs laughed each time he did it.

Jasper had left the cabin before daylight. He phoned Mr. McCracken first to make sure his purchases were ready to go, and he was assured they were. It was a forty-minute drive to the McCracken farm, and Jasper didn't want to make the man wait. Plus, he wanted to reacquaint himself with his new charges as soon as he could. The last time he had seen them was when they were one day old, wiggling around at their mother's teats with the rest of the brood. That was almost two months ago. They had changed a lot since then, but Jasper was happy to see they were still cute as hell. And just as feisty. The male was just a smidgeon larger than the female.

This was an exciting day for Jasper. It was the first time he actually felt like an honest-to-God rancher, although he had lived on the ranch for several years. Of course, maybe that was just Jasper. He hardly felt like an honest-to-God writer, either, even with several published books to his credit.

Maybe some people never feel they fit in anywhere, no matter what they do.

Jasper had two bags of hog feed the farmer had sold him to get his new acquisitions started eating right. The piglets were barely weaned, but if they missed their mother, they didn't show it. In fact, they looked like they were having the time of their lives.

After a few miles, they settled down and curled up together to go to sleep. Jasper thought they were as cute asleep as they were awake. He also suspected ranchers, *true* ranchers, didn't get this goo-goo-eyed over their livestock. And to tell the truth, he was having a little trouble thinking of Harry and Harriet as livestock at all. They seemed more like pets. And he'd only had them in his possession for less than an hour. Lord, in two months they'd probably be sharing his bed with all the dogs and cats.

At that realization, Jasper spit up a wry chuckle. Great. Just what he needed. More bunkmates. Not that a proper bunkmate wouldn't be fine and dandy, and damned exhilarating, but he would prefer one with two legs rather than four. And he wasn't talking about a chicken either. He was talking about a man. A cute man. Yes indeedy.

He laid his right hand in the cardboard box and idly brushed Harry's coat while he drove. When Harriet opened her eyes and nudged Jasper's hand for a little attention too, Jasper smiled and gave it to her.

As the miles rolled along beneath them, the piglets once again dozed off, gently snoring and snorting in their sleep. Jasper left them to it, occupying his mind with some new ideas for plot twists in the novel he was working on. He grinned when he found himself trying to think of a way to get two pigs into the story. Jesus. What an old softy he was.

After thirty minutes, Jasper left the freeway and followed a gravel back road for several miles. At long last, his turnoff finally came up, and he gratefully steered onto the private lane leading up to his cabin. At that very moment, the skies opened up again. Visibility turned to shit in three seconds flat. Jasper flipped on the wipers and leaned forward to better see where he was going. The winding, potholed lane was a trial to traverse in *good* weather. In a torrential downpour, it was damned near impossible. He laid a comforting hand over the back of the pigs when the Jeep bounced and splashed through a series of craters, all filled with muddy rainwater now, jarring the piglets and startling them so they scrambled to their feet with a snort.

They hung their front feet over the side of the box and tried to see out, their little pink snouts sniffing the air as if they sensed their journey was almost over.

By the time the Jeep splashed and scrambled and churned up the last steep hill to his front yard, Jasper was humming a merry tune in spite of the rain. He was eager to see how Harry and Harriet took to their new home. The home he had worked so hard to prepare for them. And thanks to the rain, he suddenly realized with a grin, they would even have mud to wallow around in. Pigs loved mud. At least Jasper had always heard they did.

Since the cardboard box the piglets were standing in would have disintegrated in seconds in the slashing rain, Jasper pulled his denim jacket over his head as a makeshift umbrella and carried the pigs to their new home one at a time. Harriet didn't seem to mind being carried, but Harry, when Jasper went back for him, griped and squirmed and oinked every step of the way.

Jasper was relieved when he was back at the gate to the pen and able to set the little bastard down. He watched as Harry ran straight for the hog house to escape the rain. A moment later Harriet and Harry both stuck their heads through the door and looked out at him, as if wondering why he hadn't joined them.

Jasper grinned. Soaked all the way down to his socks already, he didn't figure he could get any wetter, so he stepped inside the gate and sloshed through the mud to make sure his new acquisitions were comfortable in their new digs. He ducked through the hog house door and slid to a stop so quickly he almost fell flat on his ass.

Lying in the far corner against the newly erected wall, which still smelled of freshly cut wood and sawdust, was a man. An unconscious man. He was lying with his back to Jasper, and he was naked from the waist up. Curled up in a fetal position, he was trembling, so Jasper could see he wasn't dead. And from the lean, firm line of his back, and the nicely rounded curve of his ass beneath the sodden jeans the guy was wearing, Jasper suspected he was a *young* man. In fact, one of Jasper's first thoughts was this: if the man was as attractive on the front side as he was on the back, then he was probably a pretty good-looker indeed.

The two piglets were sniffing around the man as if Jasper had placed him there for their amusement. When Harry started chewing on the hem of the guy's pant leg, Jasper thought he had better intervene.

Stooping to avoid banging his head on the roof, he crossed the dry floor in his muddy boots and knelt at the man's side. The man didn't move, but Jasper could hear him breathing in ragged little gasps. And thank God for that much. It was unsettling enough to find an unconscious stranger on one's property. Finding a dead stranger would have been even more unnerving.

When the man made no move to indicate he knew he had company, Jasper shooed the pigs aside and leaned across the prone body to get a look at the stranger's face.

A shock of black hair lay across the man's eyes, and Jasper gently pushed it up and out of the way. He had been right. It was a young man. Probably no more than twenty. Handsome, with a strong chin and neat little ears that, at the moment, were bright red. Looking closer, Jasper saw the fellow's cheeks were flushed too.

Jasper laid his palm across the man's forehead, and sure enough, he had a fever. In fact, he was burning up. And all the while he was burning up, he was shivering from being exposed to the cold and damp. Jasper didn't like that at all. He had to get the fellow inside.

He gently gripped the young man's shoulder and gave him a shake.

"Hey, fella. Wake up. Let's get you into the cabin."

Nothing.

Jasper shook him again. "Come on, fella. If I leave you out here you're as good as dead. Either you'll die of pneumonia or the pigs will eat you. Don't think you'd enjoy either one of those options."

His stab at humor fell on deaf ears. Literally.

Planting his feet firmly beneath him, Jasper squatted to distribute the weight carefully on his back and slid his arms under the young man. With a grunt, he lifted the limp body from the ground. The man was so hot from the fever burning through him. Jasper could feel the heat through the sleeves of his jacket.

Once he was standing, Jasper was pleased to note the man lying in his arms didn't weigh much more than a minute. He was, in fact, a little guy, thank God. And by the look of his ribs showing through his pale sides, Jasper thought maybe he hadn't been eating too well lately.

"Let's get you inside," Jasper said again and headed for the door.

The young man groaned and his eyelids fluttered, but he spoke no words.

Jasper carefully ducked back through the hog house door with the man in his arms. The poor guy gave a ratcheting gasp when the cold rain hit his bare chest but did not waken.

Jasper hurried as fast as he could to the cabin porch, where he awkwardly shuffled the guy around in his arms until he could extract the door key from his pocket. When the tumblers clicked and the door swung open, Jasper quickly stepped inside and kicked the door closed behind him, shutting out the cold air.

As gently as he could, he laid the young man on the sofa, then straightened up and looked down at him.

Face up and still unconscious, the young man groaned again.

Jasper was considering whether to get the guy to his Jeep and drive him the forty miles to the nearest hospital, or whether to first get the wet clothes off him and try to warm him up before hypothermia set in. Calling an ambulance wasn't much of an option. It would probably take the EMTs a week to find the place. His ranch was hell and gone from civilization.

Trying not to panic, Jasper thought things through as calmly as he could. It wasn't *that* cold outside, so hypothermia was probably a worst-case scenario. But still, this guy was sick. *Seriously* sick. Warmth was probably the thing he needed most right now.

So with his mind made up, Jasper went to work.

The first thing he did was grab an armload of towels from the bathroom and dry the man's torso. He also tried to get the rainwater out of the man's thick black hair. Then he shucked off the guy's tennis shoes and peeled off his wet socks. When that was accomplished, Jasper fumbled with the young man's belt buckle, all the while trying not to think lascivious thoughts because the guy really was pretty damn cute. When he had the belt undone, he unbuttoned and unzipped the man's trousers and peeled them down his legs, leaving the guy naked.

Jesus, the man was beautiful! Lean, pale, perfectly formed. Strong, hairy legs. A smooth chest with just a sprinkling of dark hair trailing down from his belly button toward his dick. And speaking of dicks, even the young man's cock was beautiful, asleep as it was, nestled in a bed of crisp dark pubic hair. The man's balls lay heavy and tempting between his legs. Jasper stared at them so long he finally had to give himself a shake to stop ogling the poor kid.

And kid he damn near was. Looking at him now, Jasper wouldn't have made any bets about whether the guy was even out of his teens yet.

Beginning to feel like a first-class pervert, Jasper went to work in earnest to help the young man out. First he toweled the man off. Vigorously. Trying to get some blood moving around in his nearly comatose body. Jasper tucked a pillow under the young man's head, pulled an afghan over him, all the way from his toes to his chin, then set about building a fire in the fireplace. When the flames began to take hold and the room was starting to warm up, Jasper pushed the sofa closer to the fireplace. Then he went to the closet and grabbed another blanket, throwing that over the man as well.

Not once did the man open his eyes or seem to be aware what was happening to him. Nor did his fever appear to diminish, and that was beginning to worry Jasper. Once again he began pondering whether to call the paramedics. He supposed he could talk them through finding the place.

While he thought about that, Jasper dampened a dish towel with cool water, folded it into a neat little block, and laid it across the young man's forehead. Maybe it would help bring down the fever.

During all this, the three dogs and two cats sat against the far wall watching the proceedings. It was as if they knew they would be in the way if they got too close. But with the fire burning nicely, and the sofa situated where Jasper wanted it, it looked like their master was finally finished fooling around. So one by one, they all moved in to sniff the new visitor and welcome him to their home.

When Lola hopped onto the sofa and snuggled up beside the young man as if she already knew him, Jasper left her to it. He knew as well as anyone the comfort of a good dog was better than medicine sometimes. Lola's body heat wouldn't do the guy any harm either.

And thinking of medicine, Jasper headed for the cabinet in the bathroom to see what he had on hand. The pickings were pretty slim, since

Jasper almost never got sick. But he did find some liquid cold medicine and aspirin, which, if Jasper remembered right, might help lower the man's fever.

Before he set about trying to get the medicine down his patient's throat, Jasper thought he had better see to Harry and Harriet first.

He tipped up the collar on his coat and ducked back out into the rain. Heading for the pigpen, Jasper could already see his two new charges through the driving rain, watching him from the safety of their hog house door. He thought they looked mightily confused, as if wondering why they had been brought to this godforsaken place in the middle of nowhere and then summarily *abandoned*, for Christ's sake.

Jasper veered from his path and grabbed a bale of straw from a mound of the stuff he had purchased a couple of weeks ago and which was now stacked neatly under a tarp at the side of the lean-to. He carried the straw across the muddy pigpen and into the hog house, where he proceeded to rip it to pieces and spread it around for bedding. It would help keep the ground dry and the piggies warm as well.

Then Jasper headed back out into the rain and grabbed the upside-down bucket still sitting in the middle of the yard by the mysterious footprint (which Jasper supposed wasn't quite so mysterious now, seeing as how the man who probably made it was currently snoring in front of the fire on his goddamn couch). Bucket in hand, Jasper opened the Jeep's tailgate, tore into one of the new fifty-pound bags of hog mash, and put enough in the bucket to keep the pigs satisfied for a while.

Tucking the bucket under his jacket to keep it out of the rain, he rushed back to the hog house. Once there, he shook the mash into the beat-up old metal pan he had decided to use to feed the little guys until they were big enough to use the real hog trough he had constructed outside.

Once Harry and Harriet were chowing down and beginning to look at home, Jasper retrieved the guy's shirt, which was still wadded into a ball on the hog house floor, and headed back to the cabin, carefully securing the gate behind him to keep his charges safe.

Once inside, it was Jasper's turn to dry off. Since the young man was still sound asleep, Jasper slipped out of his wet clothes smack in front of the fireplace. Grabbing one of the towels he had brought for his guest, he rubbed himself down and took off naked up the stairs to the loft, where he grabbed some dry clothes and hurriedly pulled them on.

The fireplace was beginning to warm the cabin, and since it wasn't really *winter* cold outside, he didn't think he would need to light the furnace. Besides, as soon as the rain stopped, Jasper was fairly sure the temperature would go back up. This was just a freak spring storm. It wouldn't last forever.

Fully dressed in dry jeans and a sweater, but still in his stocking feet, Jasper thundered back down the stairs and stood behind the sofa, looking down at Lola and her new best friend.

The young man seemed to be breathing a little easier, or maybe that was wishful thinking on Jasper's part. Anyway, at some point while Jasper had been gone, the guy had draped an arm across Lola's back and was holding her like a teddy bear. Lola seemed to be eating it up too. She rolled her eyes to look up at Jasper standing above her, but she didn't move her head, which was resting gently on the young man's chest.

Even as Jasper watched, Lola closed her eyes and fell asleep. Occasionally, the man would erupt into a fresh burst of trembling, either from his fever or from the chills stampeding through him, and when that happened, Lola would briefly open her eyes to look at the stranger's face. When she was satisfied all was well, she would once again close her eyes and drift off to sleep. Jasper smiled, thinking if Lola had ever had a litter of pups before she showed up on his doorstep, she must have been a wonderful mother. For that was exactly what she was doing now. Mothering.

And frankly, Jasper had never seen a human more in need of a little TLC than this one.

Maybe it didn't make much sense, but it seemed to Jasper if Lola trusted the guy, then he should trust him too. Because, to tell the truth, Jasper had long thought Lola had more common sense than *he* did.

And when *that* thought tumbled through Jasper's head, he gave a quiet chuckle. Not because it was a weird realization, God help him, but because it was *true*.

He gave himself a shake and clawed his way back to reality.

Soup. Hot soup. He didn't know when the young man had last eaten, but he didn't think it was lately. Then Jasper thought about coming home the night before to find his cabin door open. Nothing had seemed to have been taken, but now he guessed he knew who was responsible for the break-in. And since the guy was likely starving when he broke in, Jasper couldn't seem to dredge up much resentment for what he had done. Jasper might have done the same under similar circumstances. He was sorry the young man had not simply asked for help. Perhaps then he wouldn't have stayed out in the night air and the cold rain long enough to get as sick as he was.

Lord, Jasper suddenly realized, the guy must have been huddled against the weather under the trees somewhere. Without food. Without shelter. And for how long, he wondered. Days? How had he ended up here to begin with? Jasper's cabin was hell and gone from the freeway. Hell and gone from *anywhere*. And Jasper had seen no abandoned vehicles beside his lane or the gravel road leading up to it.

Jasper wondered if maybe the guy was a hiker who took a wrong turn somewhere and ended up lost. But he hadn't been dressed like a hiker, not in jeans and a chino shirt and tennies. And even if he was lost, why hadn't he simply knocked on Jasper's door and asked for help? Why go to all the trouble of breaking into his house while Jasper was gone? And how *had* he broken in? Jasper had found no evidence of a jimmied door or window.

Well, now, that was certainly something to think about. If the guy had managed to break into Jasper's cabin without leaving any evidence behind, then he must have known what the hell he was doing. And if he knew what he was doing, what did that make him? An honest-to-God crook? Burglar? Sneak thief? What was it old George W. used to call the bad guys? Evildoers?

Jasper couldn't believe it. Of course, right on top of not believing it, Jasper also realized maybe he didn't *want* to believe it. Fact was, he liked the looks of the guy. And he felt sorry for him. And if Lola had taken to him so readily, then surely to crap he wasn't a serial killer or anything equally horrible. Just a young guy down on his luck with nowhere to stay and sicker than hell. Nobody to be afraid of, certainly. Jasper was convinced of that. That conviction ricocheted through Jasper's head for a couple of minutes. *Was* there anything to be afraid of here? Or if not afraid, at least *leery* of? He supposed he'd better do a little investigating, just to be sure. The guy would never know. He was still out like a light.

With a twinge of guilt, Jasper scooped up the man's wet trousers from the floor where he'd tossed them. He emptied out the pockets and laid everything he found on the coffee table. Quietly. He really felt bad about snooping through the guy's stuff. But still….

He quickly realized there wasn't much to snoop through. A few coins. A wet wad of one-dollar bills crumpled into a ball—no more than six or seven bucks in all. An automobile key with a Cadillac emblem on it that looked new. A wallet with a few pieces of ID inside. Social security card. California driver's license. Supermarket discount card. A couple of scraps of paper with something scribbled on them he couldn't read, and a store receipt so faded Jasper couldn't make heads or tails out of it, either.

And that was all.

The Cadillac key was a little perplexing. If the guy had a Caddy, where the hell was it? Why was he on foot? Had it broken down somewhere? Was that why the man was here? But if it was, it still didn't explain why he had chosen to hide in the trees long enough to make himself so ill. If it took a downpour to make him seek shelter, and even then only in a hog house, then there must be a pretty good reason for it. And Jasper was beginning to have a hard time believing the reason was strictly legitimate.

Something was definitely fishy here.

Once again, Jasper picked up the driver's license and studied it.

Timothy Sebastian Harwell, it read. Jasper counted back from the guy's birthday and realized, yep, twenty years old. In fact, next week he would be *exactly* twenty years old. He really was almost a kid. Jasper checked out the address on the license. It was a San Diego address, but Jasper didn't recognize the street. Could have been anywhere in the city.

He turned his eyes back to the young man's picture and smiled. The kid was a photogenic little shit, no two ways around that. Jasper's driver's license picture made him look like a Neanderthal. (He really should have shaved the morning they took it.) But Timothy Harwell's picture was gorgeous. The guy even had a big grin on his face. And it was a very nice grin too. Jasper found himself grinning back. That was the moment when Jasper decided to trust the guy. He was too sick for Jasper to fear him anyway. Jasper didn't think the young man could even stand up, let alone hold him for ransom or anything equally contentious. And if threats of bodily harm did come into play, Jasper felt reasonably sure he could pound the guy into a bloody pulp without too much trouble. Jasper was a head taller and twice as muscular, for heaven's sake.

Jasper looked over at the guy sprawled out on the sofa like a dead thing.

"Well, Timothy Sebastian Harwell," he whispered to himself, making the dogs perk up their ears. "What exactly did you do to get yourself in this pickle, huh? Something illegal, maybe? Why else would you be hiding out in my woods?"

No response, of course. The guy was out cold. Still, he looked so damned innocent. And, at the moment, pathetic. *Truly* pathetic.

Jasper reached out and pushed the thick black flap of hair out of the young man's face again. He removed the damp cloth he had placed on Timothy's forehead and dried the skin with his shirt cuff. Timothy's eyeballs rolled around under his lids, but that was the only response Jasper got. The young man's skin was still hot to the touch. Maybe even hotter than it had been earlier.

Christ. Poor guy. Soup! Get the guy some soup, dipshit! He needs food and fluids and medicine. Don't just sit here pondering and petting! Do something to help!

Softly, so as not to disturb either the patient or the dog, Jasper headed for the kitchen. On the way, he tossed his own and the stranger's wet clothes into the washer by the back door. Then he tossed in the guy's tennis shoes as well and started the thing up.

He moved to the cupboard, found a can of soup that looked nutritious, opened it with a can opener, poured it into a bowl, and tossed it in the microwave. While it heated, he filled the teakettle and set it on the stove, then turned the flame up all the way so the water would heat quickly. He grabbed a serving tray, which he never used, and when the soup was hot and the water boiling, made a cup of tea and placed everything on the tray, along with a shitload of paper napkins, since he suspected he might be pouring the stuff down the young man's throat and that could get messy.

Jasper scooped up the tray, headed for the living room, and stopped in his tracks three feet in.

Timothy Sebastian Harwell was staring at him from the sofa with the biggest, brownest eyes Jasper had ever seen. At the moment, the look in those eyes expressed considerable confusion.

"Hi," Jasper said, gathering his wits about him and moving to the coffee table, where he carefully set down the tray so as not to slosh the soup. "You're awake."

The young man's eyes never left Jasper's face. His lips parted as if he intended to say something, but no sound came out.

Jasper perched himself on the edge of the sofa beside the young man and leaned close.

"I'm sorry, Tim. Are you trying to say something?"

A horrible shudder trembled through the man's body, almost like a seizure. His hand came out from beneath the blanket and clamped onto Jasper's arm. The grip was astonishingly strong. It took a concerted effort for Jasper not to wince.

Still, the young man did not speak. His eyes were bright with fever as he stared at Jasper's face, but Jasper had the oddest feeling the man wasn't really looking at him; the man wasn't actually seeing *anything*.

Jasper laid his free hand on Harwell's forehead to check his temperature again, and it was almost like laying one's hand on the side of a pot-bellied stove when a damn good fire was burning inside. His fever was worse, or seemed to be. Jasper was no expert, but he was starting to get a little scared here.

He watched as the young man erupted into another uncontrollable shudder, and this time his teeth clenched tight and he gave a gasp of pain.

Jasper cooed some nonsense words of comfort while he shook out a couple of aspirin from the bottle. He tried to poke the pills between the young man's lips, but the kid's teeth were still clenched. Jasper couldn't get the medicine inside.

Then Jasper had a better idea. He laid four aspirin on the coffee table and mashed them into powder with the bowl of a spoon and, with the heel of his hand, scooped the powder into the tea. He got himself better situated and lifted the young man's head enough to spoon some of the tea into his mouth. This time it worked. The tea slid between the kid's clenched teeth, and spoonful by spoonful, Jasper finally got most of the liquid down his patient's throat.

By the time he was finished, the rictus of shuddering had passed. Again, the young man opened his eyes and gazed at Jasper. This time there was awareness in them, and Jasper smiled to see it.

"Hi," Jasper said with a gentle grin, resting the palm of his hand along the patient's cheek.

The young man lifted his hand and covered Jasper's. Then he wove his fingers through Jasper's and held on like a drowning man clutching the side of a boat.

"Thank you," he hissed.

"You're welcome." Jasper smiled. "Let's get some soup in you too, okay?"

But by the time the words were out of Jasper's mouth, his patient was once again sound asleep. It might have been Jasper's imagination, but he thought Timothy was at least breathing a little easier. Maybe the liquid had helped. And the aspirin wouldn't hurt either, once it had a chance to work. Jasper decided to wait a while before trying to get some soup down the man. Sleep was probably as important as food at this point.

He started to pull his hand away and rise, but the young man tightened his grip on Jasper's fingers—in his sleep. Jasper waited a minute and then tried again to extract them from the young man's grip, but the guy was holding on for dear life.

Jasper didn't know what to do.

Finally, he made himself as comfortable as he could, perched as he was on the edge of the sofa with the young man's hip pressing into his leg, and waited. And while he waited, he studied Timothy's handsome face.

He studied it for what seemed like ages. In fact, more than an hour passed.

When Jasper woke up, his head was resting on Timothy's chest. He jerked awake with a start. Christ, he had dozed off! Jasper lifted his head to look at his patient.

And lo and behold, this time his patient was looking back through clearer eyes. He was no longer trembling and his cheeks were less flushed too. Maybe the fever was going down.

Jasper gave what he hoped was a welcoming smile, and much to his amazement, Timothy Sebastian Harwell smiled back. It was weak, but it was most definitely a smile. And a beautiful smile it was too.

Jasper's heart gave a tiny lurch to see it aimed in his direction.

Then Jasper thought maybe the guy wasn't completely back to reality after all because of the words he uttered. They didn't seem to make a whole lot of sense.

"Beautiful…," he said, "…no shirt." And something else that sounded like "bucket".

And with that, the young man's eyes closed again. But this time when he tumbled into sleep, there was less misery on his face. He looked almost peaceful. At least Jasper thought he did.

Jasper sat speechless, trying to analyze what the man had said. The meaning behind the words. Had he meant what Jasper *thought* he meant? Then Jasper smiled. Well, *there* was an interesting plot twist. Maybe.

With his paw no longer being held in a death grip, Jasper gently laid his hand across Timothy's forehead. He was no expert, but it certainly seemed the fever had diminished a bit, although the young man's skin was still hot to the touch. Thankful for that much, Jasper stiffly rose. He had been sitting in an awkward position too long. Taking the tray, he headed back to the kitchen. When his patient awoke again, Jasper would try to get some soup down him.

Until then, Jasper thought, he would do some pondering while the poor guy rested. Later, when he woke up, Jasper would try to get the man cleaned up a little bit. He smelled like he hadn't bathed in a few days. Once again, Jasper wondered how long his guest had been hiding among the trees before he crawled into the hog house to get out of the rain. He knew the man had been there yesterday. The footprint he'd found the day before proved that. And there was also the indisputable fact of the break-in, although again, satisfied nothing had been taken, Jasper wasn't inclined to hold a grudge about it. What sort of schmuck holds a grudge against a hungry man searching for food?

Jasper scurried around doing this and that and finally parked himself at the kitchen table with his own cup of tea and a bag of cookies. He sipped his Earl Grey and listened to the rain pepper the roof. It sounded like it was going to be coming down all day, not that Jasper minded. Idly patting Jumper's head as the dog sat beside him staring up at him and begging for crumbs, Jasper once again tried to imagine how the young man might have found his way to this lonely mountain. But more importantly—*why* he had found his way here. The more Jasper thought about it, the more it bothered him.

The guy might be cuter than hell, but still, something wasn't right. And once his patient was on the mend, Jasper was determined to find out what it was.

Jasper revisited the words his young charge had uttered moments before.

"Beautiful... no shirt." And what was that other thing he said. Bucket?

Jasper clipped off a wry chuckle. Maybe the guy was still out of his mind after all. Jasper thought it best not to make too much of the young man's words, nor to get any amorous ideas into his head. Not on the basis of one delirious statement from a sick stranger about how Jasper looked while sitting half-dressed on a goddamn bucket. Delirious people were known to say all kinds of strange stuff. Jasper figured it would be better if he forgot what Harwell said completely. That would be the adult approach.

Jasper's face twisted into a self-deprecating grin. It was nice to know that once in a while, at least, his common sense could still override the influence of his dick. Not often. But occasionally.

Maybe he wasn't a totally desperate slut after all.

Chapter FOUR

JASPER was vaguely astonished to realize he had a flair for this nursing business. He really did.

He also had a hard-on. A big one. And it was being strangled to death in the crotch of his blue jeans.

His houseguest was laid out naked in front of him while Jasper gave the guy a sponge bath. Jasper had to. Timothy Sebastian Harwell was starting to stink.

The young man had slept like a dead thing through the entire night. Jasper had trudged up and down the staircase so many times to tend the fire and look in on his patient that, along about three in the morning, he curled up on the recliner by the sofa and slept there, leaving his bed to the animals. He didn't really get that much sleep, what with his patient moaning and the fire crackling and the rainstorm pounding the cabin roof.

He finally gave up trying to sleep, pulled on some clothes, grabbed a flashlight, and ran through the mud to check on Harry and Harriet. They were sound asleep under a mound of straw, all snuggled up side by side. Rather than wake them, Jasper ran back through the rain and ducked back into the cabin, shaking himself dry like a dog.

It was now well into the wet, wet morning and Timothy had been sleeping for the better part of a day and a night with only brief moments of wakefulness. The dawn had materialized around an ugly gray sky, which was still vomiting vast amounts of rain onto Jasper's mountain. During all that time, Timothy had not uttered another word, aside from those three or four largely unintelligible words he had coughed up the day before. In fact, during the morning's waking moments, Jasper wasn't sure if the guy's eyes were focusing at all. He lay there looking straight up at the ceiling, sometimes shivering with cold, other times sweating bullets from the fever that still tore through him. When the chills hit, Jasper could hear his teeth clatter all the way across the cabin. Eventually, Timmy would fall asleep again, and Jasper was always grateful when he did. Somehow he worried less about his patient when the man was sleeping. Awake, there was too much pain on his face, too much struggle to breathe. Asleep, at least, Jasper knew he wasn't suffering.

It was Jasper who finally took the initiative in getting the guy to the toilet. He suspected Timmy needed to go. And he was right. All Jasper had to do was wait for one of the man's waking periods in which to execute his plan.

Along about eight o'clock in the morning, with the first flutter of the man's eyelids, Jasper had scooped him up like a baby and carried him off to the bathroom, where he carefully set the guy on the commode so he could do his business. Timmy (which was what Jasper was calling him now, because he *seemed* like a Timmy) had been so humiliated by the experience, he had sat there weeping even while his body took the common sense approach of doing what needed to be done.

Timmy was so weak he couldn't clean himself afterward, so Jasper used a series of washcloths to clean the young man's bottom, and again Timmy started to weep.

Jasper had cooed and tsked and tut-tutted the whole thing away, trying to make Timmy feel less embarrassed, but he wasn't sure if he'd succeeded. And Jasper had to concede if their roles were reversed, he would be just as mortified as Timmy. Still, bodily functions took precedence over squeamishness. Jasper was sure Timmy would have been even more horrified if he had relieved himself all over the couch.

On rubbery legs, Timmy had been able to walk back to the sofa with Jasper holding him up, but the minute he lay down, he was once again out like a light. Or pretending to be because of the shame he felt over the bathroom ordeal. And even if he was pretending, which Jasper was pretty sure he was, he figured it gave him the perfect opportunity to clean the guy up. Jasper didn't want to see Timmy crying from embarrassment again, so he had no qualms whatsoever about sponging the guy down while he slept. Or pretended to sleep.

And now it was Jasper's turn to be embarrassed. He hadn't expected to find this nursing business such an all-fired turn-on. It wouldn't be so bad if the little guy wasn't so damned cute. But he was. And he was still burning up with fever, his hot skin more arousing than it would have been anyway. Jasper tried not to linger. Just get the job done and go on to something else, like finally getting some more soup inside his patient. But while trying to be gentle as he worked over Timmy's body, Jasper was aware of feeling somewhat erotically charged. He couldn't help it.

And apparently, Jasper wasn't the only one feeling a wee bit aroused. While Jasper soaped Timmy's crotch, he felt distinct movement under his hand as the young man's cock gave a lurch and started swelling, pulsating to the rhythm of his beating heart. Jasper was hypnotized by the transformation. Timmy's dick going from flaccid to erect was one of the most beautiful things he had ever witnessed in his life.

But still Jasper felt like a perv. The guy was practically on his deathbed for Christ's sake, and here Jasper was washing his boner. And a substantial boner it was too. Thick. Uncut. Luscious. Still, Timmy was weak already. If Jasper actually stroked him to ejaculation, the man would probably drop dead on the spot, his last ounce of strength shooting off into the morning air.

Jasper dug down deep and found a modicum of restraint tucked away somewhere in his abdomen. It was a funny thing, actually. He had spent his whole life never knowing it was there. He chuckled at that thought. God, he was a putz.

In the end, there was only one way for Jasper to get the job done. He simply had to look away while he ran the soapy cloth over the young man's flesh, then look down at the rag as he wrung out the soap and away again as he sponged Timmy down with clear water to wash away the suds, ignoring as best he could the bobbing cock beneath his washcloth. When Jasper finished washing and rinsing the boy from the waist down, he toweled him dry and breathed a sigh of relief as he covered the boy up all the way to his belly button. Then Jasper executed the same procedure on Timmy's torso, which was still an erotic experience, but at least Jasper didn't have to look at that tempting cock laid out in front of him.

With the young man's torso washed and dried, Jasper tucked the blankets around his patient and sat there on the edge of the sofa gazing at the guy. God, what a trial that was. Jasper's hands were shaking, and his own erection was still begging for a little attention, which he refused to give it. Toddling off to the kitchen to whack off would have truly been too perv-like to contemplate. So Jasper sat there by the young man's side long enough for both their hearts to stop pitter-pattering excitedly inside their chests.

After a while, the young man's body was once again rattled by an explosion of shivers, then the shivering stopped and his fever flared up. But soon, even the fever seemed to recede. While Timmy didn't speak, he did moan occasionally. And once, just once, he reached out and stroked the hair on Jasper's forearm, as if to say "thank you for being here," or maybe just to reassure himself he was not alone. Jasper tried to think of what comforting words to say in response to the gentle, needy touch, but then another round of teeth-clattering chills set in, and the moment was lost.

While that gentle moment lasted, however, Jasper had enjoyed the man's touch. Enjoyed it a lot. Too much, maybe.

He gathered up his wash pan and cloths and towels and headed for the kitchen. Once there, he threw the linens in the washer and rinsed out the metal pan and hung it on the wall outside the back door. Then he stood at the door watching the rain come down, all the while fingering his cell phone, turning it over and over in his hand.

Jasper was still undecided about calling the paramedics. His patient didn't seem to be getting any worse, but Jasper couldn't see him getting any better, either. His greatest fear was that Timmy had a burgeoning case of pneumonia and needed some antibiotics to knock it out. But he wasn't coughing. You coughed with pneumonia, didn't you? The worst symptom the man exhibited, aside from the fever and chills, was his labored breathing. And that had never abated. Jasper could hear him all over the house as he fought to breathe. Could it be the guy just had a horrific case of flu, complicated by the fact that he had been lying out in the hog house, half-dressed, during the worst rainstorm Jasper had seen in a decade? Would a simple case of the flu, no matter how serious it was, make a man gasp for air like that? He wondered.

Okay, Jasper told himself, *I'll give the guy until tomorrow morning. If he isn't better by then, I'll either drive him down the mountain to the hospital, or have the EMTs come and pick him up.*

Closing the outside door to shut out the rain, Jasper moved to the door that opened into the living room. He stood there with his shoulder to the jamb, feet crossed, watching his poor, pathetic patient shivering across the room. The fireplace was doing its job. The room was nice and toasty. But the heat didn't seem to be getting inside the guy where it belonged. Jasper wondered what he could do about that.

More soup. It was the only thing he could think of, and in truth, Timmy had probably consumed less than a cup of the stuff even though Jasper had tried to spoon it down him half a dozen times already.

Well, so what? Maybe it was time to try again.

He once again heated the bowl, set up the tray, and moved everything to the coffee table, perching himself on the edge of the couch as he had done so many times before.

This time Jasper was shocked to see eyes studying him from under those thick black eyelashes the kid had. He not only looked awake, he looked fairly alert too. Jasper was so shocked he damn near dropped the tray.

"Well, damn," Jasper said. "Hello." Jasper reached over and laid his palm across his patient's forehead. Unless he was suffering from a bad case of wishful thinking, Jasper thought the guy's skin felt noticeably cooler.

The young man's face twisted into a weak smile while Jasper felt for a fever. He swallowed with a grimace, as if he had a sore throat. Then he said the first words he had spoken to Jasper all day that made a lick of sense. "You carried me in here, didn't you." It wasn't a question. It was a statement. And there was considerable gratitude in the way it was said too. At least Jasper thought there was.

"Yeah." Jasper nodded, releasing the guy's forehead and pressing the back of his fingers to Timmy's cheek, again gauging his temperature. "You were out in the hog house. Had to bring you inside before you lowered the property values."

For the umpteenth time that day, a tear leaked from the young man's eye. "Thank you," he said softly. "I think maybe I would have died if you hadn't."

"Yeah," Jasper said again, patting Timmy's arm in an awkward, conciliatory sort of way, when what he really wanted to do was pull him into his arms and give him a good hug to let him know everything would be okay. "I think maybe you would have too."

Timmy's eyes closed of their own volition. The young man couldn't seem to stop them. "I—I have to sleep. I'm sor—" And he was out once again.

Jasper smiled as he tucked the blankets around the man, for all the world like a doting mother. It took him a minute to realize he was smiling. But when he did realize it, he smiled even wider. Thank God the guy was better. What a relief! Maybe the fever had broken. Jasper wasn't sure. But at least it had gone down. And that was a very, very good thing. To prove to himself the fever really had lessened, he laid his palm softly across Timmy's forehead one more time. Yep. Definitely cooler. Still warm, but nothing like it had been.

Once again, Jasper pushed the guy's thick hair up out of his face. He let his fingers linger in it for a second, and then with a sigh, he pulled himself to his feet and headed for the cupboard by the window—where he kept the booze.

Jasper needed a drink. This nursing shit was kind of nerve-racking. Especially with all the sexual tension going along with it. At least there was sexual tension on *Jasper's* part. He wasn't so sure about Timmy. Maybe the guy's erection had simply been a knee-jerk reaction to having his dick washed down with a soapy rag. Maybe Jasper's gentle touch really had nothing to do with it at all.

Bummer.

Yep. He definitely needed a drink.

HOURS later, the rain had slackened a bit, but it was still pelting down pretty hard. Jasper kept reliving the feel of Timmy's dick growing hard beneath his hand, and the memory was driving him nuts. He wasn't sure why, but that had been one of the most erotic moments of his life. Hands down. To take his mind off of it, Jasper threw on a plastic poncho and slopped his way through the mud to check on Harry and Harriet again. If a torrential downpour, an acre of mud, and a couple of tiny porkers couldn't take his mind off sex, nothing could.

Harry and Harriet seemed to be doing just fine. They were still burrowed under the straw like a couple of gophers, snoring and snorting in their sleep, when Jasper poked his head through the hog house door. One of them, either Harry or Harriet, had poked a foot through the straw and it was twitching like crazy. Jasper wondered what pigs dreamed about, if anything. He quietly poured more feed into their pan and snuck off without waking them, content in knowing they were settling into their new surroundings with a minimum of PTSD.

Back at the cabin, Jasper once again started to worry about his patient. Jesus, the guy was sleeping so much. But his skin was cooler and his sleep seemed less restive, so Jasper begrudgingly left him to it. Maybe the kid's body knew what he needed better than Jasper did.

Once again, much to Jasper's consternation, Timmy slept through the entire day.

At sundown, when the rain was easing and this side of Jasper's mountain was sliding into darkness, the young man finally opened his eyes.

Jasper was sprawled out in the recliner, twiddling Jumper's ear and trying to jot down notes for his upcoming novel while juggling two sleeping cats that had taken up residence on his lap. Bobber was laid out on the rug in front of the fire, soaking up the heat, and Lola was cuddled up next to Timmy on the sofa. Both dogs were snoring like a couple of buzz saws.

With the cabin growing darker by the minute, Jasper was just thinking about throwing the felines off his lap so he could go around and turn on some lights when he glanced over at Timmy and found the young man staring at him.

Jasper blinked in surprise. In the orange firelight, his patient looked like he was burning up with fever again, but Jasper quickly realized it was a trick of the light.

Actually, the guy looked a hell of a lot better. And Jasper felt a broad grin creeping across his face when he realized it.

"Well, hello there, young man. Back to the world of the living, huh?"

Timmy's voice was crackly from disuse. "Not—sure. What time is it?"

"Don't you mean, 'what day is it'?"

"Why? How long have I been here?"

Jasper moved to the sofa and perched his ass on the edge of it. He laid a hand across the young man's forehead. The fever was gone.

Timmy rolled his eyes up to look at Jasper's hand, and Jasper realized he had probably been touching the guy long enough. He pulled his hand back and laid it in his own lap out of harm's way.

"Let's see," he said, trying to cover his own embarrassment for a change. "You've been in the cabin for two days. I'm not sure how long you were out in the woods making yourself sick by not asking for help. As for the hog house, you couldn't have been parked in there very long. Hell, I just built it."

"It's crooked," Timmy said.

And for the first time in two days, Jasper laughed. "Jesus, kid, are you an architect or something?"

"No. And I'm not a kid, either."

Jasper pursed his lips and nodded. "You're right. Sorry. But why *were* you out there in the woods, if you really *were* out there, which I'm assuming you were. I mean, you were the one who broke into the cabin, right?"

Timmy closed his eyes as if he really didn't like the direction the conversation was taking. "Sorry. I… was hungry. I tried not to take very much."

"It's okay, Timmy," Jasper said with an easy smile. "I wasn't accusing you of anything. But it would have been simpler if you had just knocked on my door and asked for help."

"Maybe," Timmy said. And after a beat of silence, he asked, "How did you know my name?"

Now it was Jasper's turn to look guilty. "I went through your pockets. Found your wallet. Don't hold it against me. It's not every day that I find an unconscious traveler in my hog house."

Timmy lifted the covers high enough to peek under them, then he tucked them more firmly under his chin. "I'm naked. Where are my clothes?"

"They're in the washer, what's left of them. Your shoes too. They were soaking wet, and I was afraid you were coming down with pneumonia, so I peeled them off you. Like I said, there wasn't much left of them anyway. If it ever stops raining, I'll hang them out on the line to dry. By the condition you and your clothes were in, it looked like you'd had a rough couple of days."

If Jasper was hoping that would encourage the guy to explain why the hell he was out there sleeping in the hog house, he was soon to be disappointed.

Timmy just said, "Thanks. I guess I was kind of a mess. You gave me a bath, too, didn't you? I seem to remember…."

Jasper jumped up, trying not to look embarrassed but fairly sure he was failing miserably at that too. "Yeah, well, you were starting to stink. But now that you're clean and wide awake, let me get you something to eat. Stay there and I'll bring it to you."

"Thank you," Timmy said again. "I am kind of hungry. And… I'm not sure I can get up. Sorry to be such a wuss."

"You're not a wuss," Jasper said and started toward the kitchen to prepare the guy a bowl of soup. And maybe some instant mashed potatoes. But before he got out of earshot, Timmy asked, "Where's the bathroom?"

"You don't remember?" Jasper asked, turning back.

Timmy looked confused. "No. I—"

"Come on," Jasper said. "I'll help you."

"But I'm naked."

"You're also weak as a kitten," Jasper said. "I won't look. Promise."

God, he was such a liar.

He helped the man to his feet, and with his arm around Timmy's back and his hand tucked in Timmy's armpit to hold him up, Jasper helped him to the bathroom. Once he was sure he was safely seated on the commode, Jasper closed the door behind him and headed to the kitchen to fix his patient something to eat.

His fingertips were aflame with the feel of Timmy's skin.

For the first time, Jasper truly realized how short the young man was. The top of Timmy's head came about to Jasper's chin. But that didn't bother Jasper so much. What bothered him was the velvet heat of the man's flesh. My God, it felt like sun-warmed satin. And his fever was almost gone, so that must be how the man felt *all the time*. Once again,

Jasper found himself trying to discourage a blossoming hard-on before it could creep down his pant leg and embarrass the fuck out of him when it came time to help Timmy back to the couch. Not sure he would win the battle by then, Jasper tugged his shirttail out of his jeans and let it hang down to disguise the evidence of his ill-timed lust. Jesus, didn't his dick have any sense of restraint at all?

And wasn't his dick concerned at all by the fact that it didn't know what the guy was doing hiding out in Jasper's trees to begin with? There was certainly something fishy there. And it was something Jasper would have to get to the bottom of. The last thing he needed or wanted was to find himself harboring a criminal. Although, if Timothy Sebastian Harwell was indeed a criminal, then he was the cutest one Jasper had ever seen.

When Harwell was stronger, Jasper would learn the truth. Either that, or show the guy the door. After all, he certainly had some explaining to do. For one thing, why the car key when he didn't have a car? And how had he been so adept at breaking into Jasper's cabin without leaving any evidence behind if he hadn't had a little experience in that line of work to begin with? And what sort of experience exactly? *Legal* experience? Seemed unlikely, to say the least.

And one more question. If he was a criminal on the lam, why did he look and act so goddamn cute and innocent? And why, pray tell, was Jasper falling for it hook, line, and sinker? Jasper wasn't that hard up, was he?

Well, maybe Jasper would omit that last question. If he were a woman, he would probably be thinking his biological clock was ticking, but being a man, well, he couldn't really blame it on that. And he knew he couldn't interrogate Harwell either. Not yet. The man was still far too sick to be hounded. But still, Jasper wanted some answers. And come to think of it, maybe the guy would talk more freely if he wasn't naked.

Duh.

That got Jasper moving. He rummaged through his dresser in the loft until he found a pair of pajamas. They were a gift from his ex-wife about a thousand years ago, and it was so typical of her to give him pajamas. She knew damn well Jasper always slept naked. He'd never worn pajamas in his life that he could recall. And just to prove his point, the damn things were still in the store wrapper.

Jasper ripped the plastic off and shook them out. They were hell and gone too big for Harwell, but it was the best Jasper could do on the spur of the moment.

He carried them to the bathroom, trying unsuccessfully to shake out the wrinkles en route. Jasper rapped gently on the door and tossed the pj's inside.

A moment later, he heard a muffled "thank you."

EVEN while sitting on the commode, bending over to retrieve the pajamas from the floor made the blood rush to Timmy's head. The walls whirled around him, and for one horrible moment, he thought he might fall flat on his face.

When his vision cleared, he looked at what Jasper Stone had tossed through the door. *Good God*, Timmy thought, *two or three of me will fit in these things. If I'm actually strong enough to walk, I'll probably walk right out of them and make myself naked again.*

Maybe that was the guy's plan. Yeah, right.

He pressed the pj's to his face and breathed in, hoping to find a trace of Stone's scent in the fabric. But they felt and smelled brand new. Timmy doubted if Jasper had ever had them against his skin at all. And wasn't that a damn shame.

Timmy could tell his fever was about gone, but he was still so ill he could barely think. Why his sex drive was still in gear was a mystery, because if the opportunity to partake of sex with Jasper Stone, or anyone else for that matter, ever actually arose, Timmy was pretty sure he wouldn't be up to the task. Hell, he could barely swallow without gasping for air like a guppy.

He still wondered if he had pneumonia. And if he did, he wondered what he could do about it. Bed rest, he supposed. Antibiotics might help, but Timmy had no intention of letting Stone haul him down off this mountain and lug him into an emergency room. Suddenly, Timmy's whereabouts would be known in a dozen different circles. Hospital records. DMV records, maybe, because they'd have to do a background check on him to see if he had insurance before they'd admit him as a patient. Police might be involved as soon as Stone told the doctors how Timmy came to be in his care. All kinds of shit could hit the fan.

And God knows where the meanest man in Tijuana had spies. Everywhere, probably. Timmy had a sneaking suspicion they were all on the lookout for little old Timothy Sebastian Harwell. The unluckiest turd in the bowl. Always was, always would be.

His life was such a mess!

Timmy pushed his arms through the sleeves of the pajama top because he was starting to shiver again. It wasn't that cold in the bathroom. The shivering was just part of his sickness, he knew. The flannel pajama top made him feel a little warmer. A little more protected.

Still sitting, he tucked his feet in the pj bottoms and pulled them up to his knees while he finished piddling around on the toilet, all the while wondering if he had the strength to stand up again.

Being helpless was a new experience for Timmy. He had always taken care of himself. Always. Maybe he didn't always do it with a great deal of *intelligence*, but at least he was his own boss. He was the one in control. He knew right now, right this very minute, he had the least amount of control over his whole situation than he had ever had over any situation in his whole stinking life. Oddly, for one of the first times ever, he was humiliated by the stupid act that had put him in this mess. He liked Stone. And he was horrified to think of the man finding out why Timmy had descended on his mountain in the first place.

At the moment, there was some sexual tension ricocheting between the two of them. Timmy sensed it as surely as Jasper Stone. And Stone *did* sense it. Timmy could see it in the man's eyes. Had felt it in the man's touch when Stone was bathing him.

All that would end the moment Jasper found out why Timmy was here. The realization made Timmy's heart ache, as if he didn't have enough things hurting already.

Goddammit, Timmy wanted the man to like him. That's all. Jeez, was that so much to ask? It's not like he was asking for a long-term relationship or anything. But a few hours of carnal pleasure (after he was feeling up to it) wouldn't do any lasting damage to anybody's sense of propriety. A few gentle words bandied back and forth wouldn't kill anybody either. The guy was a hunk, after all. And a sweet hunk at that. All Timmy wanted to do (later) was get his hands on the man and make him moan. In a good way, of course. And maybe let Stone coax a few moans out of him too.

He struggled to his feet and pulled the pajama bottoms up to his waist. Looking down at himself, he gave one of those moans he had been thinking about. Well, maybe not quite. This was more a moan of mortification. These butt-ugly pajamas hung all over him like a forty-foot flag on a ten-foot pole. And he'd been right. If he didn't watch what he was doing, he would be walking right out of them.

That is, if he could walk under his own steam at all.

On trembling legs, he managed to get to the bathroom sink—which was like two feet away—but even that was almost asking too much of his battered nervous system. While running his hands under the faucet and soaping them up with a bar of Ivory he found in a soap dish, he made the mistake of looking into the mirror.

Jesus God! He'd seen dead people with more color than he had. And his hair was sticking straight up off the top of his head as if his brains had exploded. Note to self: when trying to look attractive, don't lay around sick on someone's couch for three days with wet hair.

He dried his hands on a towel, then tried to walk to the door. He took three steps forward and had just managed to pull the bathroom door open when his strength simply petered out. With a cry, he lunged forward and hit the floor so hard all five of the man's animals stampeded across the cabin in different directions.

With his cheek against the carpet, Timmy got a sideways view of Stone's blue-jeaned legs and work boots rushing toward him. Timmy tried to laugh it off, to let the man know he was okay, just clumsy, but before he could do so much as chuckle, he was once again unconscious.

He never knew when Stone scooped him off the floor and gently laid him one more time upon the sofa by the fire. He didn't feel Stone's gentle hands try to arrange the humongous pajamas that were all twisted around him. And he didn't know when Stone once again tugged the blankets up, tucked them beneath his chin, and went quietly back to the kitchen to let the man sleep.

SOMETIME later, Timmy felt warmth beneath his hand and knew the dog was back. The beagle mix. She was lying at his side, just as she had done for the past two days. And as she had done out in the woods too. She seemed to like lying next to him, and Timmy found that sort of loyalty kind of humbling. He had never owned a dog in his life. Now, among all his other regrets, he was beginning to regret that too.

Jesus, had he ever done *anything* right?

As the evening deepened and Timmy swam in and out of consciousness, he gradually became aware of a change in sound, a softening of the noises around him. The cabin grew oddly silent but for the crackling of the fire. It took a while for his fevered mind to understand what the silence meant.

It was simple, really. The rain had finally stopped.

Chapter FIVE

TIMMY wasn't the only one who noticed a sudden hush in the thrum of background noise that had resonated through the cabin for the last couple of days. Often those changes in ambient sound take a while for the mind to grasp. Like the ticking of the clock beside Jasper's bed. Sometimes it was annoyingly loud, but more often, he didn't hear it at all. It was just there. Like the beating of his own heart. Jasper opened his eyes to the new sound level sometime around three in the morning. At first he couldn't understand what was different. He knew the rain had stopped. That had happened earlier. But now it was something else. There was a hush in the air he couldn't quite understand.

Then he realized what it was. His patient was breathing easier. Like the noisy old clock beside his bed, the sound of Harwell fighting to breathe was the sort of monotonous, unbroken sound that ceases to register after a while. But when it stops, and the silence comes rushing back in like a percussion wave, you notice it right away. Jasper had been listening to that rasping, agonized sound for two days and nights. And now, like magic, it simply wasn't there anymore. The man was no longer gasping for air with every intake of breath. Jasper crawled from bed, eliciting a teeny growl from Bobber, who didn't appreciate being disturbed no matter what the reason.

Jasper gave the old dog a reassuring pat on the head as he swung his bare legs out of bed. Grabbing his bathrobe from the back of the chair, Jasper slung it around his nakedness and, on bare feet, quietly navigated the stairs down to the living room.

The room was lit only by the smoldering coals in the fireplace. Jasper gently laid a couple more chunks of firewood on the coals, then turned to squint through the darkness at the sofa where his patient lay.

Timmy's breathing no longer sounded like an old school bus grinding up a hill. He was breathing easily and smoothly. Jasper stepped closer and laid his hand softly against the young man's cheek. The fever was gone. Timmy's skin was cool to the touch. Cool and bristly. He needed a shave.

Jasper felt his own heart lighten at the man's improvement. Maybe he wouldn't have a corpse on his hands after all.

He jumped when Timmy spoke.

"I'm feeling better, if that's what you're wondering."

Jasper smiled, although he knew Harwell couldn't see it. "I'm glad. I thought you might be. You're breathing better. Did you notice?"

"Yeah," Timmy said. "I was just lying here thinking about it. I'm still pretty weak, but I don't feel so sick. I wonder if maybe you saved my life."

Jasper could feel a blush rising to his cheeks. "Well, I wouldn't go that far. All I did was save the pigs from having to put up with you."

They both laughed.

"Well," Jasper said, "if I can't get you anything, I'll go back to bed. I know you're tired."

"No, I'm okay. I've just been lying around too long. I need to sit up for a while."

Jasper heard the young man's bedclothes rustle. He was slowly hauling himself up to a sitting position. Judging by the moans and groans, the man obviously still had some hurt going on. Jasper went to a desk in the corner and flicked on a lamp. He settled himself into the recliner, and for the first time, the two men actually looked at each other.

Jasper saw a handsome young guy with tousled black hair in a pair of pajamas that would have held three of him. His eyes were at half-mast from having just awoken, but there was a look of relief on his face. Probably because he was no longer as sick as a dog. He looked like he knew he was on the mend, and Jasper was as happy about it as Timmy was.

From across the room, Timmy saw a man slightly older than himself. Handsome, brawny, with curly, mussed-up hair and a shadowy beard darkening his honest, open face. He also saw a strong, hairy chest peeking through the V of the bathrobe and muscular, hairy legs poking out from the bottom.

Timmy tried not to stare, but it wasn't an easy thing to do. Jasper Stone was just his type, and about the sexiest man Timmy had ever seen in his life. To take his mind off that, he tilted his head to the side and made a show of listening to the quiet night. "The rain stopped. It's not pounding on the roof anymore."

Jasper nodded. "Now we'll just have to wait for the mud to dry up."

"Not a big fan of mud, huh?"

"Not really."

The tone of the conversation shifted from light to serious in a heartbeat, and it was Timmy who shifted it. "I'm sorry I dumped myself in your lap like this. I didn't mean to. It just kinda happened."

Jasper steepled his fingertips under his nose and nodded. He kicked the footrest up on the recliner and made himself more comfortable. "Would you mind telling me *why* you dumped yourself in my lap? You're lucky to be alive, you know. You could have died out there. Hell, you damn near died *in here*. Seemed like it, anyway."

Timmy shrugged. As if it was no big deal. "Just hiking, you know. Took a wrong turn. Ended up lost. Stupid, really." He studied the flames in the fireplace because he couldn't bring himself to peer at Jasper's face. It was an honest face. People with honest faces can spot bullshit a mile away. Or Timmy always imagined they could. Being a fairly proficient liar, he was tuned in to things like that. He wasn't particularly proud of it, but he was.

Jasper didn't believe Timmy's story, but he suspected this was not the proper time to really grill the guy. Even now, after sitting up for just a few minutes, Timmy was already looking tired. His voice was weaker, hoarser, like sick people's voices get when they're about done in. If there were questions that needed answering, they could certainly wait.

Except for the one question foremost in Jasper's mind. *That* one he would really like answered.

"Timmy, is there anyone we should call to let them know you're okay? *Somebody* must be missing you, worrying about you. Work, maybe? Family?"

Timmy couldn't have looked more startled if a rattlesnake had materialized in his lap.

"Why? Has someone been looking for me?" He leaned forward, as tense as a bowstring. His brown eyes burned into Jasper's as he waited for a response.

"No," Jasper said calmly, ignoring the quickening of his own heart. He had hit a nerve and he knew it. "Were you expecting someone to come knocking?"

Timmy shuffled around, trying to look nonchalant, trying to regain his composure. Jesus, he almost blew it there. "No... no. No one is looking for me. Why would they be?" Timmy wilted back into the couch. All this lying was wearing him out. Usually, it didn't bother him at all. Of course, now he was only running on about three cylinders, if that.

"You're not looking so good all of a sudden," Jasper observed. "Maybe you should lie back down. Get some sleep. We can talk tomorrow."

The man was right, of course. Timmy could feel his energy draining away even as he listened to Stone's words. A shame, really. Here Timmy was about to get a little flirty. Now he knew he didn't have the energy even for that. The innocent question Jasper had asked about anyone looking for him had zapped the strength right out of him. He needed to be by himself for a while to figure out how to handle all this. Should he tell Jasper the truth? Hell, no. The man would throw him out on his ear, and Timmy needed to lie low for a while until he could decide what to do.

He flashed an innocent grin in Jasper's direction, hoping to minimize the damage. "I think you're right. I need to sleep. I really am sorry to be such a pain in the ass."

Jasper shook his head. "I shouldn't be bugging you with all these questions. I'm sorry. Go to sleep. Your female is waiting for you."

Timmy looked down at Lola cuddled up at his back. He had to scootch her over to make room for himself on the sofa. She didn't even wake up when he slid her sideways.

"My female." Timmy grinned. "There's a first." And he sprawled out with his back to the dog, resting his head on his hand and staring into the fire. Jasper had already turned out the light. Timmy wondered what the man was making of that last comment. If anything.

"Good night," Timmy said, when he heard Jasper's footsteps climbing the stairs to the loft behind him. "Thank you, Jasper."

"You're welcome, kid. Good night."

Timmy thought there was a smile in the man's voice, so maybe he hadn't done as much damage as he thought he had. That was a relief. At least he hadn't lied his way back out into the cold quite yet. But he also knew Jasper hadn't bought that bit of bullshit about hiking and losing his way.

Timmy thought of that one nasty-ass foster home back in Indiana where he stayed for a while when he was a kid. What was it the old man used to say before he came at Timmy with a switch to beat the lying out of him? Oh yeah.

"That dog don't hunt, son. That dog don't hunt."

God, Timmy had hated that cruel, Bible-spouting old asshole.

Timmy closed his eyes against a rush of weariness that seemed to come out of nowhere and slap the crap out of him. It hit him with such force, he actually went cross-eyed for a minute. Sometimes even when he *wasn't* sick, those miserable childhood memories would floor him, sending him into a spiral of depression. For comfort, and to feel her welcome heat, he rested a hand on Lola's side. Somehow, it eased his mind.

Nope, Timmy decided, dragging himself back to the present and listening to the squeak of the man's bed above his head. Jasper was no fool. He hadn't bought Timmy's pack of lies at all. What astounded Timmy was the fact that the man was too nice to say so. So basically, Jasper Stone was sexy *and* nice. Wow. In Timmy's eyes, that was about the most lethal combination there was.

Timmy's weariness of mind and body finally got the upper hand. He dozed. Even the aches pounding through him from whatever it was he suffered from couldn't keep several unchaste thoughts from tap-dancing through his head as he closed his eyes.

But soon even those thoughts were lost. Timmy slept like a dead man. And it was just what he needed. Above his head, Jasper lay awake until dawn, staring at the ceiling and wondering why the man below had felt the need to lie.

What exactly was Timothy Harwell covering up? And why was Jasper so damned attracted to him, even when he knew he was being played for a sap?

Clinging to the very edge of the bed because Jumper and Bobber and the two cats had commandeered the middle of it, Jasper gritted his teeth and girded his loins. So to speak. Tomorrow he'd get some truthful answers or Harwell would find himself sleeping in the woods again.

Maybe.

JASPER was dressed for the day and enjoying his morning coffee on the front porch, as he often did. All his animals were snoozing on the plank floor around him except for Fiji, who was pestering an alligator lizard out by the Jeep. And that was what *they* often did. Jasper could hear Timmy showering and moving around in the bathroom. The young man had made it there with no help from Jasper about thirty minutes ago, and except for one brief moment when Timmy stuck his head through the bathroom door and humbly asked if Jasper had an extra toothbrush (which he did), Jasper hadn't seen the guy since.

Jasper was happy to see Timmy looked a little stronger this morning, but he obviously still wasn't out of the woods. While he did make it to the bathroom under his own steam, he didn't do it with any sort of bounce in his step. In fact he had to hold onto something every step of the way, even while pleading with Jasper to let him do it himself. Timmy's dark, handsome eyes had that world-weary look sick people's got, and Jasper still wasn't sure a trip to the emergency room would be such a bad idea.

The dawn had opened up on a clear California sky. Not a rain cloud anywhere in sight, and after the last two days of torrential downpours, that was a blessing indeed. The trees of Endor that surrounded the cabin were still shedding themselves of the rain, shaking themselves off like happy giants in the freshening breeze that blew up the hillside. Jasper could hear the flurry of pattering drops tapping onto the carpet of pine needles below their sparkling, rain-washed limbs. The birds were having a gay old time too. Singing and flitting around. Apparently they were as happy as Jasper the rain had finally stopped. The temperature was back to normal, too, and it was going to be a hot day. Humidity would be up as well, what with all the moisture the sky had dumped on the mountain and foothills. But that was okay. At least the mountain would be drying out. He wouldn't have to slop through mud for the rest of his life.

While Jasper nursed his coffee and waited for Timmy to make an appearance, he looked down at the side of his rocking chair yet again and studied his two new acquisitions.

Harry and Harriet were sniffing around the three dogs, trying to be friendly, while the three dogs were trying to figure out what the hell these two annoying creatures were. Apparently, they had never seen pigs before in their lives.

The piglets had been so happy to see Jasper that morning when he took them their ration of mash, he hadn't the heart to leave them behind afterward. They looked so pathetic, staring after him with their little white snouts stuck through the gate and those big sad eyes watching him like a hawk, he had backtracked, swung the gate open, and laughed as they trundled along beside him back to the cabin for all the world like a couple of playful puppies.

After a while, a nervous alliance was reached between Jasper's many charges. Dogs, cats, and pigs. When they all lay down and fell asleep together, Jasper knew a satisfactory détente had been forged. Now they were friends. Great. It was just what he knew would happen. Now he had two more pets. Even Guatemala, the tabby cat, found the piglets acceptable company and proceeded to clean his bottom quite contentedly while Harry snored and twitched and grunted in his sleep next to him.

Jasper was still trying to figure out what to do about his uninvited houseguest. He didn't mind having the guy around, and he didn't mind helping a stranger out, either. The only thing that worried him was the mystery needing to be explained.

And he didn't like being lied to. He didn't like that at all.

How could no one be looking for the young man? How could Timmy be on foot way the hell out here in the middle of nowhere without so much as a backpack and a decent pair of hiking boots? If he had nothing to hide, why had he hung around the woods for two or three days without making his presence known? And why had he found it preferable to break into the cabin to find something to eat the minute Jasper roared off down the hill in his Jeep rather than simply asking for a little help like a normal person would?

Well, one way or another, Jasper was determined to get to the bottom of things today. For all Jasper knew, the guy could be a fugitive from justice. Because Harwell was cuter than hell didn't mean he was a saint. And because the possibility he wasn't a saint was a bit of an added turn-on wasn't an acceptable reason for keeping the guy around, either. Or was it? *God*, Jasper thought, *I really am a slut.*

He chuckled into his coffee, then sat up straighter when he heard the bathroom door squeak open inside the cabin.

A minute later, Timmy peered through the doorway. Jasper noticed he kept a solid grip on the doorframe to hold himself up. He looked even smaller than Jasper remembered him, still swathed in the pajamas that were a good five or six sizes too big for his small frame. But mainly that impression came from the fact that Timmy was sort of… drawn *in* upon himself. As sick people sometimes are. As if they're shielding themselves from further pain. Or every movement is a misery to contemplate. He was clutching a fistful of waistband to keep the oversized pajama bottoms from sliding off his ass.

"Morning," Jasper said with a smile, since the guy looked like he needed a smile about now.

Timmy nodded in greeting and squinted out past the porch rail to take in the view. He had to clear his throat a couple of times to get his voice to work. He hadn't used it much lately.

"It's beautiful here," he said. He tilted his head and stared off into the woods. "Hear the doves?"

"Yeah." Jasper grinned. "They go at it all day long in the trees. Sound like owls to most city people, but you knew they were doves right away. How come?"

Timmy shrugged. "Spent some time on a farm when I was a kid." He tilted his head at the other rocking chair. "Mind if I join you?"

Jasper started, appalled by his own lack of courtesy. "Oh crap, Tim. No. I mean, yes. Have a seat by all means. You shouldn't be standing there anyway. You still look awfully weak. Sit for a while, then I'll go fix us both some breakfast. Want some coffee?"

Timmy carefully stepped to the rocker and eased himself into it. By the time he was seated, his legs were shaking. That's how weak he was. Jasper saw it too.

"No coffee. Thanks. Never much cared for it." His voice was still only about two notches above a whisper. His weariness seemed to have settled all the way down to his bones.

"I'll get you some juice then. Won't take a minute." Jasper carefully set his coffee cup on the porch rail, then jumped up and disappeared into the cabin. He was back in less than a minute with a tumbler of cold orange juice. He handed it to Timmy, fighting the urge to reach out and feel the man's forehead. He supposed he had done that enough lately. Timmy was probably getting tired of it. Although Jasper sure as hell wasn't. This time he decided to hand out a little free advice instead. "You probably should stay in bed another day. You don't look too good."

Timmy tucked a leg under himself and sat in the chair like a kid, rocking gently, sipping his juice, holding the glass with both hands. His eyes were wide and bright over the rim of the glass. The man sure did have an angelic face, Jasper thought. Even now, it made Jasper's heart ache a little bit to look at it.

He went back to his own rocker, sidestepping all the animals as he went.

He caught Timmy staring at the floor with a bemused look on his face. When Jasper was at last situated comfortably in his rocker, had retrieved his cup of coffee from the porch rail, and had it tucked comfortably under his chin, Timmy said, "I thought I was getting better, but maybe not. Either I'm hallucinating or there's a couple of pigs sleeping in amongst your dogs and cats. Cute little guys too."

Jasper laughed. "Those aren't hallucinations. They are the beginnings of a fine herd of Yorkshire hogs. As soon as they hit puberty, they'll get started on that, I reckon. Right now they're pretty much, umm, pets."

"Pets?"

"Pets. I just decided that this morning. Or they did. I'm not quite sure which of us it was. Anyway, now they're pets. Apparently."

Timmy gave Jasper a long, searching look. He didn't look too convinced by whatever it was he was looking at. "So you're a hog baron then."

Jasper spit up a good guffaw. "Hell, no! I'm a writer. The hogs are a sideline. I just thought it would be fun to grow my own pork sausages for a change. I won't be eating *these* guys, of course. They're too much like family already. But in a year or two their descendants might be tasty." He looked down fondly at Harry and Harriet, who were still snorting and twitching in their sleep. "Or they will be if these two ever grow up and start fucking."

Timmy studied the man across the porch. Jesus, Jasper Stone really *was* nice. Timmy didn't run into many nice people in his line of work. He found himself wanting to spill his guts. Tell Jasper everything. But caution prevented him from doing it. Caution and maybe a little common sense. While Timmy was drawn to this man in just about every way imaginable, he also knew he *needed* him. He needed Jasper to let him stay. For a little while. Until he was on his feet; until he was stronger; until the hounds of hell that were no doubt nipping at his ass right this very minute lost his scent.

Until he could figure out what to do about this mess he had gotten himself into.

Jasper Stone had simpler things on his mind. "I'll get your clothes dried today so you can walk around without the threat of your pants falling off. Sorry those pj's are so big. I suspect they would even be too big for me. A gift from my wife. Bitch never did know how to shop."

Timmy's eyes widened a little. "Oh. So you're—" He had started to say *straight*, but he stopped himself in time. He wasn't sure why. "—*married*, then."

His host seemed to find that amusing. "Nope. Was once. Never again. Sorry. I should have said *ex-wife*. As in ex-*life.*"

Timmy stared into Jasper's eyes. They seemed to draw him in. God, the man was handsome.

Finally, Timmy said, "She probably left because of the pigs."

Jasper tilted his head back and laughed so hard he slopped coffee in his lap. While his head was tilted back like that, Timmy had an urge to stumble across the porch and press his lips to Jasper's scruffy, unshaved neck. The urge was so strong, it almost made him gasp. He felt his cock move around in those baggy-ass pajama bottoms, and he knew his dick had found the man's laughter as intoxicating as Timmy had. Good to know after everything he had been through, being sick and all, that a certain below-the-equator body part was still functioning. And judging by the sudden ramrod stiffness down there, it was functioning fine and dandy. Yessiree. He set his empty glass on the porch rail and laid his arms in his lap to hide his hard-on from his host, although he surely didn't want to.

Rather than speak, Timmy simply smiled at Jasper's laughter. When Jasper opened his eyes and saw Timmy's smile, the blood rushed to his head. Timmy's smile broadened when he saw the blush creep across Jasper's face. And then, strangely enough, Timmy felt it creep across his face too.

When Jasper finally spoke, all he said was, "I guess you'll live. Your color seems to be coming back."

"Yours too," Timmy said, and again his voice was husky. This time it wasn't the sickness. It was hunger. Hunger for the man across from him. And Timmy was reasonably sure the man knew it too.

In fact, a moment later, when Jasper hurriedly excused himself and headed through the front door to, in his words, round them up some breakfast, Timmy knew it for a fact.

He knew it by the sizable bulge in the crotch of Jasper Stone's blue jeans.

While the man puttered around the kitchen, rattling pans, clattering silverware, and probably hiding his embarrassment, Timmy sat on the porch and smiled.

Damn. He couldn't remember the last time he'd been this turned on. And if that wasn't a sign he was mending, he didn't know what was.

Chapter SIX

JASPER busied himself trying to look busy, banging the skillet down on the stove, slamming and reslamming the refrigerator door, grabbing this, grabbing that. What the hell just happened out there? Where had that surge of longing come from? One minute he and his visitor were bantering back and forth and laughing and having a perfectly normal conversation, and the next thing Jasper knew, his cock had taken over, and he was pretty sure Timmy's cock had sprung to attention too.

Wow. Jasper had never felt such an incredible rush of sexual desire in his life. And the guy wasn't even *well* yet! Hell, Timmy was still so weak, a good fuck would probably kill him.

Jasper stood stock still in the middle of the kitchen and chuckled quietly. Sick or not, the guy sure knew how to turn up the heat in a conversation. Or maybe Jasper's imagination had done that all by its little self. He wasn't sure. With a carton of eggs in one hand and a gallon milk jug in the other, Jasper gazed down at the hard-on still straining against his zipper, begging to be unleashed upon an unsuspecting world. It really wanted to wreak some mayhem. It really did.

"Stay where you are," he muttered down at himself.

And behind him, Timmy said, "Who you talking to?"

Jasper plunked the eggs and milk on the counter. With his back to Timmy, he grabbed a dish towel and pretended to dry his hands. When he was finished, he poked the towel under his belt and spread it out like an apron. Of course it was really there for another reason, and Jasper figured Timmy knew what that reason was. Still, some things are better left unmentioned.

That was Jasper's opinion, anyway.

He turned and motioned to the table. "Sit down. I'll scramble you some eggs. If you can't wait, there's the toaster. Make yourself some toast to tide you over. Jelly's in the fridge."

"I can wait," Timmy said, reluctantly dragging his eyes away from the dish towel at Jasper's waist. And what he suspected was hiding behind it. He shuffled barefoot to the kitchen table and pulled out one of the straight-backed chairs. He was still clutching the waistband of his pajamas with one hand to keep them from sliding to the floor. He lowered himself into the chair and gave a sigh. Sexual tension be damned; he was still as weak as a newborn. A hearty breakfast would do him good. Looking at Jasper wouldn't do him any harm either. Lord, the man was gorgeous.

Timmy smiled as he said, "You're a good man, Jasper Stone. Taking me in like this. Feeding me. Putting clothes on my back." *Making me horny*, he failed to add, although he really wanted to. And he was gratified to know that horniness seemed to be afflicting *everyone* this morning. *More* than gratified actually.

Jasper had six things going at once, and a hard-on was only one of them. He didn't fool around when he cooked. In seconds the kitchen was filled with the delicious scent of bacon crackling and spattering in the skillet. English muffins were heating up in the toaster, and in another skillet, frozen hash browns were browning nicely in a puddle of bacon grease and smelling like a little bit of heaven.

All the aromas combined to make Jasper's mouth water. There was something else in that kitchen making his mouth water, too, but he was trying not to think about Timmy sitting there three feet away in a pair of pajamas that could be *sneezed* off the guy, leaving nothing but a buck naked Timmy Harwell perched on his kitchen chair. Wow. *That* thought didn't help Jasper's boner disappear.

But in among all the sexual tension and the randy thoughts, Jasper was also beginning to feel a little put upon. He still didn't know one damn thing about the man sitting at his breakfast table, and that was starting to bother him. He decided to go about fishing for information in a different way. He was a writer. Surely to God he could be imaginative enough to get the answers he wanted.

While everything cooked and the kitchen filled with a mixture of heavenly aromas, Jasper refilled Timmy's glass with juice, then plopped down opposite the man. He gave Timmy what he hoped was a charming smile, trying to lower his defenses.

"Like I said, Tim, I want you to rest today. You still don't look so good." *That's a lie. The man looks scrumptious!* "I'll dry your clothes, and this evening I'll drive you home. I assume you live in the city."

Timmy nodded. He was dragging his fingertip through the ring of moisture left by his glass of orange juice, mindlessly drawing circles on the tabletop. Puttering. Avoiding eye contact. He looked like he was deep in thought, and Jasper became a little more suspicious than he already was. When Timmy finally said, "Okay," Jasper nodded and went back to the stove to flip the bacon and stir the hash browns. Muffins popped out of the toaster, and Jasper stood at the counter buttering them up.

Thank God, his hard-on had gone away. That was a relief. He tugged the dish towel out of his pants and tossed it in the sink.

Behind him, Timmy said, "I'll be ready when you want me to go." But even as he said the words, he knew he was lying. He *couldn't* leave the mountain. Not yet. He'd have to find a way around it. But not now. Later. Later when he was a little stronger. A good meal, a few more hours of sleep, and maybe then he could conjure up a plan for changing Jasper's mind about throwing him off the ranch. A smile tickled his lips. He had a pretty good idea how to go about it already.

Even while he thought those thoughts, Timmy was surprised to find a considerable amount of guilt rumbling around inside him. Guilt about not being straight with Jasper. Guilt about not telling him the truth. Guilt about *lying*. He wondered if he would be feeling the same guilt if Jasper was ugly as sin and weighed five hundred pounds. Probably not. Timmy had used people before. He didn't make it a way of life, using people, but the need had arisen now and then in the course of his twenty years on the planet. Funny thing, but Timmy didn't remember ever feeling guilty about it before.

Still....

His thoughts were interrupted by Jasper laying a plate in front of him heaped with a fine-looking breakfast. Timmy mumbled thanks, and they both dug in without another word.

Jasper smiled as he watched the kid eat. Kid. He had to stop thinking of the guy that way. He wasn't a kid. He was a young man. There was a difference. He had to stop calling him Timmy too. Timmy was a kid's name. He was Tim. *Tim.*

Jasper studied Tim while they ate. The man was so engrossed in his food, it was an easy thing for Jasper to do. Once in a while, Timmy would look over at him and grin, but then he would duck his head and go back to shoveling in the food. He looked like he hadn't eaten in a month.

Timmy's color had returned, and Jasper could see now that the man's skin tone was darker than his own, like maybe there was a Mexican ancestor in the woodpile somewhere. His hair was thick and black and it needed a cut. Or maybe Timmy liked it long. Either way, *Jasper* liked it long. It looked great on the guy, even if Timmy—*Tim!*—did have to push it out of his eyes every two minutes.

There was a brushing of dark hair across the back of the man's hands where they peeked out of the too-long pajama sleeves, and Jasper fought the urge to brush his fingers over it. Tim's hands were big and capable looking, with broad white nails trimmed short. In fact, for such a little guy, Tim's hands almost looked out of place. Like they'd been stuck on the wrong person by mistake.

Tim's eyes were dark, dark brown with a sunburst of gold in the center of the irises that rimmed the pupils, catching the light. It made Tim's eyes a magnet. They drew Jasper in every time they were even remotely aimed in his direction. There was a smudge of weariness below Tim's eyes, but Jasper figured that would go away when he got his strength back. The lashes bordering those gold-flecked eyes were the thickest and longest Jasper had ever seen. There probably wasn't a woman on the planet who wouldn't happily kill for those eyelashes.

The top button of the pajama shirt was unbuttoned, and Jasper was drawn to the triangular indentation at the base of his houseguest's throat. He found himself wondering how that spot would taste if he were to lay his tongue there. And if Tim would tremble with desire when he did.

When his dick stirred and threatened to come back to life in all its glory, Jasper forced himself to stop staring at the man across the table and concentrate on his food. And he succeeded reasonably well.

When his plate was empty, Jasper hauled himself to his feet with a contented groan and gently laid his plate and utensils in the sink.

"Got things to do," he said. "You go on eating. When you're done, go back to sleep. Later, we'll see about getting you home."

...tains the following 4 items and is sent by Nov 27,

...ey may have a different return address.

New Upgraded European & American Explosion Quantu... ×1

Black

Women's Vibrant Red Pointed-Toe Stiletto Heel Sandals ... ×1

Label size: CN 35(US 4.5) / Magenta

Timmy nodded and watched Jasper walk out the back door. He bit back a smile when a parade of dogs, cats, and pigs followed the man outside. Jeez, what a menagerie.

The minute the back door had slammed closed behind them, Tim's smile faded. A worried expression crossed his face, then a look of determination.

He knew one thing. He wasn't going anywhere. Not yet. By the time the sun went down, Jasper Stone would know it too. And when Tim got done with the man, he wouldn't mind at all.

It was then Tim started thinking about all the things he would do to Jasper Stone. *With* Jasper Stone. And in just a few hours, too, if his plan panned out.

He shoved in another forkful of hash browns, bit off a chunk of muffin, and felt a drop of moisture form at the tip of his hard-on even while he ate. He resisted the urge to take his cock in his hand and rub that moisture around with his thumb. My God, sick or not, he was horny as hell.

Tonight was going to be fun. He could hardly wait.

But he had a few things to do *before* tonight too. The thought made him a little nervous. If Jasper caught him in the act, it wouldn't be pretty.

He'd have to be careful. But that he could do. Timothy Harwell had spent his life being careful.

Well, until the goddamn Caddy Escalade had crossed his path.

THE days-long downpour had made a mess of the ranch. The whole place was swimming in mud. There were branches torn from the surrounding trees when the storm was at its peak, and Jasper casually grabbed up the ones in his path, tossing them out of the way. Only a sharp, if amused, word of rebuke prevented Jumper from immediately chasing the branches down and dragging every one of them back to Jasper's feet.

Not quite sure what to make of the dog's antics, Harry and Harriet went off to explore their new home, snorting, snuffling, and grunting along like a couple of old men. Jasper kept an eye on them while he went about his work. You never know when a mountain lion or coyote might get the urge to supplement his breakfast with a bit of bacon. Even if the bacon was still a baby.

Behind the cabin, near the lean-to, Jasper ran across three or four shredded shingles that had blown off the roof during the storm. Stepping back and shielding his eyes from the morning sun, he scanned the roof and found where the shingles had once been. Crap. He'd have to fix that before it rained again. He was fairly sure he still had a few leftover shingles in the shed out back. The hole in the roof was at the very edge of the eave. He supposed that's why it hadn't created a leak inside already. Still, it would get worse if he didn't repair it. A little roofing work would give him something to do to take his mind off the sexy bastard still lounging around inside his cabin in those baggy-ass pajamas, looking like a million bucks and refusing to give up his secrets, the little shit.

The writer in Jasper hated the last sentence that had gone gallivanting through his mind. However, since he was busy with other endeavors he didn't take the time to do a mental edit job on it, as he so often did with other unwieldy thoughts. All writers are a little strange that way, Jasper suspected. At least he certainly was. Editing thoughts. Seeing them as they would look on paper. Tightening them up.

Okay, fine, he told himself, pushing the question of thought-editing out of his head for the time being. He had more important things to worry about. Like fixing the roof. And repairing some of the other damage the ranch had sustained, thanks to the storm. Then and only then, maybe on toward evening, he would try coercing Harwell to part with a few of his secrets. At the very least, Jasper would like a believable explanation how the man got to his lonely mountain in the middle of nowhere. And as long as the law wasn't after his ass, Jasper figured he'd be satisfied with whatever explanation the man gave him.

As long as it wasn't another lie. Jasper didn't have much patience with liars. Even cute ones.

He stopped dead in his tracks and remembered the sight of Tim laid out naked before him as Jasper gave him a sponge bath. The feel of the young man's fevered skin, the heat of it. A sparkle glinted in Jasper's eyes when he recalled Tim's cock, heavy with blood, shifting beneath the washcloth in Jasper's hand. My God, that was something! Jasper closed his eyes and let the memory flood through him. Finally, with a tsk, he gave himself a shake and brought himself back to the present. He looked down at the branch in his hand, and this time when he threw it, he gave Jumper a click of his tongue and the dog shot out after it like his tail was on fire. The big black dog scooped the branch up in his teeth in midflight, spun like a top, and headed straight back for Jasper, grinning all the way and dragging that damn branch along with him, proud as hell and having the time of his life.

Jasper laughed.

Using every ounce of willpower he possessed, Jasper ignored the hard-on poking down his pant leg as best he could. Determined, he set out to get some work done. But, like a favorite plaything, Jasper kept the memory of Tim's naked body in a special drawer inside his head, accessible any time he wanted to revisit it. And during the course of the day, he revisited it often.

And always with hunger in his heart.

TIM found Jasper's guns in the second closet he rummaged through. A nice slide-action Remington .22 rifle that wouldn't stop anything bigger than a goat, but would probably work well enough on a pissed-off human if the need arose. And a .38 Special with about the same stopping power as the rifle. The sort of guns Tim would expect a rancher to keep around for rattlesnakes and other nasty varmints.

Tim checked to make sure both the rifle and the revolver were loaded, which they were. He found extra cartridges on a shelf above his head, then put everything back exactly where he found it.

If things went downhill—and Timmy wasn't thinking about Jasper now—he felt a little more secure knowing he could arm himself at a moment's notice. Not that he knew much about guns, only what he'd read. But he knew enough to point and shoot and reload the fuckers. And he would have no qualms about putting a bullet through the meanest man in TJ, or one of his minions, if they came calling. Why should he? After all, Tim knew damn well they wouldn't hesitate putting a bullet through *him*.

Boy, some people don't like being robbed at all. Downright testy about it. Twits. Relieved to know he now had some firepower at his fingertips if anyone managed to track him here to Jasper's ranch, which he figured was a long shot, Tim quietly closed the closet door, took a grip on his pajama bottoms so they wouldn't tumble down around his ankles, and headed back to the couch.

The fire was out in the fireplace, but with the sun once again beating down in all its Southern California glory, now the rain clouds had moved along to pester someone else, the cabin had warmed up nicely. Without bothering with a blanket, Tim collapsed on the sofa cushions with his hands behind his head and looked up at the ceiling as he drifted off. He smiled when Lola hopped up beside him and made herself comfortable.

The breakfast had done him a world of good. He actually felt halfway decent now. He supposed that clenched it. He'd had the flu, not pneumonia. Pneumonia would have taken a hell of a lot longer to run its course. And while he was still weak, he wasn't nearly as miserable as he had been for the past two or three days, and he knew he had Jasper to thank for that.

And he *would* thank him. Not just sexually, either.

After all, knowing where to grab those guns at a moment's notice might just save Jasper's life as well as his own. That would be a pretty good thank you right there.

He hoped it wouldn't come to that, but you never knew. It very well might.

Of course, if it weren't for him, Jasper would never be put in harm's way to begin with, but Tim tried to ignore that bit of logic. Too much guilt to be found along that road.

Way too much guilt.

He thought of Jasper's body, Jasper's strong, hairy chest, the kindness in Jasper's eyes. The gentleness in Jasper's hands when he was bathing him. Tim was looking forward to this evening when he put the moves on the guy. He really was. There was some interesting terrain to explore on that man, and Tim was in an exploring frame of mind.

When he finally slept, he slept with the tiniest smile upon his lips.

And that's how Jasper found him hours later when he went inside for lunch.

JASPER tiptoed through the living room, quietly pulled together the makings of a sandwich, grabbed a soda. Remembering his promise, he stopped what he was doing long enough to hang Tim's clothes and tennies out on the line to dry. That accomplished, Jasper went back into the kitchen and gathered up his lunch, carrying it all outside so Timmy could rest without Jasper banging around disturbing him.

He was surprised at how disappointed he had been to find Tim fast asleep. It would have been nice to pass a few pleasantries back and forth. Maybe inquire about how he was feeling. Get another glimpse of those strong, capable hands and that intriguing triangular hollow at the base of the man's throat.

Jasper wasn't a fool. He knew he was working himself into a state of infatuation with the man conked out on his couch. Looking the way Tim did, it was hard for Jasper not to. And while Tim was really a complete mystery to Jasper, he still found himself being sucked into the man's orbit, wanting to get closer, hoping Tim would like having him there. Needing to talk. Needing to touch. Needing to take it all the way. To rip those stupid pajamas off the man and feel him naked and hard and hot against Jasper's own eager flesh. Timmy's slight frame would be all but lost in Jasper's arms. But it would be protected there too. Savored. Worshipped. If Timmy wasn't as turned on by Jasper as Jasper hoped he would be, maybe Jasper's own hunger would be enough for both of them. He could carry the man to orgasm, he knew that much. He could sense Tim's need.

Outside, Jasper polished off the sandwich, drank the soda in one sustained gulp, and laughed at himself. What a romantic fool he was becoming! He was as bad as Lola, wanting to be next to the guy every blessed minute. Maybe what he really needed was a bit of sexual release. No maybes about it, actually. Well, there was no reason he couldn't hit a few bars that night after he drove Timmy back into town. Maybe even ask the young man to join him, if he felt up to it.

Whoops. There he went again. Still trying to find ways to get close to the guy.

In a surge of determination, Jasper shucked all thoughts of Timothy Sebastian Harwell and gathered up some roofing nails, some crisp new shingles, and a hammer. He tossed everything in the backyard, then went to fetch a ladder. It dawned on him that pounding a bunch of nails into the roof after warning himself not to disturb his houseguest probably wasn't the brightest thing he'd ever contemplated.

But what the hell. Even if it did wake Tim, maybe that would give the man the urge to come on out and strike up a conversation. That would be nice.

With that thought in mind, Jasper grabbed up the first shingle, positioned it properly on the southwest corner of the cabin roof, and, with a mischievous glint in his eye, pounded the shit out of about six roofing nails to keep it in place.

If that didn't wake his houseguest up, nothing would.

But apparently, and much to Jasper's disappointment, it didn't.

He finished the roofing job and did a few other tasks. He got Harry and Harriet resettled in their pen, since he really couldn't have them living in the house for the rest of their lives, and once that was accomplished, Jasper headed for the shower. The day was winding down by now. He had accomplished a lot around the place, and he was tired. Still horny, but tired.

Passing through the living room, Jasper saw Tim was still asleep on the sofa. He must have showered, though, because his hair looked damp, his face shiny and clean.

Jasper resisted the urge to lay his hand over the man's forehead to test for fever.

Tugging himself out of his dirty clothes, Jasper went about cleaning up before dinner. And before driving Harwell home. He wasn't too thrilled about it, but he couldn't have a complete stranger living in his house for the rest of his life any more than he could have a couple of pigs living in it.

God, why did everything have to be so complicated?

Teeth brushed but forgoing a shave, Jasper stepped naked into the shower and let the warm water wash away his angst.

A moment later, when Tim stepped naked through the shower door to join him, Jasper's angst became a little bit less angsty. Actually, it became a piece of history is what it did.

Lost forever, by God. Never to be seen again.

Chapter SEVEN

"Mind if I join you?" Tim asked.

"Uh... uh...." Jasper couldn't seem to remember the English language. Funny. He knew it a few minutes ago.

Looking down, he saw Tim was already hard, his young cock chock full of blood and standing straight up like a flag pole. It was the most beautiful thing Jasper had ever seen, bar none.

Jasper quickly recovered the power of speech. "N-not at all," he stuttered around a growing smile. He tried to sound blasé, as if Tim had simply asked him if he'd like a scone with his tea, but he didn't pull it off very well and he knew it. It's not easy being blasé when you're in the company of a twenty-year-old with a hard-on.

While his words were uttered in what was meant to be a casual voice, or as casual as he could manage under the circumstances, Jasper could hear his old pumper thudding away beneath his ribs like Poe's telltale heart flopping around under the parlor floor. *Bambam bambam bambam.* Sweet Jesus.

Tim smiled, closing the shower door behind him. "You can call me Timmy, by the way. I kind of like it when you do."

Jasper was squinting under the shower spray. It was limiting his vision, and he wasn't happy about that at all. He stepped forward out of the deluge and wiped the water from his eyes. Suddenly, in the cramped shower stall, their two bodies were a whole lot closer than they had been before. Jasper could feel his dick swimming upstream like a salmon. Lengthening. Reaching out. Stretching upward. Jasper watched in wonder as the hair on Timmy's legs flattened beneath the rushing water, while the hair on the young man's head was quickly plastered to his face. And suddenly, he looked even younger than he already was.

"Timmy," Jasper said, as if tasting a new flavor of ice cream. He pulled his eyes from the young man's cock and smiled at the amused look he found in Timmy's eyes.

Timmy blinked, pushed his dripping hair off his forehead, then reached for the bar of soap and lathered up his hands. As he did, their two erect cocks bumped against each other, and Jasper gave a tiny gasp.

Timmy looked down. His white teeth flashed beneath a truly handsome smile. "I'll get to that later," he said. "That okay with you?"

"Hell, yes," Jasper smiled back. "I—"

"I what?" Tim asked, eyes wide and innocent. He replaced the soap in the dish and laid his lathered hands atop Jasper's chest. His fingers slid through the matted hair there. He seemed to enjoy what he was feeling. He was exploring, just as Jasper had imagined himself exploring earlier.

Jasper cleared his throat. He had to. It was the only way he could talk. "I don't mind," he clarified, which was probably not necessary since it was no doubt written all over his face.

"I didn't think you minded," Tim said, and his hands began to move.

Such a rush of desire raged through Jasper's body that he reached up with both hands to grab the showerhead before his knees collapsed beneath him. While Jasper's arms were stretched high above his head, Tim reached up, eyes wide with lust, to feel the underside of Jasper's biceps. The skin there was so smooth and firm and bulging, Tim, too, began to tremble. Then he dragged his soapy hands downward, scraping his fingernails through the hair in Jasper's armpits. When Jasper closed his eyes at the sensation, Tim leaned in and pressed his lips to Jasper's throat. The top of his head nestled quite comfortably under Jasper's chin. That's how short he was.

Jasper lowered one arm and snaked it around the young man's waist, pulling him close. Their bodies melded against each other. Tim stood on tiptoe to slide his cock over the soapy water sluicing down Jasper's stomach. Their hard thighs pressed together. Timmy's balls were tight against his groin, and Jasper could feel them pressing against his dick, shifting in their sack, both firm and incredibly soft at the very same time.

Hard nubbins of passion that made Jasper want to swoon feeling them pressed against his own.

Tim reached down and clutched Jasper's cock in his soapy fist. It was a handful, and Timmy laughed. "Wow." His fingers circled Jasper's glans, and now it was Jasper stretching up on tiptoe to slide his dick deeper into that heavenly fist.

Timmy dropped to his knees in front of Jasper and let the shower spray bounce off the top of his head as he pressed his lips to Jasper's belly button, relishing the feel of the slick hair and the hot, solid flesh against his mouth. Jasper reached down and caressed Timmy's thick hair, running his fingers through it, sweeping it from Timmy's eyes.

Timmy slid his tongue down Jasper's torso until it met the thatch of dark pubic hair surrounding Jasper's bobbing cock. He tasted it, tugged at it with his teeth, nudging Jasper's cock aside with his cheek as he foraged. He slid farther south and pressed his lips to the underside of Jasper's cock, smiling to see that the man before him was uncircumcised. The heavy foreskin encircled Jasper's glans, the top of which peeked out from the sheath of flesh, red and eager and plump, slit oozing crystal precome that was begging to be licked away.

Obligingly, Timmy sucked away the pearly drop. Then he pulled Jasper's foreskin back to fully expose the glans. Jasper's cockhead was fat and perfect and incredibly tempting. Timmy popped it into this mouth, and Jasper damn near fainted as he grabbed the sides of Timmy's head to hold him still.

"Oh God," he said. " Don't move. Please. Wait."

Timmy followed orders and held his head perfectly still while Jasper ever so slowly slid his cock deeper into that hot velvet mouth. Jasper shivered uncontrollably from his feet all the way to the top of his head. He stood on tiptoe, every muscle in his body straining. Timmy smiled around Jasper's cock, and when Jasper felt that, he laughed out loud and relaxed a little bit.

"Oh Jesus, kid, you're killing me!"

Jasper felt his cock slide from between those talented lips. Timmy held Jasper's dick to his cheek when he answered, still stroking, still manipulating. It was almost as if he couldn't bear to be parted from it.

"Don't die just yet." Timmy grinned up at Jasper's bug-eyed face. Timmy giggled as he tried not to drown in the shower spray. God, he loved the feel of Jasper's cock against his face. "I've got plans for you, Jasper. Good plans. Important plans. So don't fucking die."

With that, he slid Jasper's rock-hard dick back into his mouth, and Jasper had to squeeze his eyes tightly shut and bite down on his tongue so he wouldn't cry out, it felt so good.

When Jasper spoke, his voice was a mere shimmer of sound. That's how turned on he was. "You really know what you're doing, don't you." It wasn't a question. It was a statement of fucking fact.

"Oh yeah," Timmy sighed, and Jasper felt his cock slide deeper into the young man's mouth and bump the back of his throat. It was exactly where Timmy wanted it to go. Then, to Jasper's astonishment, Timmy opened his mouth wider and slid Jasper's cock all the way into his gullet.

Jasper's knees damn near buckled. This was a first. Until now, deep throating was always an unimaginable concept. Now it was—wow. Reality. He could feel the corona of his cock, as engorged as it had ever been in Jasper's life, pop in and out through the muscular ring of Timmy's throat. He could feel Timmy's uvula dragging across his slit. Timmy caressed his balls with gentle fingers, directing his cock. His other hand slid up between Jasper's legs to massage his asshole as he gulped down Jasper's dick, taking it ever deeper with every thrust.

Jesus God, this kid was good.

Jasper snapped out of heaven long enough to realize he should be doing a wee bit of reciprocation. Nobody likes a head hog. Give a little, take a little—that's the name of the game.

Jasper freed his cock from Timmy's hungry throat and bent to scoop him off the floor by his armpits, like he would a toddler. He brought him all the way up to where Timmy's feet were off the floor and their faces were at equal height. When he got Timmy right where he wanted him, Jasper roughly splayed his lips over Timmy's mouth. Their tongues found each other, and Timmy slid his arms around Jasper's shoulders, holding him as tightly as he could as his mouth fought for dominance, which Jasper let him have.

Timmy's strong, fuzzy legs wrapped around Jasper's waist, relieving Jasper of a little of the young man's weight, although in truth the kid weighed practically nothing.

Oh, but Lord he could kiss. And suck cock. Mustn't forget that.

Awkwardly as hell, Jasper wangled around to turn off the shower. Still clutching Timmy to his chest, Jasper's strong hands cradled Timmy's ass, holding him aloft, pressing him against the shower wall. Timmy's cock was still sliding across Jasper's chest, and Jasper loved feeling the hardness and the heat of it there. Impatient to get into a more comfortable position, Jasper gave the shower door a clumsy kick. It flew open, and he carted the kid, still dripping wet, all the way through the cabin and up the stairs to the loft.

There Jasper stood him gently on the floor and, using a towel he had grabbed on the way, knelt before the boy and gently dried his strong legs and gorgeous crotch. With gentle movements, he wiped away the moisture from Timmy's dick and balls, and when Timmy's pubic hair was nice and fluffy, Jasper buried his face in it as he handed over the towel and let the kid do the rest of the work.

Jasper felt the towel sweeping across his hair, his back, as Timmy's groin trembled against his face.

Like a man at prayer, humbly and adoringly, Jasper took the young man's cock into his mouth for the first time, and he was pleased to hear Timmy gasp. His cock slid into Jasper's mouth so easily. So smoothly. It was like it had always been meant to go there. Like it was *home.* Jasper accepted every beautiful inch of it, relishing the taste of the precome practically flowing from the boy's urethra. God, he had never seen anyone drip so much in his life. And it tasted delicious. Salty, sweet, perfect. Jasper's own cock was dripping again too. He could feel it.

And suddenly he wanted the boy to taste him, just as he was tasting the boy.

He dragged his lips across Timmy's balls in a gentle parting movement, then rose to his feet. Scooping the boy into his arms once again, he laid Timmy across the bed. Then Jasper stood there looking down at him, admiring him, and while he did Timmy reached up to cradle Jasper's cock. He gave it a gentle stroke and watched, wide-eyed, as a fat drop of crystal liquid formed at the tip of the bulbous head.

Like a child, but like a man, too, Timmy leaned his head back and stared up into Jasper's eyes as he licked the precome away from Jasper's dick. Jasper smiled gently down at him, stroking a pattern across the young man's cheek with his thumb. Timmy twisted his head enough to kiss the thumb that stroked him.

Then Timmy sat up and once again sucked Jasper's cock deep into his mouth.

Hungry for the boy, Jasper lay down on the bed beside him but faced in the opposite direction. For the very first time, they played their dicks across the other's faces simultaneously. Strong hands massaged trembling thighs, noses nestled into fat, come-filled balls, hard-as-iron cocks bopped and bounced around and dripped juices all over the place.

It took every ounce of willpower Jasper possessed to form a coherent sentence. When he did, he asked for exactly what he wanted. He did not hesitate.

"Come for me, Timmy. Please. I have to taste you. Shoot for me."

Timmy reached down and splayed his hand along Jasper's bristly jawline. The clean scent of the man's balls was in his nose, and it was the most heavenly fragrance Timmy had ever breathed in.

"We'll come together," he said. "We'll try, anyway. I hope you're close, because I sure am."

And Jasper laughed. "Don't wait for me. I'm ready to explode now!"

They both closed their eyes as they once again dipped their cocks into each other's mouths. Timmy's tongue massaged Jasper's glans, sucking hard, begging for his come, and Jasper did the same to Timmy, nipping at the flesh beneath his glans on the upstroke of every suck.

In seconds, they were both trembling. Both on the verge of coming. Both as eager as they had ever been in their lives to witness it happen to the other man, not just experience it themselves. This time, and maybe for the first time, they really wanted to *share* the experience. Come together. Make love. Be *one*.

When Timmy rasped, "I'm going to come!" Jasper slid his mouth away and pressed his lips to the base of Timmy's cock. With his chin buried in Timmy's balls, he slid his fingers across Timmy's slit, and at that very moment, he felt Timmy give way.

The come flew out of him like fireworks on the Fourth of July. His ass came off the bed at the second squirt and the semen shot even higher. Jasper quickly slid his mouth over the head of Timmy's cock and was just in time to catch the final volley. Jasper had never seen anyone come so much in his life.

"You!" Timmy pleaded, hungrily devouring Jasper's cock yet again.

And in moments, Jasper exploded in orgasm. He tried to pull away from Timmy's mouth and Timmy let him. Jasper watched his thick come splash across Timmy's eager face, the young man's smile buried in a glob of white liquid he lapped away like cream with the tip of his tongue.

Jasper stroked his cock and squeezed even more come out of it, smearing it over the boy's cheek, the boy's mouth, smiling when Timmy shot his tongue out to plead for more.

He was still hungry. They both were.

They sucked at each other's cocks until both cocks had softened inside their eager mouths. When they were totally spent, they collapsed against each other, face to crotch, fingers clasping, still shaking from what they had experienced together.

Perfect sex. That's what it was. And strangely enough, they both knew it.

"I'm not leaving," Timmy said.

And Jasper answered, "No. No, you're not."

And then they slept. Maintaining the same position, they slept long into the night.

When Jasper awoke hours later, he found Timmy softly stroking the hair on Jasper's stomach. Planting quiet kisses there. Retasting. Re-exploring.

Jasper's cock was asleep at first, but in moments it began to move. And once again Timmy slipped it into his mouth and took it all the way down his throat.

Jasper felt Timmy's young cock shift against his cheek, swelling, hardening. He gently stroked it until it stood up proud and firm, then he happily popped it into his mouth. Oh, so slowly both men's hips began to move. They savored the taste of each other's juice as it leaked from their hard cocks. Each was as happy as the other to be exactly where they were, at that precise moment, doing exactly what they most wanted to be doing. Pleasing. Being pleased. And when they came within seconds of each other yet again, it was like a gentle afterthought, a retelling of what they had experienced before. But even more beautiful this time. With less passion, maybe, less intensity, but more sweetly satisfying.

This time when they fell exhausted into each other's arms, still petting, still cuddling even as they dozed, they slept until the sun was well above the top of the mountain. The morning was almost gone when they spoke their first words. After the pronouncement of the night before, which Jasper did not regret for a moment, he figured the same words needed to be said again. Now. Right now. And so he said them.

"You're still not leaving. Not today."

And Timmy smiled.

JASPER liked the fact that their mornings were already becoming almost routine.

He set the eggs and sausage in front of Timmy, and Timmy nodded his head in thanks. Jasper played his fingers through the young man's hair, straightened the collar on those gigantic pajamas the guy was still wearing, and then leaned across the table and planted a kiss on the top of Timmy's head. "How are you feeling?" he asked. "I probably should have let you sleep last night. Instead of, you know…."

Timmy grinned. "You shouldn't have done anything except exactly what you did. What *we* did. I, for one, had the time of my life. I didn't hear you complaining much either."

Jasper grinned.

Timmy reached up to grasp the hand that stroked his hair. He pressed the palm of it to his lips. Again he savored the smell of the man before him. Along with the smell of sausage and eggs and butter that still lingered on Jasper's fingers, the man himself smelled delicious. An intoxicating mixture of butch and breakfast.

Timmy's kiss felt like butterflies against his skin, and Jasper smiled at the softness of it. He couldn't believe how gentle Timmy could be. Or how incredibly giving he was in bed. Or how beautiful.

But still—there were secrets that needed to be delved into. One night of incredible sex didn't excuse the lies the man had told Jasper the day before. He still didn't buy that bit about hiking and getting lost and—

"What?" Timmy asked.

Jasper shook his head as he drew back his hand and pulled out a chair. "Eat your breakfast. We can talk later. You still look a little peaked."

Timmy cast him a lopsided smirk. "I came about ten times last night. Why wouldn't I look peaked?"

"You came twice."

Timmy shrugged. "Yeah, but each time it was more than a quart."

And Jasper threw his head back and laughed. "Okay. You win. You can look peaked if you want. And it's all my fault, I suppose."

Timmy forked a sausage patty and hauled it to his mouth. "Hell, yes. Totally your fault. Sitting there half-naked on that bucket the other day. Giving my mind, weakened from disease, dastardly ideas."

Their eyes met over the table. Jasper gave the man a wink. "I seem to recall it was you who first trespassed into my personal territory when I was taking a shower. Talk about dastardly ideas. And then you took my dick into your mouth and, well, that pretty well set the tone for the night."

Timmy gave a happy nod. "Sure did."

Jasper gazed more closely at Timmy's face. It looked like the bottom half of it was as raw as an uncooked steak. "What's wrong with your skin? It's all red. Especially around your mouth."

Timmy scraped a gentle paw across his chin. "Rug burn. Well, *beard* burn, I should say. Kissing that scruffy face of yours is like dragging your face over a parking lot filled with broken glass. Worth it, though. Every fucking minute of it."

Jasper was appalled. "Jesus, Tim. I'm sorry. I'm gonna go shave right now."

"Don't be stupid." Timmy laughed. "Eat your breakfast. *Then* shave. I wouldn't be lying if I said I'd like to see that stubble of yours gone. I like to feel some skin when I'm smooching. Not bushes."

It was Jasper's turn to laugh, although he still looked guilty. "Fine. First I'll eat, then I'll shave. Then maybe—" He looked down at his plate, then up at the ceiling, and finally straight into Timmy's eyes. "—then maybe we can see if it makes kissing me any easier."

A hot flame rose in Timmy's dark eyes. His cheeks flushed. "Eat fast then, fucker. And shave even faster. I can't think of anything I'd rather do than get my hands on you again."

Jasper felt himself blush too. And it was an odd feeling. He was reasonably sure he hadn't blushed since he was twelve. "You know, Timmy, it was your mouth that really did the trick. Not that your hands weren't—"

"Eat!" Timmy commanded.

And Jasper bent to do exactly that. Their knees touched under the table, and Jasper felt a warm glow spread all the way through him from his patellae to the tips of his ears.

He wondered what Timmy was feeling. If anything.

AT THE first brush of Jasper's knee beneath the table, Timmy placed his bare foot over Jasper's instep. The other foot he played up and down Jasper's blue-jeaned calf.

God, the man was beautiful. And so open.

Timmy knew if he wanted to, he could play this guy for everything he had.

And at that realization, his thoughts darkened. Suddenly he felt… sick. Sick all over again. He couldn't believe it. One minute he was great, and the next minute he was ready to fall out of his chair and sleep on the kitchen floor. His thoughts swam in a murky pool of guilt and nausea and shame and—and simple sickness. He felt worse than crap. And it had hit him out of nowhere.

"I'm sorry, Jasper. I think… I think I'd better lie down for a while."

Jasper threw his napkin on his plate and jumped to his feet. "I knew it! I knew you were doing too much! I knew I should have let you rest last night!"

Timmy stumbled to his feet. His fork fell to the floor. "No, I—"

But Jasper wasn't listening. He took Timmy's arm and led him, not to the couch, but to the stairs leading up to the loft.

"You need to sleep in a proper bed," he preached. "I'll keep the animals out and let you get some rest. When you wake up, we'll eat. And maybe... talk. Okay?"

Timmy didn't know why his energy level had tanked, or why he suddenly felt so horrible, but he had a suspicion Jasper was right about fooling around too soon after being as sick as he was. He *should* have been resting last night. But God, the man was so hot. His body was so perfect.

His come....

Jasper eased him down onto the bed, and once Timmy was on his back, in one swift motion Jasper peeled the pajama bottoms from the young man's slight frame and tossed them across the room. He bent over the bed, unbuttoned the shirt, and slid that off Timmy's back as well. It flew through the air to join the bottoms in a crumpled pile in the corner.

"Now sleep," Jasper said, making a concerted effort not to get rambunctious with Timmy's naked body spread out before him. God, he was just so beautiful. Jasper pulled the blanket chastely up to Timmy's chin and tucked it in neatly.

Timmy looked up at the man hovering over him. The whites of Timmy's eyes were pink, the smudges under his eyes darker. He looked like a man in desperate need of sleep. "I'm sorry about breakfast—"

"Hush," Jasper said. He laid a gentle hand along Timmy's cheek and bent to press his lips to the young man's forehead, gently, so his stubble wouldn't scrape the skin any more than it already had. Jasper smelled the clean scent of his shampoo in the mop of thick black hair that tumbled across the pillow. "Sleep, Tim."

The boy smiled. "Timmy," he said. "Call me Timmy." Then he closed his eyes.

Timmy took refuge in the darkness behind his eyelids, glad to be alone for a minute. Shutting out the day. Shutting out Jasper. He had the strangest feeling he was going to cry. What the hell was that all about? He felt like a fool. That's what it was, of course. That's *all* it was. How could he be having the best sex of his life one minute, and then be as weak as a puppy the next? He hoped Jasper didn't think he was faking, because God help him, he really wasn't.

Before Timmy could carry that thought any farther down the road, the darkness swept in, and he slept the dreamless sleep of the truly weary.

Jasper sat in the corner by the window, quietly dividing his time between the notes in his lap concerning the novel he was currently writing and the man in the bed across the room. After a while, he slept too, with his chin upon his chest, his notes slipping one by one from his lap and drifting softly to the floor with a whisper of sound.

And in that quiet way, the day slowly slid to sunset. Evening shadows gathered.

Even while Timmy slept, Jasper's heart felt a little more attuned to the boy in the bed. A tenderness burned inside him he had not yet recognized. Had not yet noticed, actually.

Even Jumper sensed a change in his master as he lay at Jasper's feet and watched the room darken around them.

It was a long while later when Jumper lifted his ears at a sound he heard outside the cabin walls. It was a new sound. A sound he had never heard before.

Jumper clambered to his feet. With Bobber and Lola at his side, for they had now *all* heard the noise, the three dogs left the two sleeping humans behind and thundered down the stairs like an avalanche. In the living room, they flew into the seat of the recliner by the window, squeezing in together and jostling each other to get a decent view. When they were satisfied, they pressed their cold noses to the windowpane and looked out.

A soft growl erupted from all three throats.

Then they started barking. And they did it with a will. The two cats stampeded under the couch and disappeared, horrified by the racket, and from behind them, they heard their master's footsteps clomping down the stairs, his voice screaming for them all to shut the hell up for Christ's sake.

When Jasper saw the three dogs staring through the window, still quivering in excitement but momentarily silenced by his command, he pulled up short. Something was wrong.

He thought of the guns in the closet but refused to do more than give them a whiff of his attention. Unarmed, and determined to stay that way, he stepped to the front door and pulled it open. The three dogs tore outside, practically knocking him off his feet

Tucking in his shirt, Jasper rubbed the sleep from his eyes and followed them outside into the gloaming.

And there Jasper found nothing. No trespassers dressed like Neanderthals and dragging clubs made of mastodon femurs behind their sorry asses. No mountain lions stalking Harry and Harriet, hungry for baby pork chops. No slavering, marauding hordes of Sasquatches stomping through the backyard and chewing up the begonias for roughage. Nothing.

After their maniacal stampede through the front door, the dogs quickly calmed down. They sniffed around for a while, took off into the trees, and just as quickly returned, then seemed to forget what they were doing and started chasing each other around the yard. Jumper said "excuse me" for a minute to the group and took a poop by the new fence. Bobber stomped through a mud puddle and would need to be toweled down before being let back inside. And Lola looked at her two canine companions, then aimed a disapproving scowl up at Jasper as if to apologize for her brethren and returned to the house.

There Jasper would find her in the loft getting a belly rub from a newly awakened Timmy.

Lucky bitch.

Chapter EIGHT

SINCE he was feeling kind of left out, Jasper perched himself beside Timmy and Lola on the bed. Timmy smiled up at him all sleepy-eyed and handsome, and Jasper got a funny sensation deep inside. Like maybe something had melted. His heart? Liver? Electrical wiring? What? Jasper wasn't a romantic. At least he didn't think he was. Maybe he was coming down with whatever Timmy was only now recovering from. Or maybe it was simply a pang of lust he'd felt. Jasper figured no one could fault him. Just looking at the man was a heart stopper.

Timmy, meanwhile, was feeling a little nervous. His first thought when he heard the dogs yowling was that he'd been discovered. And he didn't care what Crazy Horse said. This was *not* a good day to die. He faked a yawn for Jasper's benefit so he would appear a little *less* nervous. "The dogs were going nuts. What was it?"

Jasper shrugged. "Don't know. Coyote maybe. We get them up here. Nothing to worry about. How do you feel?"

Timmy thought about that as the worry lines disappeared from his face. "Better, I think. I'm starting to get the feeling I've been laying around too long. Guess that means I'm well and it's time to get up and stop goldbricking."

Jasper beamed himself into a smile. "You *look* better." He slipped his hand under the cover enough to slide his fingers over Timmy's chest. The skin there was smooth and sleep-warm and Jasper had a sudden desire to purr like a cat, it felt so good.

Timmy rolled over onto his side facing Jasper. He folded himself into a fetal position and rested his head on Jasper's leg. He looked up at

Jasper with languid, lazy eyes. Contentment oozed out of every one of Timmy's pores. He held Jasper's hand between both of his and tucked all three of them under his chin.

His voice was still a little rough around the edges, either from having been sick or from sleeping too much. Or both. "How come you're so nice to me, Jasper?" A tease of laughter shined in his dark, sleepy eyes. "Do you only get laid by the people who climb up your mountain and pass out in your hog house because they're too sick to go any farther? Is that why you're so appreciative? Aren't there any healthy people willing to help you get your rocks off?"

Jasper grinned. This was a side of Timmy he had never seen before. An impish side. He liked it. "Yeah, but they don't do the job as well as you do. You don't have a gag reflex, do you?" He asked the question like a doctor asking a patient about his bowel movements. Matter-of-factly. Clinically unapologetic. And totally out of the blue.

The question was such a surprise, Timmy howled with laughter. The blood rushed to his face as he pulled the cover over his head. Lola sat up in the bed to see what was going on and just as quickly dropped back down with an audible plop. It was only the humans acting up. Still, her tail started wagging. She liked seeing the humans happy.

"You're embarrassing me." Timmy laughed from somewhere under the bed linens. He peeked out, his hair poking up all over the place. "And in answer to your question, it depends what's going down my throat."

"So how do you…?"

"Do it?" Timmy grinned. "Practice. Lots and lots of practice. Feel better?"

Jasper groaned. "No. Worse actually. How much practice are we talking about? And what was I, you little shit? Just another lesson? Lab work? Final exam? What?"

Jasper leaned down, pulled the covers away from Timmy's face, and planted a playful kiss on the young man's lips. But it wasn't only a kiss. Jasper was also testing Timmy's temperature. Or at least he told himself that was what he was doing. He might have been kidding himself. Maybe it was just a fucking kiss. Lord knows it felt good enough to be one.

When Timmy's hand came up to the back of Jasper's neck and held Jasper right where he was while Timmy kissed him back, Jasper thought he'd died and gone to heaven. Jeez, this guy was something else. The kiss lasted for what seemed like hours, and every minute of it was a wonderment. To both of them.

Finally, because the dog was trying to squirm in between them to get a kiss of her own, they pulled gently away from each other, but not far enough away their eyes lost contact. There seemed to be some sort of magnet holding them together. They both felt the draw.

Jasper was getting that funny melting feeling inside again, but at least he now knew Timmy's fever was gone. Timmy's mouth had tasted so good, Jasper's own temperature had shot up instead. Great. Now he had a fever and Timmy didn't. Plus the crotch of his jeans seemed to have been stuffed with cabbages or something, they were suddenly so tight.

He grinned to himself. Those pesky hard-ons. Always popping up when you least expect them. He wondered if Timmy had one. Then he saw the bulge under the blanket at Timmy's crotch level. Yep. The sweet young man had a boner indeed. Hmm.

Jasper used most of next year's willpower in the act of not peeling off his clothes, throwing the blankets across the room, and burying his nose in Timmy's ass, which seemed to be a destination he would really like to visit all of a sudden. Either that or climb the man's dick like Mt. Everest. Either location would provide excellent sightseeing opportunities.

Instead, and much to his own surprise, he said, "Come on. Get up. You have to be starving by now. Let's get you fed. Then we need to talk."

He yanked away the covers after all, leaving Timmy naked on the bed. God, what a sight. The man was magnificent. And his cock looked delicious.

Timmy's eyes opened wide in a parody of innocence. It was a *parody* of innocence because at the same moment, he grabbed his dick and gave it a gentle stroking, and *nobody* can pull off innocent while pumping a hard-on. Can't be done. It's like Heidi cradling a dolly in one arm and a dildo in the other. Simply looks wrong.

"Just talk?" Timmy cooed, making a little pouty face. "Is that all you want to do?"

Jasper laughed. "For now," he said, heading for the stairs. And *that* pretty much used up the *rest* of his will power.

During his marriage Jasper had always resented his wife's intrusion into his quiet enjoyment of dinner. And breakfast. And lunch. Since she never shut up, he could never simply eat and enjoy his food.

So it came as a surprise to Jasper to suddenly realize he actually looked forward to sitting across the table from Timmy. Quiet, talky, morose, chipper—it didn't matter what mood Timmy was in. Jasper was fascinated by each and every one of them.

This evening, Jasper was pleased to note, Timmy was in a talkative mood. While they chowed down on stew and burgers, Timmy, still swaddled in Jasper's baggy pajamas, rattled on about Lola and the ranch and how thankful he was to be feeling better. He kept telling Jasper he had never been that sick before in his life, and Jasper believed him.

At one point, Timmy reached out and touched Jasper's arm. "I want to tell you something," he said. Jasper was shoveling in a tossed salad prior to attacking his burger. "Stop just a second and listen to me, okay?"

Jasper sensed something momentous was about to be said. Something from the heart. He stopped cold, fork poised halfway to his mouth.

Timmy's eyes were solemn. "I just want to say thank you. And I mean it. Thank you. No one has ever taken care of me like you did."

"Never?"

"Never."

Jasper cocked his head to the side. "Surely when you were a kid—"

"Never," Timmy said again.

And sadly, Jasper believed him.

Not wanting to pry into the man's childhood, Jasper confided, "I almost took you to the hospital, you know. I thought for a while you were going to die on me."

"Thank God you didn't," Timmy said, rolling his eyes. "No insurance. I'd have been in debt for the rest of my life. Dying would have been better." He didn't mention the other reason he didn't want to go to the hospital; namely, a trail of paperwork that could lead his pursuers directly to him. He suspected there were few corridors the meanest man in TJ couldn't follow him down. The man had a long reach, or so Timmy had heard. Timmy had also heard he had an army of flunkies at his beck and call, and none of them were what you'd call gentle people.

"If the hospital saved your life, would that really have been so horrible?" Jasper asked. "Debts can be repaid. Death is just, well, death. It sucks a whole lot worse than a few unpaid bills."

He was surprised to hear Timmy say, "Yeah. I suppose. But I don't like owing people. I already owe you. That's enough."

Jasper frowned. "You don't owe me anything."

"You're wrong," Timmy said. "And now I'm going to ask you to let me owe you something more."

Jasper wasn't sure he liked the sound of that. "Like what?"

"Remember when you said I couldn't leave quite yet?"

Jasper laid his hamburger in his plate and stared at Timmy from across the table. He stared hard, looking almost angry. "I remember it every five minutes. You said you'd stay for a few days. I hope *you* remember. I'd hate to see you go, Timmy. I'd like to… get to know you better, if you'll let me." Then his face softened. His own words seemed to have startled him. Their intensity. Their *need*.

Timmy reached across the table and laid his hand over Jasper's. "That's what I'm saying, stupid. I really would like to stay a little longer. I like being with you."

"Then what's the problem?"

"No problem. I'd just like to borrow your Jeep so I can run into town and pick up a few clothes."

A warning bell jangled in Jasper's head. "I'll take you."

Two little creases materialized between Timmy's eyes. He didn't look happy with the way the conversation was going. "I'd rather go on my own. Would you let me do that? I won't steal your Jeep. And I have a license and everything."

"Kid, I don't care about the Jeep. And I know you have a license. I nosed through your wallet, remember? I'm just worried you won't come back. And if you don't come back, I won't know how to find you."

Timmy smiled a gentle smile. His thumb stroked the hair on the back of Jasper's hand. Jasper felt that thumb stroke all the way down to his stomach.

"You have to trust me if we're going to be friends, Jasper. Will you trust me? I won't be gone more than a couple of hours. I promise."

Jasper was feeling a little put upon again. He was also feeling the first twinges of panic. What if the man really *didn't* come back. And it wasn't the Jeep Jasper was worried about either. Fuck the Jeep.

"The clutch sticks" was all he could think to say.

Timmy grinned. "When I get back, I'll fix it. I can do more than stick a dick down my throat, you know. I'm actually a pretty good mechanic. Please, Jasper. Let me do that much, at least. It would be a start for paying you back for everything you've done for me. And judging by the way you build crooked fences and lopsided hog houses, I don't think I'd like to see you dismantle an automobile."

At that Jasper *did* laugh. Timmy was absolutely right. He wouldn't know where to start.

But while Jasper laughed, Timmy grew somber. When Jasper saw the seriousness on his face, he stopped laughing as if someone had pulled a rug out from under his feet.

"What's wrong now?"

Timmy reached his other hand across the table and scooped up Jasper's hand between both of his as he had done in the bed earlier. He stared deep into Jasper's eyes, and Jasper's heart did a somersault.

"Tell me," Jasper gently prodded. "What's wrong?"

While continuing to hold and stroke Jasper's hand, Timmy tore his eyes away and stared out the window. There was a flush on his cheeks, and Jasper realized he was embarrassed. That realization made Jasper hurt a little. He didn't like it at all. The man had absolutely nothing in the world to be embarrassed about.

Apparently, Timmy felt differently.

"I'm not used to being so genuinely liked, you know. I keep wondering how long it will last. I keep wondering when you'll get tired of having me around. Is it just sex, or are we actually becoming friends. To tell you the truth, I'm a little confused by it all, Jasper."

"Don't be," Jasper said. "And don't analyze it. And don't doubt it either. I *do* like you. That's all that needs to be said about it. If we end up being friends, well, hell, what's wrong with that?"

Timmy's voice was small and timid. "I think we're already friends. Don't you?"

Jasper was touched by the simplicity of Timmy's words. He also saw an opening, and he took it. "Yes. And friends don't keep secrets from each other. Just tell me one thing. Is it the law you're running from, or is it… something else?"

Timmy's eyes opened wide. His lips narrowed. "I'm not—"

And now Jasper took Timmy's hands into *his*. Softly, he said, "Please don't lie to me again. It isn't necessary. Tell me the truth. If we're going to be friends, let's at least start it off with honesty. I don't really care what brought you here, Timmy. I'm just glad you're here. And if there's anything I can do to help you, I will. But you have to tell me the truth. I can't remedy a lie. No one can."

Timmy's eyes darted hesitantly about the room. He knew Jasper could see what he was doing. He was stalling for time. Thinking things through. His eyes shot to the refrigerator, the stove, the clock over the sink. He didn't bother looking through the window anymore. It was too dark to see outside. The only thing to be seen there was his own reflection staring back at him from the dark glass, and that was the last thing he wanted to see.

Finally he came to a decision. Jasper was right. He didn't deserve to be lied to any more. But Timmy wasn't ready to give up *all* his secrets, either. Jasper might turn his back on him if he did, and the thought of that happening made him a little sick all over again. He liked Jasper. He didn't want to lose him yet.

He took a deep breath and decided to tell Jasper the truth. Just not all of it.

"The truth is, I live in a shithole hotel below Broadway I'd be embarrassed for you to see. I have a job, Jasper. I'm not a bum. But it's a crappy job. I flip burgers. That's all I do. I flip burgers. It barely pays the rent, which I pay by the week. If I'm away from the hotel too long, they'll go in and take my clothes for payment. Then I'll really be in a fix. I've already lost my job. I've been gone, what, four days? Five? They bitch if I'm two minutes late. So that's me, Jasper." He forced himself to look at Jasper head on. "Right now I'm without a job. I'm probably homeless. Staying with you is no longer something I'd *like* to do, but something I *need* to do. At least until I find another job. So there you have it," he finished at a gallop. "The truth you wanted. Not too pretty, is it?"

Jasper gave him a reassuring smile. There was sympathy in the smile, but there was a thank you in it too. A thank you for speaking the truth.

"None of that bothers me, Timmy. The hotel, the job, none of it. I like *you*. Not for what you do or where you live but for who you are." He chuckled. "And because you're gorgeous."

Timmy offered him back a weak smile. He was not too impressed, actually, with Jasper's flimsy stab at humor, and Jasper was sorry he'd made the joke.

Kindly, Jasper said, "All those things can be fixed, Timmy. I know they're scary right now, but I'll help you get back on your feet. I promise I will. We'll find you a job. The thing is—I still don't know why you came to be here on my mountain in the first place. Tell me what brought you here and I won't pry any more. I swear. But this I need to know. Whatever the reason, I'll help you with that too. I will."

Timmy stared at him, silent. There was shame in his eyes, and that shame made Jasper ache inside. He wondered if he was doing more harm than good. Was he opening a schism between the two he would never be able to repair? God, he hoped not.

But still, there were things *he had to know.*

"Is it the law, Timmy? Is that who you're hiding from? Just answer me that."

And Timmy said, "No." After a moment, he added, "Not this time. This time it's worse than the law."

"Jesus, Timmy, what can be worse than the law? Explain it to me," Jasper urged. "Let me help. And why was there a Cadillac key in your pocket? Where's the car? It was yours, right? So where is it?"

Again Timmy said, "No. It wasn't mine." Stubbornness pushed aside the shame in Timmy's eyes, and he stared back at Jasper almost in anger. "I've told you all I can. You'll just have to trust me. Will you do that? Yes or no."

Jasper was exasperated by Timmy's stubbornness, but he knew who was holding all the cards here. If he didn't back off, he would lose Timmy forever. He could see it in the man's eyes. He was about to get mad. He was about to rebel at Jasper's intrusions. And that scared the shit out of Jasper. He couldn't bear the thought of Timmy simply walking out of his life as though he had never been in it. He wanted a chance to get to know the guy, maybe see if a real friendship could be forged out of this weird situation. It was becoming clearer by the second if he wanted Timmy to hang around, Jasper would have to play by Timmy's rules. Maybe later they could sort things out, get to the bottom of the big mystery, find out who Timmy was really running from.

Get an honest dialogue going. Maybe even something more.

Jasper sighed. Against his better judgment, he fished into his pocket and tossed a key onto the table.

It was the key to the Jeep.

JESUS, Timmy had never seen so many potholes in his life. And every one of them was filled with water and damn near two feet deep. It was like the Land of a Thousand Lakes, for Christ's sake. Timmy had to roll up the side windows on Jasper's old Jeep so he wouldn't be tsunamied right out of the cab every time he splashed into one.

He still couldn't believe Jasper let him take the Jeep. And thank God he had. Timmy had things that needed to be done. Timmy could never have let Jasper see the dive he lived in. Not that Timmy was actually going there. He had no intention of showing up at that shithole of a hotel. Ever again.

But even if he had, it would have ruined everything for Jasper to see the joint. Jasper was a decent human being. Timmy was… not so decent, and he damn well knew it. Timmy would take every precaution he could to keep his past out of Jasper's line of sight. The thought of Jasper looking down on him and wondering what he'd gotten himself into, messing with a guy like Timmy, made Timmy's heart ache. And that was a new feeling for him.

Hell, a week ago, Timmy wouldn't have known he even had a heart.

But he certainly knew it now.

And it was a strange, strange realization. Timmy had never known such kindness and affection from another human being as he had received at the hands of the man who nursed him back to health. Even their lovemaking was, well, *lovemaking*. A little too tender, a little too *connected*, to be thought of as hump sex. Timmy was no stranger to meaningless sex. Hell, it was practically a way of life with him. But what he had experienced with Jasper was so much more than that. It floored him to realize how much he genuinely liked the guy, and how much he wanted to be with him. Even now, having been gone a grand total of twenty minutes, Jasper was feeling like something was missing in his life. Something he'd grown to enjoy having around. Something he really liked looking at.

That something was Jasper.

Timmy could still feel Jasper's fuzzy, strong body against his. The heat of it. The carefully subdued strength. Could still feel Jasper's big gentle hands when he gave him the sponge bath that first day. Could still see the light of kindness that sparkled in Jasper's eyes every time he looked at Timmy. And the look of concern too. The worry about his sickness, the constant checking of Timmy's temperature. The taste of Jasper's lips. The taste of Jasper's come.

Timmy's eyes dimmed when a surge of passion welled up inside him. He had to take a firm grip on the wheel so he wouldn't turn the damn Jeep around and fly back to the ranch to jump Jasper's bones all over again. And to think, when this all started, when Timmy woke up out of his delirious dreams and realized he was being nursed back to health by the hunk on the bucket, he had thought of Jasper as nothing more than a sap. A do-gooder. A cute one, sure, but still just a Good Samaritan Timmy could take advantage of. Timmy appreciated the help, he supposed, but he appreciated the chance to elude his pursuers in a safe, warm hidey-hole even more. That feeling didn't last long, though, did it?

Timmy had to wonder now who the real sap was. He seriously doubted if Jasper was sitting around with a hard-on mooning over *him*.

Timmy impatiently adjusted his boner and drove on.

A ways down the lane, he looked off to the left where two wheel ruts headed off into the scrub. If he hadn't known they were there, he would never have seen the tire tracks at all. He glanced through the tunnel of battered bushes in the direction the tire tracks headed to see what he could see, but there was nothing. No glint of chrome. No flash of black. No sparkle of glass.

Relieved, Timmy drove on. Jasper's old Jeep clattered and banged through the potholes with such force, Timmy wouldn't have been surprised if the motor had simply fallen through the bottom and disappeared in a gurgle of mud.

It was with an immense sense of relief that he finally maneuvered the Jeep to the end of the lane and bounced up onto an actual fucking road. He imagined the Jeep shaking itself off like a dog, and with a slip of the clutch and a grinding of gears, they were off.

Timmy headed straight for the glow of city lights he could see way the hell off in the distance. He only had three stops to make, the first the tiny clapboard garage he rented from an old lady on Pike Street. That's where his tools were. And some of his clothes, too, enough to get by with, at least. And some other rather important stuff. His face twitched into a smile at *that* thought. It surely did.

He had no intention of retrieving his belongings from the hotel downtown. Fortunately, there was nothing he couldn't live without among his belongings at the hotel. And Timmy had no doubt whatsoever the man pursuing him had one or two of his goons parked in the dusty-ass lobby, waiting for him to show up.

Well, they'd be waiting a long time.

He turned onto Pike Street, maneuvered into the only parking space in sight, and sat there for fifteen minutes watching the garage next to the big Victorian house the old lady owned. As usual, there was no outside light on. Even the house was dark, the old lady already in bed at barely nine o'clock.

When he was sure there was no one lurking in the shadows, or in any of the cars parked around him, Timmy stepped from the Jeep and slid into the darkness as silent as a cat, garage key in hand.

It took him twenty minutes to move all his belongings from the garage to the Jeep. Clothes, tools, everything. He worked diligently and quickly until he was satisfied there was nothing left behind to give away his presence to anyone who might come snooping around.

Jeep loaded, he headed back to the house one last time and slipped a crisp new hundred-dollar bill under the old lady's back door.

He suspected he would never see her again. Too bad. She was a nice old broad.

And as for the money? There were more hundred-dollar bills where that one came from.

Oh yeah. There surely were.

Still flying under the radar, he hoped, Timmy's next stop was an all-night gas station at the edge of the freeway. There he purchased a two-gallon gas can and filled it from the pump, stowing it in the back of the Jeep. Before he left, he also purchased a Bic lighter and a bag of chips. He was hungry. Slipping onto the freeway and checking his rearview mirror every few seconds to make sure he wasn't being followed, Timmy headed back to the ranch.

Only one more stop along the way. He wasn't exactly sure where that stop would be, but he would find the perfect spot. He was sure of it.

Only then would he and Jasper be safe from the man who was chasing him.

TWO hours after Timmy left, Jasper heard the clatter and clunk of his Jeep banging its way back up the mountain. He almost fainted with relief. It was the happiest sound he'd ever heard. The man had actually returned. He hadn't stolen Jasper's car and disappeared forever. He hadn't played Jasper for a fool and trodden all over his good intentions. And he sure as hell hadn't made Jasper sorry he had helped the guy in the first place. In fact, Jasper was still stunned by his good fortune in having Timothy Sebastian Harwell choose *his* hog house to pass out in to begin with.

He lit the candles on the mantle over the fireplace when he heard the car door squeak open and slam shut outside. He decanted the bottle of wine that had been sitting in his cupboard for over a year as he listened to the footsteps crossing the porch. And while the three dogs stood inside the front door, trembling with excitement and wagging their tails all over the place, as eager for Timmy to return as Jasper was, Jasper ran a hand over his smoothly shaved face to make sure he hadn't missed any spots with the razor.

While Timmy was gone, Jasper had come to the rather astonishing conclusion he didn't much care what stroke of cosmic good fortune it was that brought Timmy to his mountain; he was just glad the man was here. Really glad.

Jasper, it need not be said, was in a romantic mood. He hoped to hell Timmy was too.

Chapter NINE

JASPER wasn't disappointed. Timmy walked through the front door and directly into his arms as though he had been gone a week, surprising not only Jasper, but Timmy himself.

"You came back" was all Jasper could think to say. He spoke the words with his lips buried deep inside Timmy's mop of hair while he held him tight in a bear hug. With Timmy's head tucked under his chin and the young man's slight body completely enveloped in Jasper's arms, Jasper had the oddest sensation this, this moment *right here*, was one of the better moments of his life.

Timmy grinned, loving those burly arms around him, loving the wind of Jasper's breath in his hair, loving the broad, strong chest against his face. "Yeah, I did," he said. "Didn't think you could get along without me."

Jasper didn't answer because he was a little bit afraid Timmy was right, and he wasn't quite ready to admit it. Not yet. Not even to himself. Because of Jasper's silence, Timmy was suddenly embarrassed by the way he'd rushed into Jasper's arms, and he backed off. He squatted down, and the dogs came to get their portion of his attention. Timmy gave each of them a good neck rub and then groaned to his feet like an old man.

He averted his eyes, looking around the cabin as if he'd never seen it before. Saw the two cats, Guatemala and Fiji, perched on a windowsill and gave them a finger wiggle of greeting. By way of response, Guatemala yawned and Fiji licked his own ass. The cats weren't big greeters. Timmy brushed some dog hair off of his jeans, then pushed his hair out of his eyes for the hundredth time. Finally, he focused his attention on Jasper again. He was blushing, and he knew it.

To cover the fact, he gave Jasper a punch in the arm. "I didn't steal your Jeep, either. I brought it back. Most of it anyway. The parts that didn't fall off in the potholes. Thank you for trusting me."

"You're welcome. The lane's a little rough."

"Yeah. Like Hitler was a little cranky. And your Jeep's a piece of shit, Jasper. The clutch is going out, just like you said, but that's only the icing on the cake. Everything under the hood is on its last legs too."

"That's probably why you didn't steal it, huh?"

Timmy was startled for a second. Then he decided Jasper was kidding. No way he could know the truth.

"Bingo," Timmy said, trying not to grin but not succeeding very well. Again, he looked around the cabin. *My God,* Jasper thought, *he's trying to look butch.* And it was true. Timmy was doing that Sal Mineo-Marlon Brando-James Dean bad boy with a motorcycle thing. Trying to look tough. Trying to look… *distant.*

Jasper hid his smile. He wasn't fooled by Timmy's act of macho aloofness one little bit. He'd seen how the man rushed into his arms after walking through the door. And he thought he had a pretty good idea what all the blushing was about too. It was about Timmy showing more feelings than he was really ready to show. Jasper understood this because he was feeling exactly the same way.

When the silence ran on too long, Timmy gave Jasper's arm another punch. If the kid didn't stop it soon, Jasper was going to turn him upside down and spank his ass.

That thought made the blood rush to Jasper's crotch like someone had opened a flood gate.

He rubbed his arm, even going so far as to make a little hissing sound, pretending Timmy's punch hurt like hell, although it didn't. He might as well play along. "If you don't like my Jeep, then you'll just have to fix it, I guess. You're the mechanic in the… *house.*" He almost said "family," but quickly changed it. He wasn't sure why. To cover his discomfort, he asked, "How you feeling?"

Timmy was relieved to be back in normal conversational territory. *Safe* territory. "Good. I think I'll live." Again the blood rushed to his face. "Thanks to you." He looked down at his shoes, embarrassed all over again. Jesus, he kept saying sappy shit. What the hell was wrong with him tonight?

Jasper nodded, looking serious. Looking… pleased. "You're welcome." And after a pause that wasn't quite as uncomfortable as some of the others, he asked, "Did you get some clothes?"

"Yeah. And my tools."

"You have tools?"

Timmy laughed. "Well, yeah. Don't you?"

"I have a hammer. And I think there's a screwdriver lying around somewhere."

All discomfort forgotten, Timmy threw his head back and laughed like a hyena. "And you're supposed to be the butch one!"

Jasper blinked. "Am I?"

"Well, yeah. Look at you. All those big hairy muscles and shit. But maybe it's just for show. You know, like a movie set."

Jasper narrowed his eyes. "A movie set?"

"Yeah. Like, you know, the walls are there but there's nothing inside. Just hollow structures made to look like buildings. Maybe that's what you are. Just a bunch of empty muscles with nothing much going on inside."

"Empty muscles. I see. Like a facade, you mean."

Timmy snapped his fingers. "Yeah. That's it. A facade. You're a butch facade!"

At that, Jasper picked the lad up like a sack of potatoes and threw him over his shoulder.

"I'll show you butch," he said, and headed for the stairs with Timmy laughing and screaming and kicking like a maiden snatched up by a marauding Hun. "Gee," Jasper teased. "I guess I really am the butch one. That's a nelly little laugh you've got there, Timothy Ann."

"I'm not being nelly!" Timmy wailed. "You're tickling me, you fuck!"

So Jasper tickled a little harder. As he climbed the stairs he gave Timmy's ass a resounding slap and Timmy laughed all the louder.

"Hey! That hurt!"

Jasper didn't believe it. "No, it didn't. You're laughing. Here, let me do it again. I'll show you."

"No!" Timmy pleaded. "Stop! I'm going to pee my pants!"

"That's okay." Jasper grinned. "I cleaned you up once. I can do it again."

Timmy struggled to free himself, but he was still laughing so he didn't seem too desperate about it. "Only a cad would throw that in somebody's face! Fix your own fucking Jeep!"

The next thing Timmy knew, he was flying onto the bed, where he landed on his back with a loud "Oof!"

Jasper dove on top of him before he could catch his breath. Together, they rolled around in each other's arms, and as they rolled around, their clothes miraculously seemed to fall (or be stripped) away. It was sort of like fucking magic. Suddenly, they were naked.

Breathless, Jasper held Timmy beneath him and stared into his eyes. Timmy stared right back, and when their lips came together, they heard only the pounding of their individual hearts and the echo of Timmy's laughter still bouncing around the cabin.

Gradually their hearts slowed, the laughter dissipated, and they fell into the alchemy of touch. Warm bodies. Hard cocks. Trailing fingers. Hairy legs, knotted tight. Strong arms, holding close. Stomachs pressed together. The scent of man. *Two* men. Longing for release. Longing for each other. Happy to be exactly where they were at that precise moment in their lives.

Need. The bedroom walls *echoed* with *need.*

Jasper felt Timmy's warm hands stroking his back, stroking his ass, pulling him ever closer. Lying pinned beneath Jasper, Timmy felt the safest he had ever felt in his life.

Slowly Timmy folded his legs and raised them high to wrap around Jasper's waist. He offered himself. *All* of himself. Jasper tore his lips from Timmy's neck and pulled away, far enough to see the light of hunger in Timmy's dark, eager eyes.

"Tell me what you want," Jasper whispered. "Tell me exactly what you want."

Timmy hesitated for the slightest moment. He buried his fingers in Jasper's curly hair, raised himself far enough to once again brush his lips over Jasper's smooth face. Over Jasper's mouth. Felt their cocks grinding together, making them both shiver.

Neither man was laughing now. Neither man was smiling. Only their eyes were alive with happiness. Alive with passion.

"Fuck me, Jasper. Please. Fuck me."

Jasper's voice sounded raw, grated with hunger. "Is that really what you want?"

"Yes."

"You're not doing this just for me, are you? Because you think it's what I want?"

"Do it."

"Cause I just like being with you. I don't care what we do."

"Do it!"

"I don't want to hurt you."

"If you don't fuck me right this minute, I'm going to send you down the mountain to buy a dildo and I'll fuck myself!"

Jasper gave an exaggerated groan. "Sheesh! All right. God, you're demanding. I'll fuck you already."

"Good. And be gentle. I've never done this before."

"What!"

Timmy giggled. "Just kidding."

Jasper rocked back on his knees and lifted Timmy's legs even higher. Resting them on his shoulders, he slid a gentle thumb over Timmy's opening. Jasper felt the muscles there contract, then quickly relax.

Jasper smiled. Bending in and pushing Timmy's legs wide, he laid his lips there, right where his thumb had been a moment before. When his tongue shot out to taste Timmy's core for the very first time, Timmy gave a gasp. His hands came down and his fingers crunched Jasper's hair, desperately holding him in place. Then his hips began to move. Timmy pushed himself harder against Jasper's mouth. Clutching the man tighter. Holding Jasper in place.

Jasper scooped his hands more securely under Timmy's ass and lifted him higher, making him more accessible. Timmy's opening was neat and hairless. Beautiful. Jasper slid his tongue across it, then dipped it deep inside. He grinned when Timmy cried out. Pleased with the reaction,

Jasper stuck his tongue in a little deeper. Timmy started trembling and thrusting his ass ever harder into Jasper's face, and Jasper happily accepted every thrust.

While his mouth savored Timmy's hole, Jasper reached into the nightstand and pulled out a condom. It was tricky, eating that luscious ass while ripping the condom wrapper and positioning the condom over the head of his cock, but he managed it without too much trouble. God, he was good. He rolled the condom down over his dick with his free hand and pulled his tongue from Timmy's ass at precisely the same moment.

"No—don't stop," Timmy moaned.

Jasper laughed. "Hold your horses. The best is yet to come. No pun intended."

And with that, he positioned himself on his knees once again and pressed the head of his cock to Timmy's spit-soaked hole. Without asking permission, since he seemed to have already received it, Jasper slowly eased his dick through the tight, trembling ring of muscle. He watched Timmy's face with every bit of pressure he exerted, ready to stop in a heartbeat if he saw pain in Timmy's eyes.

But what he saw was Timmy, bright-eyed and eager, watching him back. Timmy's mouth was slack with lust and his fingers were gently pulling at Jasper, urging him deeper, begging him to hurry.

Finally, Jasper felt the ring of muscle give way completely, and his fat cock head slid smoothly into the depths of Timmy's ass. Timmy arched his back and accepted every inch of it, head tilted back, eyes squeezed shut in pleasure, his strong young fingers still pulling at Jasper, pulling, pulling.

When Jasper's cock was buried to the hilt, he stopped and let Timmy adjust to his girth, to his length. The feel of Timmy's satiny hot ass relaxing around his erect cock was one of the most sensuous experiences of Jasper's life. He'd fucked before, but Jesus, Timmy was really getting into this. Jasper was almost awestruck, watching the pleasure on Timmy's sweet face. Timmy's breath was coming in short little gasps and he was smiling. *Smiling.*

Timmy released his grip on Jasper's hips. He laid one hand across Jasper's broad hairy chest, and with his other hand, he grabbed his own cock and began stroking it, slowly at first, slowly. But as Jasper's cock began to move, as Jasper slowly pulled his cock almost out of Timmy's channel, then eased it back inside to its former depth, Timmy began to stroke his cock to the beat of Jasper's rhythm. The dick in his hand was as hard as marble. Jasper watched, fascinated, as Timmy slid his fingers around the head of his own cock, trembling at the sensation. And trembling, too, at the sensation of Jasper's cock delving into his deepest parts, splitting him open, seeking his heart, seeking his secrets.

Timmy laid himself open, accepting Jasper's every thrust. Gasping and crying out now with every stab of that magnificent cock.

When Jasper's lips came down to cover his, Timmy drove his tongue inside that hot delicious mouth, seeking *Jasper's* core, *Jasper's* secrets.

Jasper broke off the kiss gently. He repositioned himself yet again on the bed, balancing on his knees, holding Timmy by both ankles now, lifting his legs high, opening them wide. He watched as his cock slid in and out of that satin envelope, sheathed in this man he cared so much for, this man he was beginning to—

But before that thought could coalesce inside his mind, Timmy gave a great cry and Jasper watched, hypnotized, as the young man's come shot straight up into the air, splashing Jasper's chin, his chest, his arm.

At that moment, Timmy's ass opened even more and Jasper quickened his tempo, driving hard now, gasping and crying out himself. Timmy released his sodden cock and grasped Jasper's hips with come-soaked fingers, pulling him deep, begging, begging.

When Jasper came, it was like the world had suddenly exploded around him. A supernova, lighting the galaxy. Over and over, he felt his juices gush from him into that heavenly heat, that heavenly void, making Jasper tremble and gasp and cry out as Timmy had done.

As his movements slowed, Timmy lifted his back from the bed and wrapped his arms around Jasper's neck, pulling them so close together they were practically a single entity.

"Don't pull away," Timmy begged. "Stay inside me."

So Jasper did, gently cradling the boy, feeling his cock grow softer, feeling Timmy hold him in place with the contraction of his muscles, accepting Jasper inside himself even now, as if the man's cock were actually a part of Timmy. A part he could not bear to lose.

But soon, in spite of everything they did, Jasper felt himself slide away. And there was nothing either one of them could do to stop it.

Timmy clutched him tightly and groaned as Jasper's cock slid through the tender ring of muscle for the final time.

Seeing the contentment on Timmy's face, his squeezed-shut eyes, his tongue licking the corners of his mouth, Jasper still could not bear to part completely from the man.

He lifted Timmy's legs again, and once more knelt inward to press his lips to Timmy's opening.

As his tongue slipped inside, Timmy sucked in a great gulp of air.

Then, to Jasper's wonder, Timmy laughed.

They collapsed into each other's arms, Timmy's spent come slathering them both. They were still trembling, but not in passion. Now they were trembling in laughter.

"We're stuck together," Timmy hissed.

Jasper giggled and slipped to the side. He scooped Timmy into his arms without resting his weight on the man. Timmy let himself be gathered up in those hard, hairy arms, and he smiled when he felt them around him.

He pressed his face into the hair on Jasper's wide chest and breathed in the man's smell.

It was the best smell in the world.

"Thank you," he muttered, his lips brushing Jasper's skin, tongue still reaching out to taste, to savor. Still yearning. Still hungry.

So Jasper gathered him up closer. He buried his lips in Timmy's hair and tenderly stroked the boy's smooth back, the gentle swell of that incredible ass, dipping his finger there to feel the heat of the boy's opening.

They lay like that for the longest time, relishing the feel of each other, delighting in the contact. Discreetly, Jasper peeled away the condom and dropped it in the wastebasket by the bed. They took turns padding naked to the bathroom, doing what needed to be done. Jasper ran down the stairs and retrieved the wine bottle and the two glasses he had laid out earlier and then forgotten in all the excitement. Back in bed, they snuggled and sipped their wine, once again pulling each other close.

Outside, the night deepened.

They finally slept. And as they slept, they smiled. Neither set of arms released the other the whole long night.

When they awoke, they knew things had changed.

THE next morning there was an openness between the two men they had not shared before. They had a history now, and they both knew it. They had gone as close to each other as two men can possibly go, and they had enjoyed every moment of it. Longed, in fact, to share it again. That first day after their long night together, neither thought of much beyond the joining they had experienced. The joinings they would experience in days to come.

If they were quiet at breakfast, it was not a quiet born of awkwardness, but of contentment. Twice, Timmy reached out to brush his fingertips over the hair on Jasper's arm, or to trail his thumb along the veins that snaked down the back of Jasper's strong hands. Each time, Jasper smiled across the table and Timmy smiled back. Words were unnecessary. Only the closeness mattered.

Jasper's writer's mind suspected it had something to do with trust. Timmy had trusted Jasper to make that special kind of love to him. He had opened himself up completely to Jasper and Jasper had not broken his trust. He had been gentle. And he had appreciated what Timmy offered, and relished every moment of the time they spent exploring it.

For Timmy's part, he no longer felt the need to be anyone other than who he really was. While there were still secrets to be kept from Jasper, they were not secrets kept in contempt. They were secrets Timmy would have shared with no one. Because frankly, he wasn't yet sure exactly what to do about them. He supposed he was hoping things would go on the way they were going. Maybe he'd be lucky. Maybe no decisions would have to be made at all about his… predicament.

So with that hope in mind, Timmy set out to enjoy the time he had with Jasper. And to do as much for Jasper as he could, because never for a moment did Timmy forget Jasper really did save his life on that stormy day when he carried Tim into the cabin and nursed him back to health. Timmy did not understand a lot of things in life because he had never lived them, never experienced them. While he was not innocent of mind,

Jasper's Mountain

he was still fairly innocent of heart. But he understood debt and the repayment of debt.

For perhaps the very first time in his young life, he was also beginning to understand happiness.

And he was learning it from Jasper.

> Dear Reader,
>
> By now, your Cock must be HORNY. If you have a condom on your Cock, You can Fuck ME.
>
> How big is your Cock? 7" 8" ---- 10"?
>
> I would like to Suck your Cock
>
> How does your CUM Taste? Sweet, Bitter, Salty?
>
> John Inman.

Chapter TEN

TIMMY'S beat-up tennis shoes and his raggediest pair of blue jeans were sticking out from underneath the Jeep. Timmy was nicely stuffed inside them. He was lying on his back atop a slab of plywood. Otherwise he would have been up to his ears in mud. A few days had passed since the storm, a week maybe, and the ground was still soggy, although the weather was warm.

Jasper was standing beside the Jeep looking down at those beat-up tennis shoes and those lean jeans-clad legs, holding a tool in his hand he'd never seen the likes of in all his life. Timmy had told him to hold it, so here he was—holding it. He was too embarrassed to ask what it was. Didn't actually much care what it was. His attention was being held hostage by a fair-sized hole in one of the pant legs that exposed a very fetching expanse of Timmy's hairy thigh. There was also a most interesting bulge in the crotch of Timmy's jeans. Jasper really wanted to reach down and grab that bulge or maybe waggle his tongue around in the pant-leg hole, but he was afraid he would startle Timmy and the engine of the goddamn Jeep would fall out and smash the guy flat.

The fact that Timmy had stripped off his shirt so he wouldn't ruin it with grease was also playing heavily on Jasper's mind. My God, the man's trim stomach and that little trail of black hair forging a path from his belly button to his belt buckle and points beyond were as enticing as the bulge. Hell, everything about Timmy was enticing. Everything.

Again, Jasper looked at the tool in his hand. What the fuck was this thing? Then he looked at the toolbox Timmy had brought to the ranch. It weighed a ton and had every tool known to man neatly stashed away inside. The weirdass tool in Jasper's hand wasn't the only one he didn't recognize. There were others that looked even odder. Martian tools. That's what they were.

Jasper gave his head a shake. Jesus, he was cracking up. He wasn't used to being this happy. It was warping his brain.

Harry and Harriet were watching the proceedings with their noses sticking through the fence, grunting and snorting out suggestions. Both Jasper and Timmy were ignoring the pigs completely. Timmy didn't figure the pigs knew as much about internal combustion engines as he did, while Jasper wouldn't have been surprised if the pigs actually knew *more* than *he* did. But he sure as hell wasn't going to admit it to anybody.

"Why don't I just buy a new Jeep," Jasper said. "This one's obviously broken."

"Oh, shut up," Timmy said. Then he reached out from beneath the chassis with a greasy hand. "Spanner," he said, all business.

For lack of a better idea, Jasper handed over the tool he was holding. He was amazed when Timmy didn't throw it back in his face. Apparently, it was exactly what he wanted. Well, wasn't that a stroke of luck. A spanner. Now he knew what the tool was called. Of course he still had no idea what the fucking thing was used for.

It had been five days since the night Timmy had driven into town. Five days since he and Jasper had shared the wine—and *other* momentous events such as, well, butt fucking. And it was a funny thing: Jasper could still feel a smile part his lips every time he thought of that night.

Timmy had not left the ranch since. Neither of them had. They had settled into an easy, friendly alliance filled with laughter and desire and an amazing amount of joy. They could go hours and never say a word, or they could jabber all afternoon and never shut up for a minute. And either scenario was as comfortable as the other. Somehow, they had managed to forge a strong friendship around their hunger for each other that was not totally bound up in sex alone. They honestly seemed to like each other, and that was an astonishing thing to Jasper. Perhaps *the* most astonishing thing of all.

Being all alone on the ranch with no one around to snoop or pry or interrupt, they found themselves falling into sex at the drop of a hat. No self-consciousness, no awkward fumblings, no false displays of embarrassment or shyness. When the mood struck, they simply acted on it. Each was a fantasy to the other. Jasper's strong hairy body was exactly what Timmy craved in a man, and Timmy's slim sexy frame and big dick and gorgeous, gorgeous ass were exactly what Jasper found most exciting.

Timmy slid out from under the Jeep and, still flat on his back, grinned at Jasper. He had somehow managed to smear a streak of motor oil across his mouth, which made him look like he'd been chowing down on a mud pie. There was also a perfectly delineated handprint rendered in motor oil in the center of his chest. And to Jasper's way of thinking, boy, was *that* sexy.

"Start her up," Timmy said. "Let's listen to it."

Jasper waited until Timmy was well away from the tires so he wouldn't accidentally pop the clutch and run over him. Then he climbed into the cab and turned the key. The old Jeep came to life like a trooper. The engine idled smoothly and quietly.

Timmy clicked his tongue as he hauled himself to his feet and dusted himself off. "For Christ's sake, Jasper, give it some gas. I want to *hear* it."

Jasper gunned the engine, and still the motor purred like a kitten. It hadn't sounded that way since Jasper turned old enough to vote. After all, he'd had the Jeep for over a decade.

"Well?"

Timmy wiped his hand across his mouth, smearing the oil further. Now there was a glob in his ear as well. He cocked his head to the side, listened to the engine for a minute, then dragged an invisible knife across his throat, motioning for Jasper to kill the motor.

Jasper did.

Timmy smiled and threw the spanner in the toolbox. He turned his attention back to Jasper, looking him up and down as he sat in the front seat of the Jeep with the door open and one long leg hanging out.

"Sounds great," Timmy said. "Let's fuck."

"Uh, sure." Jasper pointed to Timmy's mouth, then to his own. "You know, you've got—"

"What?" Timmy was rubbing his greasy hand over the crotch of his raggedy blue jeans. The bulge Jasper had spotted earlier seemed to have grown. A lot.

"Nothing," Jasper said, watching Timmy's hand slide across that bulge, forgetting about the oil stain on the man's face completely. He had a sudden overwhelming urge to be naked. "Where do you want to do it? Inside, outside, hog house roof, right here in the mud? Where? I'm not letting you in bed looking like that."

"Rules, rules, rules," Timmy moaned with a grin. He took Jasper's hand and led him to the house. "Kitchen floor okay?"

"Jim dandy," Jasper said, feeling desire rush through him like wild fire. "We'll lock out the dogs."

"Good." Timmy grabbed Jasper's belt buckle and dragged him to the house. "I like the dogs, but when they lick my ass in the middle of sex, it's a little disconcerting."

"How about when I do it?" Jasper asked.

"That's a different story."

THAT evening, as they sat on the porch, nursing beers, watching the mountain darken around them, Jasper asked a question that had been bothering him for a long time.

"How did you break into the house? I mean, how did you know what to do? It's not like you're a burglar or anything." After a heartbeat or two, he added, "Is it?"

The lie fell smoothly from Timmy's lips, and he hated himself for it. "No, Jasper. I'm not a burglar. I apprenticed with a locksmith for a few months after high school. Learned some tricks. Here, I'll show you."

He pulled a velvet drawstring bag out of the bottom of his toolkit, which was still sitting on the porch. He removed the items one by one, displaying them for Jasper's benefit.

Timmy laid the items on the porch rail in front of Jasper's chair. Jasper leaned forward and checked them out. The first instrument was about four inches long and shaped like the letter L, with a spring attached so when squeezed shut, it would automatically spring open again. The next two implements resembled swizzle sticks with different shaped tops, one with a half-diamond-shaped top and the other with a half circle on the end. The last item looked like a regular old key, only a little emaciated, as if it suffered from a severe case of bulimia. It was skinny and sharp edged but still retained the basic shape of a key.

Timmy tapped each device with a fingertip as he went along, explaining them one by one. "This little beauty shaped like an L is a tension wrench for applying torque to the tumblers inside a lock to hold them open while they're being picked. Then we have the tools that do the picking. Hook pick, shaped like a diamond; ball pick, with a circular end. And last but not least, we have the good old warded pick. Basically a skeleton key. Works about three fourths of the time on any fucking key lock you run across. The tension wrench works *every* time, just takes a little longer."

"Which one did you use on my front door?"

"This." Timmy pulled a penknife from the velvet bag. "For you I went low tech. Used this little baby. A credit card works just as well. Slip it through the doorframe, waggle the bolt back with it gently, and voila!" He pulled a credit card from the bag as if to demonstrate.

Jasper plucked the credit card from Timmy's fingertips. He looked at it. "You mean it's that easy?"

"It is if you know what you're doing. Plus you've got a cheap lock on your door. You get what you pay for, you know."

Jasper looked at the credit card more closely. "This belongs to some woman. Where'd you get it?"

Again Timmy shrugged, the lie springing easily from his lips. "Found it on the street. It's expired, you notice. Not good for anything but picking locks. Not like I stole her identity or bought a car on the poor woman's credit. Relax." This time what Timmy said was the truth. He had never used a stolen credit card in his life. Not to buy things with at any rate. He wasn't that stupid. As a lock picking tool? Well, that was a different story.

Jasper handed the credit card back to Timmy and plopped himself back down in his rocker. He quietly nursed his beer while he watched Timmy put the tools back in the bag and stash them in the toolbox.

Jasper tried to believe what Timmy had told him. He *wanted* to believe. But the longer he was with Timmy, the more he was troubled by the fact that Timmy still would not explain how he came to be on the mountain. The hiking story was a lie, and Jasper knew it.

Maybe the credit card story was true. Jasper couldn't imagine Timmy being dumb enough to leave a stolen credit card lying around in his frigging toolbox.

But what of the young man's lock picking capabilities in general? Timmy had been a little too glib with his explanation. *Apprentice to a locksmith my ass,* Jasper thought.

And there was still the Cadillac key Jasper had found in the man's pocket. Jasper had yet to hear an explanation for that.

He sank into silence and didn't really notice what Timmy was doing until he materialized at Jasper's side and planted a kiss on top Jasper's head. Jasper stopped rocking and fretting long enough to look up at him and smile.

Timmy very sweetly smiled back. "What are you thinking?"

Jasper didn't answer. He *couldn't* answer. He didn't know what to say. What he really wanted to do was simply stop doubting Timmy's lousy alibis and excuses and blatant evasions and trust the man completely. They had a wonderful thing going here. Jasper didn't know how long it would last, but he was sure as hell enjoying it so far. He tried to avoid the knowledge one day Timmy would simply have to leave. He must have another life somewhere. He'd have to rejoin it sometime or other.

But that thought, the thought of Timmy leaving, left Jasper with an emptiness inside he couldn't quite explain. Or maybe he could, but he didn't want to.

As if from outside himself, he watched Timmy's hand reach out and clutch his own. He watched Timmy pull him to his feet and take the beer bottle from his hand. Then he watched Timmy step in front of him and lay his lips over Jasper's mouth, ever so gently. Jasper closed his eyes at the sensation of Timmy's kiss. He let himself be pulled into Timmy's arms. Then, with a silent, tender look, Timmy stepped back, took Jasper's hand, and led him into the cabin and up the stairs.

Their lovemaking that night was the sweetest Jasper had ever experienced with anyone. Male or female.

As they lay in each other's arms afterward, listening to their pounding hearts settle back to a reasonable tempo, Jasper found himself wanting to say words he had not spoken to anyone for years. Lying together, still damp with sweat and sticky with come, Jasper buried his face in the crook of Timmy's neck while Timmy held him close. Stroked his hair. Cooed soft sounds that meant nothing, but to Jasper meant everything.

Jasper pleaded with himself to fall asleep before he blurted out the words he was itching to speak. Once they were said, there was no turning back.

The next morning, although Jasper wasn't a praying man, he thanked God Almighty sleep had found him before the words spilled from his lips and into Timmy's ears.

At least, now, Timmy still did not know Jasper was head over heels in love with him. And Jasper doubted he ever would.

Because Jasper knew he simply did not trust Timmy enough to tell him.

For Jasper, that realization was a sock in the gut. It filled him with a misery he hadn't seen coming. Lying in the bed, feeling Timmy's warm body beside his, Jasper squeezed his eyes shut, hoping that would stop the tears. And it did. But there was no stopping the pain.

The pain of knowing he would have to let Timmy go.

And probably soon.

TIMMY sensed Jasper's distance the minute he woke up. When he reached out for Jasper in the lazy, sleep-warm way lovers do, Jasper patted his hand and excused himself, climbing out of bed and heading for the bathroom to prepare for the day. There was none of the usual whistling and humming that accompanied Jasper's morning ablutions, either. None of the yelling out of questions and making conversation through the bathroom door. No invitation to shower together and maybe do some other stuff as well. Aside from the sound of running water and the banging of a few cabinet doors, the sounds from the bathroom were cold. Impersonal. And it saddened Timmy to hear them.

At breakfast, an odd silence hung in the air. Even the animals seemed subdued. They had picked up on Jasper's mood as surely as Timmy had.

Timmy had to admit to himself what he had fully expected to come to pass sooner or later, indeed had. Jasper was pulling away. It shouldn't have come as a surprise to him, but somehow it did.

It was time he faced the facts. It was time to move on, and Jasper was letting him know as nicely as he could.

Timmy kicked himself for showing Jasper the lock-picking tools. He shouldn't have told Jasper even a tenth of what he had told him over the past two weeks.

And what he really shouldn't have done was let himself get so close to Jasper.

While Jasper banged sullenly around the kitchen preparing breakfast, trying to look chipper but not really pulling it off, Timmy stared through the kitchen window at the bright sunny morning unfolding on this side of Jasper's mountain. It was a beautiful sight. The trees sparkling with dew, the birds swooping here and there, the cat Fiji stalking an alligator lizard across the roof of the hog house, tail and ears flat, hungry for some nice fresh lizard meat to give his day a jump start.

Timmy watched all the beauty outside as if he were watching a movie. But it was a movie he couldn't quite get into. He couldn't make himself feel a part of it. Because frankly, he was starting to feel sick all over again. It wasn't the flu this time. This time it was something way down deep. Something at the very heart of him. There was a misery growing there. And an anger too. Anger at himself. Anger at his misfortune to have ever ended up on this fucking mountain to begin with.

Anger for letting himself fall in love with Jasper Stone. The minute that thought entered his head, Timmy knew it was true. He was nuts about the guy. All the things he had found to admire in Jasper were the things he lacked inside himself. And he damn well knew it. Honesty, kindness, contentment, sweetness. Jasper was the man Timmy would have liked to have been. Timmy knew simply being around Jasper made him a better person.

And if Jasper could actually love someone like him, someone so fucked up and imperfect, then maybe it was a sign there was something in Timmy *worth* loving. Something *worth* saving.

He supposed it took Jasper's pulling away to make Timmy realize beyond all doubt he had fallen hard for the man. He had grown used to so many things these past two weeks: The way Jasper's strong arms held him close. The gentle way Jasper made love. The tenderness he showed in a thousand different little things he did during the course of a day. And now, the thought of losing all that was too much to cope with.

It was so like his luck, Timmy silently railed at himself. The day Timmy woke up ready to finally admit his love for Jasper was the same day Jasper had apparently decided he'd had enough of whatever the hell they had going on between them. Was it a love affair or was it just sex? Do you really need *love* flowing both ways to make a love affair? Timmy didn't know. And while Timmy was pretty good at reading people, this morning he couldn't read Jasper at all.

What he did know was somehow during the night Jasper had flipped a switch inside himself, cutting Timmy out. Timmy could feel it every time Jasper's eyes skidded over his, which this morning was seldom.

The kindness, the affection, he was so used to seeing in Jasper's eyes was gone.

And now that it was, Timmy knew something inside himself had died right along with it.

That something was hope. Hope that he could change. Hope that he could be happy. Hope that life would stop dealing him the shitty end of the stick. *Hope he was worth enough to be loved by a good man like Jasper Stone.*

"I'm sorry," Timmy said, while Jasper was still turning rashers of bacon in the skillet. "I'm not very hungry. I think I'll take the Jeep for a spin. Just to make sure I fixed it right. That okay?"

Jasper turned and looked at him. He knew immediately Timmy was hurt. Well, so was he.

"All right," he said, and hating himself for it, he turned back to the stove, once again pushing Timmy away.

Jasper held his breath until he heard the door click closed. Then he wiped a tear from his cheek. It had been a long time since he'd felt a tear there.

A long, long time.

And he had never felt an ache like the one that thrummed inside him now. Never.

When he heard the Jeep start up and rattle off down the lane, Jasper turned off the stove even though his breakfast was only half-cooked.

He wasn't hungry any more.

TIMMY drove and drove. An hour passed. Two. The Jeep sounded and responded great. The hum of its engine was the perfect backdrop for Timmy's thoughts.

Timmy's miserable thoughts.

As always happened when things weren't going smoothly in Timmy's life, his mind dragged him back to his childhood. As if things weren't bad enough. Somehow, to Timmy's way of thinking, that had always been the catalyst for every bad thing that had ever happened to him. His childhood. The foster homes where food and shelter was provided, but little else. The changing schools every year or two, when the state decided it was time to move him to another residence, another district. The shyness he had been crippled with as a child and had only overcome after he was out in the world, forging his own path as an adult. Taking care of himself for a change. Relying on no one for anything.

Surviving, but having to break a few rules to do it.

At moments like this, when he found himself wallowing in those horrible memories of childhood, it was always a little like stabbing himself in the gut and then twisting the knife. It was a self-inflicted wound, letting his mind drag him back to seeing himself as that sickly looking kid in the hand-me-down clothes and the jacket provided by the state. God, Timmy had hated that jacket. It was a cheap handout, and everyone knew it. It was like being branded an orphan, wearing that crappy plastic jacket. Like a scarlet letter emblazoned across his back, proclaiming him unwanted. Unloved.

Timmy could not remember a gentle hand ever soothing his childish bumps and bruises. He never remembered a hug, a kiss, the promise of someone always being there to comfort his fears when the nights were dark and the shadows held monsters. He wasn't many years beyond being that miserable, unwanted kid. So when the tears began to fall as he drove down the gravel road abutting Jasper's potholed lane, he wasn't really surprised. And he wasn't embarrassed either. He was alone; no one would see.

And even if they did, no one would care.

That last realization tore through Timmy like a jagged blade. His eyes were suddenly so filled with tears he could hardly see what he was doing. He pulled the Jeep over to the side of the road, bumping to a stop, killing the engine, and letting himself be wrapped in the sudden sad silence like a hug.

All these new thoughts were as astonishing as they were frightening to the young man who had never had to worry about anyone but himself. He had never been a cruel person—he *knew* this—but he *had* always been self-reliant. Since the only person he had ever needed to worry about was himself, the only person he had ever truly *cared* about was himself. He had few friends, and the ones he did have weren't close. He turned his bed down for no lovers. He had no family to be a part of his life. There had never been anyone—until now.

Somehow, Jasper had touched something inside Timmy. It was a touch Timmy had never felt before. But now that he *had* felt it, he knew he could never live without it again.

And he suddenly knew with crystal clarity why Jasper had pulled away this morning. *Jasper didn't trust him.* And how could you trust someone who had not been honest from the minute they came face-to-face? Timmy had lied to Jasper from the very beginning, and somehow Jasper knew it.

But Timmy could fix that. He *would* fix it.

He sat there, two hands on the wheel, staring blindly through his tears to the road winding on ahead of him. He wiped the snot from his nose and let it come. The tears, the sobs, the pain.

Even as he cried himself out, Timmy knew what he had to do.

He had to tell Jasper the truth. *All* of the truth. Everything.

God help him, this time Timmy couldn't let the demons win. This time he had to fight for what he wanted. If it took humbling himself and telling secrets he had never shared with *anyone*, then by God, he'd do it.

Because there was one overriding reality in this misery Timmy was feeling that was absolutely inescapable.

He could not let himself simply walk away from Jasper. And he could not let Jasper walk away from him. What had started as lust had meandered over into love. Real love.

And for perhaps the first time in his life, Timmy now knew exactly what he wanted. Exactly what he needed. And that something was standing back there in a mountain cabin right now, looking through the window, maybe, wondering if Timmy would ever come back at all.

Timmy had heard a lot about love during his twenty years on the planet, but he supposed he'd never really believed much of it. Maybe love is one of those things you simply *can't* understand until it's got you by the balls and won't let you go.

And since it now had a death grip on his ass that wouldn't quit, Timmy suddenly understood it perfectly.

Love. What a sneaky bitch she was. But he wouldn't fight her. Not anymore.

He wiped the tears and snot from his face and turned the key in the ignition.

This time he would fight for what he wanted. He would even beg if that's what it took. But he couldn't let Jasper go. He couldn't. Not only did Timmy love the man, he also somehow knew Jasper was his salvation.

He could change with Jasper at his side. He knew he could.

Because Jasper was worth changing for.

He looked at his red, bleary eyes in the rearview mirror, then popped the clutch, which no longer slipped, and headed back onto the road.

Already, his heart felt lighter. He could do this. He knew he could. He had seen flashes of love in Jasper's eyes during the course of the last two weeks when Jasper looked at him. Timmy knew he had.

Timmy would rekindle that fire if it was the last thing he ever did.

He ground the Jeep into gear, pulled a U-turn, and headed back to the ranch.

JASPER sat on the sofa scratching Jumper's ear while Lola and Bobber stood on the recliner, staring through the window at the trees outside. Jasper knew what they were doing. They were watching for Timmy. They missed him.

He had been gone for over an hour, but Jasper was so depressed about the way things were going, he couldn't even work up any angst about the possibility that Timmy wasn't coming back at all. Besides, Timmy's toolbox was still sitting on the porch, and somehow Jasper knew the man would not leave without that.

He'd be back. He would. But what Jasper was going to say to him when he returned was a mystery. Even to Jasper.

He knew what he *wanted* to say. He knew what his *heart* wanted him to say. But those would be words of love, and how do you speak words of love to someone when you know they've been lying to you with every breath? How do you speak words of love to someone who shuts you out and doesn't tell you what you need to know?

How can you love someone you cannot trust?

Jasper slumped back against the couch and closed his eyes. He was exhausted. Exhausted and heartsick.

And now he was beginning to worry. Timmy had been gone too long. Maybe he'd had an accident in the Jeep. Maybe—

Jumper tore away from Jasper's hand and leapt onto the recliner with the other two dogs. They stared through the window, and Jasper watched as their hackles rose and their lips pulled back in growls.

When they started barking, they were loud enough to wake the dead.

It wasn't Timmy. Jasper knew that much. The dogs wouldn't be growling if it was. They'd be wagging their tails and hopping around all happy and eager. Also, Jasper had not heard the sound of the old Jeep grinding up the mountainside.

He hauled himself forlornly to his feet, not really giving a shit *who* it was if it wasn't Timmy. Still heartsick, he stalked to the door to pull it open.

The dogs tore out around him before Jasper could step onto the porch.

Maybe the coyote's back, Jasper thought, squinting into the morning sun.

He shielded his eyes with his hand and stared out toward the trees where the dogs were headed. Then he tensed.

Once again, he thought of the guns in the closet, but he dismissed the thought as quickly as it came. It was too late.

The men were already upon him.

Chapter ELEVEN

THE two men had just stepped from the trees. When they saw Jasper exit the cabin, they raised their hands in greeting, but when they spotted the three dogs barreling down on them at a full run, their greetings faltered. One man reached inside the puffy down vest he was wearing, but at that distance, Jasper couldn't see what it was he was reaching for. However, the movement put him on alert.

It looked like a man reaching for a gun, and Jasper didn't like that at all. Then he thought maybe it was a nervous gesture. A protective gesture. The animals were so keyed up, they would probably scare *anybody* to death, although Jasper knew their ferocious display was all for show. At least he hoped it was. They had never bitten anybody yet. Not that he had many visitors to test them on.

Jasper whistled, and the dogs stopped in their tracks. They didn't look too happy about obeying, but they did.

Again one of the men raised his hand and called out thanks.

Jasper nodded, slapped his hip so the dogs would come to his side, and waited for the men to approach.

As they drew near, Jasper saw the two men were casually dressed, but not *hiking* dressed. Except for the fat down vest on the one man, which the weather was way too hot for, they looked like they had just stepped out of an Abercrombie and Fitch catalog. Stylish. A little too stylish for men their age. Neither one of them looked much under forty.

The men were trim, their arms well muscled. They wore short-sleeved shirts, neatly tucked in at the waist. Their slacks were exactly that. Slacks. Not blue jeans. Not khakis. Dress slacks. They looked as out of place out here in the middle of Endor as that stupid fucking hot vest. One man actually had tassels on his loafers, which Jasper found amusing, since the man's feet were slathered with mud all the way up to his pant cuffs. He'd have to throw those loafers in the trash when he got home. And maybe the pants along with them.

The guy seemed to know he looked ridiculous, too, and he didn't look happy about it. Like he had really loved those shoes, dammit.

Jasper tried not to smile.

One man, the taller of the two, had blond hair cut short, and the pale, pale skin and blue eyes of a Viking. His eyes were such a light blue, in fact, they were actually kind of creepy. Alien eyes. Cold. Like a lizard.

Jasper had been in the men's company for five seconds, and he already knew he didn't like either of them. One looked mean, and the other had a cruel tilt to his head. That's the best way Jasper could describe it. A cruel tilt.

That man was Hispanic and had acne scars pocking his face. A lot of them. He must have had a miserable adolescence, what with his face looking like a meat-lover's pizza and all. And it didn't look like his mood had improved much since. Nor had his face. He eyed Jasper as though he'd enjoy nothing more than ripping off his head and rolling it down the mountainside like a bowling ball.

Both men looked aggravated as hell but were trying not to show it. The pockmarked Latino was also looking bored. Bored and hot. He kept pulling a handkerchief from his back pocket and blotting the sweat from the potholes in his face.

Jasper suspected the men's anger really wasn't directed at him. It was directed at the circumstances in which they found themselves. Namely, hiking through a fucking muddy forest in the heat, then being threatened by a pack of angry dogs, and doing it all a little bit overdressed to begin with. It would be enough to piss anybody off. Embarrassing is what it was.

Jasper tried really hard not to grin at their discomfort. He didn't figure they would be too amused if he did.

When the men were within twenty feet, and the dogs were still vibrating with excitement at his feet, Jasper called out, "Can I help you gentlemen?"

Pockmarks stopped and warily eyed the dogs. Jasper's writer's brain locked onto one word for the guy. Surly.

The other man, the big blond in the stupid puffy vest, strode forward to close the gap and stick out his hand. He purposely ignored the snarling dogs at Jasper's feet.

"Hush," Jasper said again, and the dogs quieted down. Ignoring Pockmarks, he stuck out his own hand to the man closest to him, and the blond's ham of a fist closed around it like a vise. He gave Jasper's paw a really good squeeze. A lesser man might have been cowed. But not Jasper. He was no ninety-pound weakling himself. He gave back as good as he got, and he was reasonably sure he detected a flash of disappointment in the goon's face when he did.

Jasper's mind kept going back to the vest the blond man was wearing. Not much reason to wear a fat, poofy vest on a day like this—unless you were trying to cover something up. Like a big roll of fat around your gut.

Or a gun.

Jasper's heart gave a stutter. Since there didn't appear to be much fat on the blond man *anywhere*, Jasper had an uncomfortable feeling the possibility of a gun being stashed under that stupid vest made more sense.

It was a funny thing, Jasper thought. He could count the times in his life on one hand when he had disliked somebody at first glance. And here he had two at once. A twofer, each as unlikable as the other. He didn't figure he'd ever be asking either one of these men over for crumpets and tea. He'd rather sit on a pinecone.

Jasper caught himself gnawing at his lower lip and forced himself to stop.

He asked again, trying to be polite, but not *too* polite. "Can I help you gentlemen?"

Blondie aimed those cold blue eyes into Jasper's face like darts. Jasper suspected that was him trying to be charming, but it was hell and gone from charming in Jasper's book.

The other man, Pockmarks, continued to stare at the dogs. Once in a while, he also gazed up at the cabin windows at Jasper's back, as if wondering if anyone else was on the premises. That searching look, more than anything, put Jasper on the defensive. He determined then and there to tell the two men nothing. He didn't give a fuck who they were. Or what the fuck they were looking for.

Strangely enough, it never occurred to Jasper to think they might be looking for a handsome young man with thick black hair and a body to die for. The same young man tooling around somewhere in Jasper's Jeep at that very moment. And why it *shouldn't* occur to Jasper was confusing indeed, because just about every other thought inside Jasper's head was monopolized by thoughts of Timmy. Those thoughts filled Jasper's head like smoke fills a burning house.

But not now. Now, Timmy was oddly absent from his mind.

Blondie dragged Jasper back to the present. "Just out for a stroll. The car overheated back on the highway, thought we'd walk around while it cooled off. Live here alone, do you?"

"Odd question," Jasper said. "Mind if I ask why you ask it?" An uneasy feeling was starting to nag at Jasper's nerve endings. Like a little alarm bell, clanging away inside his head. His toes started to ache the way they do when you're standing at the edge of a cliff and instinctively digging in through your shoes to ground yourself. You look up at the sky, imagining all the empty air above and below you at the same time. Vertigo. That's what it felt like. Vertigo. Not much different than fear, actually.

Blondie looked around the place like those real estate guys Jasper had been dealing with lately. But somehow Jasper knew he wasn't. If he was embarrassed by Jasper calling him out on his nosy-ass question, he chose not to show it. Jasper suspected there wasn't much that embarrassed this guy. And somehow that made him like the man even less.

"Sorry," Blondie said, although he didn't look sorry. "Didn't mean to sound like I was snooping. Just making conversation, you know." Again he looked around the place. His eyes centered on the new hog house for a minute, and he tilted his head. "That thing crooked?"

"Built it myself," Jasper said, fighting a blush that threatened to rise to his cheeks. "Not much of a carpenter. If there's nothing else, I have some work to do and—"

"Probably don't get many visitors out here, do you?" That was Surly. He was still standing well away from the dogs at Jasper's feet. He carried his Mexican heritage in his voice. His accent was pure barrio. "Hell and gone out in the middle of nowhere like you are. Except hikers, maybe. Get a lot of hikers passing through? You know, like us?"

The little hairs at the back of Jasper's neck were starting to do a cakewalk. "I don't really consider you guys hikers, now do I? I mean, you're just waiting for your car to cool down, right?"

Surly narrowed his eyes. "You know what I mean."

Blondie didn't seem to like the way the conversation was going. He shot an impatient look at his buddy, then spat up an insincere chuckle for Jasper's benefit. "My friend's a little grumpy. The humidity."

He was about to say something else when something caught his eye over Jasper's shoulder. "Well now, that's quaint. You don't see that much anymore."

Jasper turned to see what the man was talking about.

"Clothesline," Blondie said, not waiting for Jasper to ask. "Makes me think of my childhood. My poor old mom hanging every damn thing she washed out on that droopy clothesline behind the house. What a pain in the ass it must have been. Kind of a thing of the past now. Wouldn't it be easier to use a dryer?"

He didn't really look like he cared much about how much trouble his mother went to hanging her laundry on the line. He was way more interested in why Jasper found it necessary to use the fucking thing.

"No big mystery," Jasper said. "Dryer's on the fritz. Haven't got around to—"

Then Jasper's heart did a little somersault inside his chest. He turned back to look at the clothesline again—and at Timmy's clothes hanging limp in the windless air right next to some of his. Two pairs of blue jeans, one Timmy's and one Jasper's, hung side by side. One pair was a foot shorter than the other. If that didn't give away the fact that there were two people staying on the premises, nothing did.

Suddenly, Timmy wasn't absent from Jasper's mind any longer. The lad was back to filling up Jasper's head like smoke, as he usually did. And suddenly, he was worried all over again. Why *was* Timmy here? What *had* brought him to this lonely mountain in the first place?

One thing Jasper did know. If Timmy was being hunted, he didn't want it to be by these two. He didn't want Timmy anywhere *near* these two apes. But somehow Jasper knew—he *knew*—Timmy was exactly what the two creeps were looking for. He felt a chill slide down his back, like maybe the temperature of his blood had suddenly dropped twenty degrees. It was a feeling he hadn't experienced for a while, but he knew what it was right away.

This time he didn't piss around comparing what he felt to vertigo. Nope. This time it was flat out fucking fear, and he knew it.

"You were saying?" Blondie asked, all wide-eyed and innocent and not fooling Jasper at all.

A bead of icy sweat dribbled down Jasper's ribcage. He bent to pet Jumper to cover his discomfort. "I was saying the dryer's on the fritz. I hate that fucking clothesline as much as your mother probably hated hers. Now then, guys, I really do have some work to do. I guess you know how to get back to your car. Down the lane the same way you came. It's probably cooled off by now, don't you think?" He glanced up at the sun climbing high in the sky. He did it more for show than anything else, but it did give him a straw to grab at. "Plus it's gonna be hotter than hell pretty soon. You really *could* die of a heat stroke traipsing around this mountain at high noon. Not to mention the rattlesnakes. The heat always brings them out too. It doesn't improve their mood any either. You wouldn't want to run into one or two of those."

"Maybe you've got a point," Surly said, slapping at something on his arm. A mosquito, maybe. He bumped Blondie's shoulder to get his attention. "Let's go. The man's got work to do."

Blondie gave another glance at the cabin windows, saw no movement, and seemed to come to a conclusion. "Yeah, best be going. You take care now," he said to Jasper. He looked down at the dogs. "And the next time someone stops by to chat, don't be so goddamn grumpy, dogs. Ain't neighborly."

He made a gun out of his thumb and index finger and aimed it at Jumper's head.

Jumper gave a tiny growl, more than ready to bite the barrel off that imaginary gun, and the guy seemed to know it. He laughed a humorless laugh and gave Jasper a cocky little salute.

"Seeya. Sir."

And with that the two men turned on their heels and started to head back the way they'd come. Then they seemed to change their minds and stayed right where they were. An awkward silence filled the air. Then the blond man spoke.

"One more question," he said with a cold smile. "Where's your automobile? Don't see one anywhere."

Again that cold chill slid across Jasper's skin. Fuck.

Jasper plastered a phony grin on his face and gave what he hoped was a hopeless shrug. "Just my luck, the damned thing started acting up. The mechanic has it." Jasper glanced at his watch, or pretended to. "He should be bringing it back pretty soon. He's a friend of mine. Knows I'm stranded without it."

"Yeah," Blondie said, matching Jasper's phony smile with one of his own. "You're kind of at the mercy of the fates without a means of getting down off this fucking mountain. You never know what sort of emergency might crop up when you'll need a quick means of escape."

Jasper spat up an unconvincing laugh. Even he didn't like the sound of it. "Yeah, well, the mechanic should be bringing it back soon. I oughta survive that long."

For some reason, Surly had moved around behind him. Jasper was about to step to the side to get both of the men in front of him again, when he saw Blondie give an almost imperceptible nod to his partner.

And that imperceptible nod was the last thing Jasper saw.

His head exploded in a burst of pain, and he managed to stay awake just long enough to watch the ground come flying up toward him.

He heard Surly mutter, "Liar," and then darkness took Jasper completely.

Chapter TWELVE

WHEN Jasper first opened his eyes, they didn't seem to want to focus. When they finally did, at about the same time his head blossomed into a magnificent flower of pain, the first thing they focused on was Timmy's face. Two of them, actually. Then his vision centered and the image folded into one Timmy instead of two. The young man was stroking Jasper's jaw with gentle, cool fingertips. That must have been what woke him. The fingers felt nice, but they didn't do much to alleviate the throbbing ache in Jasper's skull.

Timmy was talking, too, he noticed, but it took a minute for the words to burrow through Jasper's pain and make themselves heard. When they did, he heard Timmy say, "Come on, baby, wake up. It's okay. It's okay."

Jasper liked the comforting words. He liked the concern he saw on Timmy's face too. And he liked the nearness of the man. He pulled himself awake to be near him, if for no other reason. All the resolve he had found earlier about halting whatever sort of relationship he and Timmy were headed for was quickly forgotten. He had never before been so happy to see someone. The fact that this was also the man he loved didn't appear to be such a bother anymore.

"You're back," he said simply, and Timmy nodded.

Jasper started to smile, but then he saw the blood. Timmy's face was a mess.

And about the time he made that observation he also realized his movements were restricted. It took a minute to scope out the fact that some asshole had tied him to a chair.

"Well, shit," he said, looking down at his arms bound behind his back and his ankles tied to the kitchen chair legs. Gazing around through the pain in his head, he saw the chair was in the wrong room. He was parked in front of the fireplace facing the window that looked out on the porch. He could even smell the cold ashes in the grate.

The light outside told him not much time had passed. The sun appeared to be straight up in the sky. High noon. He had been out for about an hour.

"Untie me, Timmy. These ropes are killing me."

Timmy slid his eyes from Jasper's face and looked over his shoulder with worried eyes. From behind him, Jasper heard the second voice. It sounded like Blondie, the stupid twit with the overstuffed vest. "That would be a big 'no,' Timmy. Touch one of his ropes and I'll cut your fucking hands off."

Jasper watched as a tear leaked from Timmy's eye. Finally starting to get a grip on the situation, Jasper realized Timmy was on his knees in front of Jasper's chair. As Jasper watched, still a little disoriented by the pain shooting through his noggin, Timmy leaned forward and rested his forehead on Jasper's chest.

"I'm so sorry," he said. "I'm so sorry." And then he snaked his arms around Jasper's back and wept. "I didn't mean for anyone to hurt you, Jasper. I swear I didn't." And he wept even harder.

Unable to comfort him with a touch because his hands were tied, Jasper bowed his head and pressed his face into Timmy's hair. He kissed him there, hoping that would be enough. And perhaps it was. Timmy's crying slowed. He gave a shudder, then pulled back to look in Jasper's eyes once again. Timmy's face was blotchy from weeping, and there was still a smear of blood across his cheek. His ear was red and swollen too. A small cut split his eyebrow. His bottom lip was torn. It looked like he had been worked over pretty good.

"They hit you," Jasper said.

Timmy tried to grin. Jasper could see the effort caused him pain. "Yeah. You too. Aren't we a pair? Two gorillas jumped me when I came in the door. You?"

"Snuck up behind me like cowards and hit me over the head with what must have been an anvil."

Again Timmy exerted the tiniest smile, then gently rested his fingertips on Jasper's jawline. "I'm sorry."

Jasper nodded. "I know. It's all right." He gazed around the room, wincing when he moved his head too far. "Where are the dogs, Timmy?"

"They've got them locked up in the lean-to. Hear them? They're throwing a fit in there. But they're okay. If they ever do get out, though, I hope they gobble these fuckers down like Milk-Bones. Ouch. My lip hurts. How's your head?"

"I haven't had any complaints yet."

Timmy tried to laugh at that well-traveled joke, but his torn lip stopped him cold. He said ouch again instead.

A third voice wormed its way into Jasper's consciousness. It was a familiar voice, and it brought a host of memories along with it; memories and the realization how Jasper came to be in this situation: to wit, tied to a fucking chair with a hammering headache. The voice belonged to Surly, the pizza-faced prick who had snuck up behind him and conked him in the head with what, in reality, must have been a gun butt. The man was obviously somewhere in the kitchen or the laundry room, talking into a cell phone. His voice was loud and booming and brassy, and he sounded like he was really trying to control his anger.

"I can just do 'em now. I can do 'em both," Surly was saying. Growling, actually.

Jasper didn't think he wanted to know what those words meant, although he thought he had a fairly good idea.

He gave Timmy a forlorn grimace. "What did you do, Timmy? What do these guys want?" Then before Timmy could answer, he said, "I'm sorry about this morning. I shouldn't have acted like that. I was just...." But he let the words trail away to nothing. This wasn't the time to accuse Timmy of being dishonest and keeping secrets from him. Shit, their lives were hanging by a thread here. He had no idea why, but it sure as hell wasn't time to start talking about honesty with the man he was in love with. Although he decided *those* words *did* need to be said.

"I love you, Timmy. I don't know what's going to happen here, but I want you to know that much. I love you."

Again, tears welled in Timmy's eyes. "I love you too, Jasper. That's what I came back to tell you. I love you more than anything."

Blondie apparently wasn't the romantic type. "Will you two fruits shut the hell up for Christ's sake! You're making me sick!"

"Sorry," Jasper said. Then he turned his head as far as he could toward the tall blond man who was still out of his line of sight and added, "Oh, and fuck you."

"Wiseass," Blondie said. "But that ain't gonna last long. Hard to be a wiseass with a bullet ricocheting around your brain pan."

Jasper had a feeling that was probably true, but at the moment, there wasn't much he could do about it. He wished he could wipe the tears from Timmy's eyes. He hated seeing them there. He didn't suppose showing fear would get him anywhere, but maybe he could find out what was going on. At least if he was talking, he knew he was still alive. Both of them. Him and Timmy.

"So you're going to kill us, then?"

"That's up to the boss. Now, shut the hell up. I'm trying to finish this crossword puzzle. What's a three letter word for annoying?"

"You," Timmy said, and Jasper did laugh at that.

Surly had stopped talking in the kitchen. Suddenly, there he was, standing in front of them, scowling down at them like they were something nasty he had peeled off the bottom of his shoe.

"The boss is coming," he said. "That should knock the smirks off your faces."

"What?" Blondie groaned. "Now? Don't he trust us to just whack 'em and get it over with?"

"He don't want them whacked." Surly lit a cigarette and blew two thick billows of smoke out of his nostrils like a dragon. He stared down at Jasper and Timmy and blessed them with a smirk. "He don't want them whacked *yet*. Got some questioning to do first, I guess. So cuddle away, lover boys. You won't be cuddling much longer."

He gave Timmy a slap to the back of the head, just because he could, and sauntered back to the kitchen, where Jasper heard him open the refrigerator door, apparently rummaging around for something to eat.

"Buy your own fucking groceries!" Jasper called out. Then he buried his face in Timmy's hair again because it was the most comforting position he could get himself into at the moment. There was moisture on his shirt from Timmy's tears and that kind of broke his heart a little bit, but still it was nice to have Timmy close.

"Hush," Jasper whispered, trying to figure out what to do. "Hush, baby."

Once more he tried working his hands loose, but the ropes were too tight. He couldn't get any leverage. The two of them settled into an uneasy, miserable silence, Timmy still sitting on the floor in front of Jasper, Jasper tied to the chair with his arms and legs screaming for movement so he could get the blood pumping again, both of their heads hurting like motherfuckers. The two goons were both in the kitchen now. Jasper could hear the clink of silverware on plates. They were eating.

Jasper listened to the wailing of the three dogs out back. They didn't like being locked in the lean-to without food or water or Jasper to comfort them. Jasper wondered how the goons had lured the dogs in there to begin with. Food, maybe. He couldn't think of any other way they could have done it.

With the men in the other room, Jasper's eyes wandered to the closet by the front door where his two guns were stashed. Timmy was still free to move around the cabin, although he still chose to sit in front of Jasper and hold him tight. Jasper was afraid to tell Timmy about the guns. If he made a grab for them, and failed, the men might kill him. Or at least hurt him more than they already had. And Timmy wasn't familiar with the guns. Maybe he wouldn't even know how to work them right off the bat. It would only take a second of fumbling around to bring the goons down on his head before he had a chance to make a difference.

Jasper would have been surprised to learn Timmy already knew about the guns and was having almost the exact same thoughts as Jasper about trying to make a grab for one of them. Unfortunately, Timmy's assessment of the situation was precisely the same as Jasper's. So he finally made up his mind—he would go for the guns only if things began to unravel completely. If it looked like they were going to die anyway, then he'd have nothing to lose. But for now he'd wait.

They would both wait.

And wait they did.

They heard Blondie tell Surly the boss would be here in about an hour and he was hiking back down the lane to get the car as soon as he finished eating. Timmy jumped when he heard Blondie mention the lane, but Jasper didn't think much about it. They were both jumping every five seconds anyway, they were so keyed up and scared.

And besides being scared, Jasper was ticked off too. Just his luck to finally exchange declarations of love with the man of his dreams on the day they were both slated to get shot in the head. He couldn't imagine a finer example of piss-poor timing.

With the men in the kitchen, Jasper lowered his voice to the faintest whisper and tried again.

"Tell me, Timmy. What did you do? Why are these guys here?"

Timmy rocked back on his heels, hands on Jasper's knees. He looked like he was ready to make a full confession, and Jasper was relieved. At least he would know what was going on.

Timmy kept his voice so low it was a mere rustle of sound. He leaned closer so Jasper could hear him, never taking his eyes off the two men in the kitchen, whom Jasper couldn't see.

"Remember the Cadillac key? I stole an Escalade from a parking structure downtown. It had been sitting there for two days. I was watching it. Finally I… just took it."

"And where did you get the key?" Jasper asked. "Surely it wasn't sitting there for two days with the key in the ignition."

"No. I-I jimmied the door lock, and once I was inside, I found the key under the seat."

"Why would anybody leave their car key under the seat?"

Again Timmy peeked around Jasper's arm to make sure the men were still occupied. They were talking low themselves while they continued to shovel in food. It made Timmy realize how hungry he was. He hadn't eaten since last night's dinner.

"I think it was a drop-off car. Maybe they were running drugs or something. I don't know. I didn't find anything like that, but maybe the pickup had already been made."

"You mean this boss they're talking about is a drug guy?"

Timmy nodded, sucking snot up his nose. He looked like he wanted to cry again. "His name is Manuel Garcia. He runs a rinky-dink drug cartel out of Tijuana. I don't know much about him, but I know he's not exactly a sweetheart. I've got you in a serious mess, Jasper."

Before Timmy could apologize again, Jasper asked, "How do you know it's Garcia?"

Timmy gazed up at the ceiling, maybe to make the snot run backward. Jasper wasn't sure. Didn't much care either.

"There was a CB in the Caddy. Someone called as I was driving out of town. Apparently they had a LoJack on the car and could see it was moving. Whoever was talking had pulled away from the radio to talk to somebody else when I didn't answer and I heard him mention *El Poco*."

"El Poco? Doesn't 'poco' mean 'little'?"

"Yeah, I think so. Why?"

Jasper shrugged, or tried to, considering the ropes behind his back. "Just seems like an odd code name for a cartel owner. Not very respectful."

Now it was Timmy's turn to shrug. "There's nothing wrong with being little," Timmy said, a bit defensively, Jasper thought. And since he was such a little guy, he probably had the right. Timmy went on, "And maybe he doesn't know they call him that. It wasn't Garcia on the radio. It must have been another flunky like the ones sitting in your kitchen."

Jasper accepted that logic. But it didn't really get them anywhere. In fact, now that Jasper had a slightly clearer picture of what was going on here, he was suddenly even more worried than before. He had heard enough horror stories about cartel hits to *warrant* a little worry. The last thing he wanted was to end up with his head in a cardboard box sitting on the counter at UPS, being shipped to Tucson, or wherever the hell they shipped their severed heads. Still, if they were dealing with a *little* drug runner, maybe he wouldn't be such a threat. At least Jasper hoped he wouldn't.

Timmy was watching him, obviously wondering what he was thinking. Wondering if he was going to get mad, maybe. And Timmy couldn't exactly blame him if he did. Timmy had really managed to fuck up both their lives. And maybe *end* them too.

Jasper frowned. Something didn't add up. "Are you telling me this cartel guy is willing to bump us both off simply because you stole his Caddy? And how the hell did they track you here anyway? Oh. The LoJack."

"I guess. I couldn't find it on the vehicle. I looked everywhere, but they never put LoJack radio transmitters in the same place twice. When I couldn't find it, I drove the SUV off a cliff a few miles from here. I did a good job too. I set it on fire first, then rolled it on down the cliff into the ocean, where it disappeared without a bubble. The cartel guys must have centered their search at the last point where they caught the radio signal. I guess that eventually led them here. I'm sorry. I should have put more miles between me and where I dumped the Caddy. But I was getting sick then. I-I went as far as I could go."

Once again, Timmy was looking everywhere but at Jasper. Jasper knew Timmy's methods of evasion pretty well by now. And this was no time to be keeping secrets from each other. Or to be lying.

Jasper had to hiss to keep his voice down. He was also trying desperately to control his anger. "Why did you steal the Caddy in the first place? What did you hope to get out of it?"

Timmy twitched his shoulders. Jasper guessed it was supposed to be a shrug. "What can I say? I love nice cars. Didn't figure a short joyride would be such a bad thing. I meant to return the SUV before anyone knew it was gone. How was I supposed to know it belonged to the head of some fucking Tijuana drug cartel? It didn't have a sign on it."

"Is that really the truth?"

Again that little twitch of the shoulders. It was starting to piss Jasper off.

"What is it you're not telling me? Look at me, Timmy. You're still hiding something. If we get out of this mess and hope to be lovers, we have to be able to trust each other. Tell me. Tell me everything."

But Timmy backed off. Jasper could see him do it. One minute he was there in front of him, open and connecting, and the next he had withdrawn, like a battered boxer retreating to a neutral corner. A glint of stubbornness flashed in Timmy's dark eyes, and he evaded Jasper's gaze completely. Instead, he bent to press his face to Jasper's chest yet again. Probably to keep Jasper from looking at him. From seeing the evasion.

So when Timmy backed off, so did Jasper. Stubbornly, he tilted his head and closed his eyes. How could he be so stupid as to think Timmy would be honest with him? In the two weeks they'd known each other, the man hadn't been honest yet. Even now, when their lives were hanging by a thread, the guy couldn't simply come out and speak the truth. He still had to skirt around it, evade, tell half-truths. Lie.

The pain in Jasper's head and back and arms was suddenly compounded by a thundering pain in his heart. If Timmy would lie to him now, then nothing the man ever said could be trusted.

Hell, maybe Timmy didn't really love him at all.

They both fell silent, lost in their own thoughts. Jasper longed to trust Timmy. He had given him chance after chance, but once again the man had proven himself untrustworthy. Jasper knew he could never trust him again. Everything they once had between them was over now. It had to be. You can't love a liar.

Jasper steeled his heart as best he could against the knowledge he had lost Timmy and settled in to wait for whatever was about to happen. Whatever it was, it wouldn't be good. And the chances were substantial it might even be fucking fatal. Christ, what a mess.

Timmy seemed to know where Jasper's mind had taken him. He sat cross-legged before Jasper's chair, his arms still around Jasper's waist, his chin on Jasper's knee, staring sightlessly into the cold ashes on the grate. He, too, was waiting.

The loud alarm clock by the bed upstairs ticked off the seconds, the minutes.

Blondie left the cabin to hike down the lane and fetch their car from the main road where they had left it. They heard him clomping across the porch, then the sound of his shoes crunching over gravel. After that, silence. The sun scooted a little farther across the sky, shifting the shadows in the cabin. Out back the dogs quieted down, weary of barking. Waiting like they were. Waiting for Jasper to rescue them.

Jasper and Timmy closed their eyes and faced their fears alone, both knowing something had been broken between them. Still, Timmy would not release Jasper. He rested his head on Jasper's knee and continued to clutch him tight about the waist. Just holding on.

But even with the physical contact, it was as though they were once again strangers. There was coolness now between them that had not been there, even at the beginning. Both hearts were crushed to know they had lost a love neither had really thought they would ever be lucky enough to find to begin with.

But Jasper couldn't bring himself to accept the hurt silently. He felt an urge to strike back. To fling the disappointment right back in Timmy's face, if he could, before their doom walked through the front door in the guise of a crazy Mexican drug lord.

When Jasper spoke, his voice was ice. "You don't give up anything, do you, Timmy? You give only what you have to give. And even that isn't really given. It's used to serve a purpose, meet an end, complete a lie."

"No," Timmy sighed. "No. I—"

"Everything we've had has been a lie, and you know it. You didn't care about me. You just wanted a place to hide out until things got safe so you could go back to whatever sort of life you lived before you climbed up my fucking mountain."

Timmy flinched beneath Jasper's glare. The ache inside him became sharper when he saw such hurt and anger in Jasper's eyes. But the words! The words were knives. They cut the deepest.

Still, he had to be strong. For both of them. Later he would try to explain. But for now, he had to hang tough. They both did, whether Jasper knew it or not.

"Wait," Timmy whispered. "Trust me, Jasper, and wait."

Jasper merely shook his head as he looked away. "Trust," he said, as if it were a word he had never heard before. "Now I'm supposed to trust."

He closed his eyes and Timmy saw a tear leak through.

That one small tear from big, burly Jasper Stone broke Timmy's heart.

Even Jasper was surprised to feel that tear gather on his lashes. But what was he really crying for? The danger they were in? Or the loss of Timmy? It didn't take him long to understand which one it really was.

He squeezed his eyes tighter still and tried not to think anymore. It simply hurt too much. He missed Timmy already, and the man was still inches away. But in his heart, Jasper knew, Timmy was a *world*, a *galaxy* away. Whatever connection they once had was irretrievably severed. Nothing connected them now but pain and disappointment. And Timmy's goddamned lies.

What seemed an eternity later, they heard the sound of not one, but two, automobiles. Peering through the front window and shaking his head to clear away the tears, Jasper saw a beige Toyota and a black Caddy town car lumbering up the lane. Both automobiles looked like they might have started the day as clean as a whistle, but now they were splattered with mud all the way up to their rooflines after splashing through the potholes in Jasper's lane.

Timmy didn't look through the window at all. He kept his forehead pressed to Jasper's chest, his eyes closed.

He was praying for a little luck. And for Jasper's forgiveness.

Chapter THIRTEEN

"About time," Surly grumbled as he stomped through the living room and flung open the cabin door. He didn't even bother glancing at his two prisoners. The big guy was tied up and the little guy was a wuss. They were no threat. He stepped out onto the porch and waited by the steps.

The moment Surly's back was through the door, Jasper once again thought of the guns in the closet. Was there time? Could Timmy grab them and maybe lock the goons outside until he could untie Jasper's bonds? Could they keep them at bay until they could call the police and try to get some help out here?

But already it was too late. Jasper knew instinctively there simply wasn't time.

Jasper slumped in his chair, and at the sound of a car door, he and Timmy turned their attention to the window. Resigned to their fate, they stared through the glass as Blondie climbed out of the beige Toyota, which looked to be a rental. He was no longer wearing his stupid puffy vest, Jasper noticed. Guess he didn't feel it necessary to hide his gun anymore, because there it was as plain as day, stuffed in a shoulder holster under his armpit. Blondie adjusted his clothes, like maybe he didn't want to appear a slob in front of the boss, and stepped around to open the driver's door to the town car.

"Oh shit," Jasper muttered when he saw a man who could only be Manuel Garcia—El Poco—grunt his way out of the front seat and lumber to his feet, all the while looking around like a fucking tourist.

The man was a mountain. *El Poco my ass,* Jasper thought. *He must weigh three hundred pounds.* He wore black slacks, crisply creased, and a red guayabera with black stripes going down the front. There were so many yards of fabric in the shirt it might have been used as a pup tent. The man also wore a red ascot, puffed up at his throat, making him look somewhat like a fat bullfrog. Outside of the movies, Jasper had never seen *anyone* wear an actual ascot. And now he knew why. They made you look like a pompous twit.

Garcia's massive head was totally hairless, and as Jasper watched, the man pulled a handkerchief from his back pocket and rubbed it down like a bowling ball, removing the gleam of sweat from his skullcap.

Garcia prissily refolded the handkerchief and stuffed it into his pocket. Apparently in no hurry, he stood with his hands on his hips and stretched his back as he gazed around the property. If the circumstances had been different, and he wasn't about to get a bullet in the brain, Jasper would have laughed when he saw Garcia tilt his head to the side as he looked in the direction of the hog house.

"Yeah," Jasper muttered, rolling his eyes. "It's fucking crooked. I know."

Timmy turned away from the window and gazed up into Jasper's eyes. Try as he might, Jasper couldn't ignore that pleading look.

"Please don't stop loving me," Timmy said, and again, before he could prevent it from happening, Jasper's eyes misted over. A lump formed in his throat.

He returned Timmy's gaze for about a dozen heartbeats, all the while thinking of a hundred things he wanted to say. But in the end he just said, "Kid, I think the question of who loves who is about to be rendered moot." But he did say it with a bit of a smile, which gave Timmy hope.

"We'll be all right," Timmy said. "I know we will."

This time Jasper said nothing. He was finding it a little hard to share Timmy's rosy outlook on the situation the little shit had gotten them into.

He turned back to the window and saw the two men, Garcia and Blondie, were now trudging toward the cabin. Blondie was hanging back about two steps, like an obedient Japanese wife. Surly stepped aside as they approached to allow Garcia passage up the steps to the porch. The man was broad. He needed a lot of room. Fucker was like a cruise ship pulling into port. Maybe he needed a couple of tugboats to keep his ass headed in the right direction. Jasper could hear the front steps groan beneath his weight.

When he came through the door ahead of the other two men, the room darkened as if an eclipse had blocked out the sun.

Jesus, Jasper thought. *This guy seriously needs to cut back on the frijoles. Maybe try a salad for a change.*

To Jasper's surprise, Manuel Garcia—aka El Poco—slammed the door in the goons' faces, shutting them outside on the porch. Jasper wasn't sure if that was a good thing or a bad thing, although he certainly enjoyed the surprised look on Blondie's face when the door came swinging toward his puss.

Garcia stood inside the door, looked around the room as he once again tugged the handkerchief from his back pocket. This time he used it to blow his nose. He blew it with enthusiasm, making a loud honk reminiscent of a Canadian Goose heading south. When he was finished, like before, he prissily refolded the handkerchief into a neat little square and slipped it into his back pocket. Only then did his eyes come to rest on Jasper and Timmy—Jasper tied to his chair by the fireplace and Timmy sitting before him, one arm still clutching Jasper's waist.

Garcia assessed the situation quickly. After locking eyes with first Timmy, then Jasper, he resignedly slid his eyes back to settle them on Timmy's face.

"So you're the thief, then." He had the unmistakable lilt of a Mexican accent in his words. But he also sounded well educated. His words were concise and perfectly articulated, his eyes alert—two bright diamonds peering out from a sea of blubber, missing nothing. One could imagine a lively intelligence thudding around inside that massive cranium. Yet for such a big man, Garcia's voice was high-pitched. Almost feminine.

Not sure what to say, Timmy simply nodded.

"You're a pretty one," Garcia said. Then his eyes slid to Jasper. "You boys are looking awfully cozy sitting there. One would almost think you are lovers."

Garcia stepped forward and, looming over them both, brushed his fat fingers through Timmy's hair.

Jasper blushed in anger. "Don't touch him! And don't call him a thief!"

Garcia blinked, and a lazy smile spread across his face, which at the moment was flushed from the heat and humidity. And the three hundred pounds of lard beneath his skin. "So, señor. You're feeling protective of your little friend. How gallant."

He reached back and slapped Jasper with his open palm like a woman. Jasper was so surprised, it took him a second to realize the noise of the slap was far worse than the pain. It smarted a little, but that was all. The man wasn't really trying to hurt him. He was merely trying to put him in his place. Jasper wasn't sure why, but again he gathered hope from this. Maybe they still had a chance this wouldn't go as badly as expected.

Maybe they would actually survive.

Garcia spoke as if the slap had not occurred at all. He smiled down at Jasper. "You're a handsome man, señor. If you control your anger, you might stay that way a while. All right?"

Jasper nodded, still furious but well aware his options were limited. "All right."

Again Garcia reached down to play his fingers through Timmy's hair. Timmy closed his eyes at the touch as if a snake had slithered across his skin. Jasper bit his lip and said nothing.

Garcia's eyes slid back to Jasper and he grinned, satisfied. "There, now. See? It's not so difficult being cordial. And I surmise by the surprise that flashed across your handsome face when I called your little friend a thief, that maybe you did not know. Maybe he is not only a thief but a liar too. Heh? Would that surprise you too?" He spotted sorrow in Jasper's eyes at the words. "No. I see it wouldn't surprise you at all. It would seem your little friend has been keeping secrets from you."

Jasper forced himself to look away, to stare through the window. He saw Surly leaning up against the beige car smoking a cigarette. He couldn't see Blondie. Off tormenting the dogs maybe, or kicking the pigs. Jasper wouldn't be surprised by anything he did, the prick. Him and Surly both.

He looked back at Garcia. The man's taunting words wouldn't be half so humiliating if Jasper could tell himself they weren't true. But how could he? Timmy had lied from the very beginning. He was probably lying even now, when both their lives were hanging in the balance.

Garcia stepped away from Jasper and Timmy and plucked a surprised Guatemala off the bench in the corner. He held the cat to his chest and gently stroked her fur with his fat fingers, which, considering the man's line of work, seemed surprisingly gentle. He had clear fingernail polish glistening on his fingertips, which, under different circumstances, Jasper might have found amusing. Jasper could hear the purrs start up right away from Guatemala. If he had been hoping for a little more loyalty from his fucking cat, he was sorely disappointed.

Still stroking Guatemala's neck, Garcia settled his eyes yet again on Timmy.

"Tell me first why you stole my automobile. Did you think you could sell it? Make some money for drugs?"

Timmy's eyes narrowed. "I just wanted to drive it. And I don't take drugs."

Garcia looked down at the cat. "I did not think you did. Your eyes are too clear. I do not take drugs either. A filthy, soul-destroying habit if there ever was one."

"But you sell drugs," Jasper blurted out, unable to keep quiet. "What does that say about you?"

Garcia did not seem to mind the interruption. He merely smiled, as if bemused by Jasper's simplicity of thought. "I am a businessman. I provide a product. Nothing more. What does it say about a man like you when he falls in love with a thief and a liar? One would think a writer would have a better grasp of personalities. And don't look so surprised. I don't just blindly rush into situations without doing a bit of research first. You have six books to your credit, none of which made much money. You're once divorced, from a *woman* no less, and now you've set your sights on this little car thief. One would think you might do better."

"Love doesn't give us choices," Jasper said. "Love just does what it does. Like you, I guess."

Timmy looked up at him with wide, grateful eyes, but Jasper could only look away. He wasn't ready for Timmy's gratitude. Maybe he never would be.

Garcia chuckled. "I have never been compared to love before, señor. I'm honored. And your boyfriend is flattered too. Look at that adoring face staring up at you." And strangely, there was no mocking tone in Garcia's words. Only, perhaps, envy. Or maybe it was only an act. Jasper was beginning to suspect El Poco wasn't as harmless as he pretended to be.

Timmy turned away from Jasper's face to the mountain of flesh looming over him. "Let Jasper go. He doesn't have anything to do with this."

Garcia pressed his fleshy lips to the top of Guatemala's head. The cat closed his eyes and purred all the louder. "My goodness. A selfless act. One does not expect such offerings from thieves. And if I do this for you, little one, then you will tell me where my automobile is?"

Timmy faltered. "Well—"

"The car is destroyed," Jasper said.

Garcia's piggy eyes narrowed to two fat slits. He dropped the cat without warning, and Guatemala hit the floor hard then took off running. "Destroyed?" Garcia asked, calmly and without rancor. He seemed only vaguely interested as he gazed from one to the other, then back again. "In what way is it destroyed, gentlemen?"

"Burned," Timmy said, wondering all the while if it would be the last thing he ever said.

And while Garcia didn't look too happy with what Timmy had said, he still didn't look like he was quite ready to kill them yet. Or so Timmy hoped.

Jasper was less encouraged. He detected a ruthless determination in the fat man's eyes he didn't trust at all. He suspected there was lava rising in the bowels of that fat mountain, and he prayed to God he wouldn't be around when it erupted.

Garcia still spoke softly. Unhurriedly. "I want you to answer my next questions very carefully, pretty one. Very carefully indeed. How badly did you burn it?"

Timmy sighed. Shit. "It's a charcoal briquette."

"A charcoal briquette. So it is totally destroyed, then."

"Yes."

"And where exactly did this burning take place? I think I would like to see the… remains."

"You can't," Timmy said, grateful to have Jasper so close, knowing Jasper still loved him. At least he was fairly sure that was what Jasper meant when he was talking about love.

"You can't see the remains because there aren't any."

Garcia seemed to find the conversation fascinating. "And how can that be? Metal does not burn to ash. Explain to me how there can be no remains."

Timmy puffed out a billow of air and tried to ignore his hammering heart as he said, "I drove it off a cliff. I set it on fire first and it was still burning when I rolled it off a cliff into the ocean. It disappeared completely. Trust me. The car is gone. Totally destroyed. I'm sorry."

"You're sorry." Garcia laughed. And still laughing, he gazed at Jasper. "Your boyfriend is sorry."

"We're both sorry," Jasper said. "Maybe I—"

But Garcia cut him off. He stepped forward swiftly and backhanded Timmy across the face. For a mountain of blubber, he could move pretty fast. Timmy's head snapped back, and he fell to the floor beside Jasper's chair. This time the slap was obviously meant to hurt. And by the stunned look on Timmy's face, it most certainly had.

"Goddammit!" Jasper bellowed, and Garcia held a fat finger of warning up to Jasper's face.

"Shut up, señor. Do not interrupt me again." He turned his attention back to Timmy, who was pulling himself back to a sitting position and leaning on Jasper's knee. His face was bright red, and a ribbon of blood was trailing from his nose. Tears slid along his cheeks, and suddenly, his hands were shaking. The slap had obviously rattled him. He hadn't been expecting it. Jasper longed to reach out and comfort Timmy, to give him strength, or sympathy, maybe, but of course he couldn't. He could barely move. He had never felt so helpless in his life, and he detested the feeling.

Garcia stared at Timmy as if staring would make him speak the truth. "If you burned the SUV, how did you get here?"

"I hitchhiked," Timmy said.

"Why?"

"To be with Jasper."

Garcia gazed from Timmy to Jasper, then back to Timmy. "So you already knew each other."

"Yes," Timmy answered without hesitation.

Oh Christ, Jasper thought. *The kid's going to start lying again. We're never going to get out of this mess.*

"I'm sorry about the Caddy," Timmy offered, knowing it wouldn't do any good but not having too many other options at this point. "If I could buy you a new one, I would."

"Very noble," Garcia mocked. "But I do not care about the Cadillac. It was stolen to begin with. I care only about what was *inside* it."

Timmy looked confused. "But there was *nothing* inside it."

Garcia gave a nasty leer. "In that you are wrong." He turned to see Surly and Blondie standing on the porch, peering through the windows on either side of the front door. They had their hands up to their faces to shield the sun from their eyes and better see inside. Garcia made an impatient flapping gesture and the two men quickly backed away to give him privacy.

"Morons," Garcia muttered to no one in particular.

Then he rounded on Timmy. "Tell me why you destroyed the Cadillac. What was the point of that?"

"I knew the SUV belonged to you because I heard someone mention your name on the CB that was in it. The last thing I wanted to do was get on the wrong side of El Poco, but I figured it was a little too late to make amends. I knew you were tracking me by the LoJack installed somewhere on the Caddy. I looked for the LoJack to remove it but couldn't find it, so to wipe out my trail, I destroyed the whole shebang. If it's any consolation, it was a great drive. Ran like a dream."

Garcia didn't sound amused. "No consolation at all, I'm afraid. But I hope it will be consolation enough for you when I have my men blow your head off."

Garcia plopped his gigantic ass down on the sofa and Jasper heard a spring pop. The man stared at Timmy as he wiped the sweat from his head with his handkerchief again.

"I'm going to level with you two. I am gay myself. I have a wonderful harem of young men down in Tijuana just waiting to do whatever I ask of them. Poverty is a wonderful aphrodisiac. I give them shelter and food, and they give me their youth. Nice exchange, don't you think?"

Jasper and Timmy said nothing, although Jasper decided he now hated the man more than he already had, which was saying something. They waited silently for whatever Garcia was getting at.

"I am a reasonable man. And a sympathetic one. I do not wish to destroy this love affair you two have embarked upon, but I will if I don't start getting some answers."

He swiveled his eyes back and forth from Timmy to Jasper, then he settled them on Timmy. "I see a lot of young men like you, little one. Hungry. Doing whatever they can to survive. And I understand it. I was hungry once myself. But as you can see, I satisfied my hunger quite well." He laughed and patted his gut. Then he pulled a small foldable knife from his trouser pocket and, flipping it open, proceeded to dig underneath his thumbnail with it, fat folds of concentration forming across his forehead.

Timmy and Jasper both stared at the knife in Garcia's hand. Neither of them thought for a moment he was actually cleaning his nails. They weren't that dumb.

Garcia seemed to appreciate the fact that their sole attention was centered on the knife. He smiled and held it up for their benefit. The handle was creamy white, the blade caught the light like a flame. "Pretty, no? Ivory and steel. Very sharp, very dangerous. Small, but lethal." His smile broadened as he took in their rapt attention. He went back to scraping the blade beneath his nail.

Once more he centered his attention on Timmy. "I'm going to ask you some questions, little one, and I expect the truth. If you lie to me, I'll start cutting off body parts until I get the answers I like. Do you understand?"

Timmy swallowed hard and nodded, not trusting himself to speak.

"Good," Garcia smiled. It was the same smile a cobra makes before it strikes. "Why were you so interested in my automobile? The truth now. You do not wish to see me angry."

Timmy released Jasper's waist and looked down at his hands. Jasper followed where Timmy looked and saw Timmy's hands were shaking. He wasn't surprised. Although he couldn't see his own hands, since they were tied behind his back, he could nevertheless feel them shaking too.

"I thought the Caddy was beautiful," Timmy explained. "I wanted to drive it. That's all. I just—"

"You just love fine automobiles, señor. How discerning of you. But being poor, the only way you can drive them is to steal them."

"Y-yes. Although I prefer to call it borrowing."

"Do you? I was always taught when you borrow something, you return it. Since my car has not been returned, I will continue to call it stealing. You understand? Of course you do. Now then, how long did you watch the Cadillac before you made your move?"

"Almost two days, off and on."

"Did you see who parked it there in the parking structure to begin with?"

"No."

"And where were you when you were watching the automobile? What was your vantage point?"

"I was in my hotel room across the street. It's a residential hotel, and I live on the third floor, the same floor the Caddy was parked on. It was right there. Right across the alleyway. I could almost touch it."

Garcia chuckled but it was mirthless. "And touch it you did. A fact which you undoubtedly regret at this very minute."

"Yes, indeed."

Again, Garcia chuckled, but it died in his throat when he asked, "Did you see anyone else enter the car during the time you were watching it and building up the courage to… *touch* it?"

Timmy's eyes widened. He saw the opportunity and took it. "Yes. One man entered the Caddy while I was watching it."

Garcia stopped fiddling with his nails and tilted his bowling-ball-sized head to the left, narrowing his eyes to study Timmy more closely. "Really" was all he said.

And Timmy nodded. "Yes."

Garcia leaned forward, closing the knife and placing it on the coffee table. "And what did that one man do?"

"He took a case from the back of the Caddy."

"What sort of case?"

"A black case. Like a suitcase. A little one."

"I see." Silence rang through the cabin, punctuated by the tapping of Garcia's fat fingers on the coffee table. Finally, he spoke.

"Didn't you think it strange that after two days someone would finally take something from the automobile without actually driving it away?"

Timmy shook his head. "No, but—"

"But?"

"But, well actually I did think it was strange."

"And why was that, little one?"

"It was strange because he had to lift the back floorboard up to get what he was after. He took it from the tire well by the tailgate. It seemed like a funny place to keep a suitcase."

Garcia ignored that comment. "How did he get inside the automobile?"

"He had a key, I guess."

"I see. What did he do after he retrieved the suitcase?"

"He carefully recovered the tire well with the floor panel and wiped his fingerprints from the back door handle. I thought that was strange too. Then he quickly walked away. He didn't go into the front of the cab."

Garcia was looking like he couldn't decide if Timmy was lying or telling the truth. This was obviously information he had not expected at all. And Jasper had to admit, if Timmy was lying, he was doing an excellent job of it, although for the life of him Jasper couldn't figure out how the hell Timmy thought this would help them.

"Would you recognize this man if you saw him again?"

And at that Timmy laughed. The sound of it surprised everyone in the room. "Shit, yeah, I'd recognize him. Hell, he's standing out there on the porch. Pizza Face. Pizza Face is the one who took the suitcase."

Garcia didn't bother looking toward the porch. He merely steepled his fat index fingers and poked them under his blubbery chin as he stared at Timmy. His eyes were coldly calculating. He was obviously thinking things through.

"You're playing a very dangerous game, little one. Trying to turn the general against his own troops is a very dangerous game indeed."

Timmy's eyes were wide and leery. They were also determined. He suspected this was as close to death as he had ever come in his twenty short years, and he didn't much care for the feeling. Still, he had dealt his own hand. He had to play it. There was still a chance....

"If you don't believe me, ask Pizza Face," Timmy said. After a beat of silence, Timmy added, "Why? What was in the suitcase?"

Jasper stared from Timmy to Garcia and back again. Jesus, he could feel the sweat dribbling down the small of his back. And as if things weren't bad enough, now he had to pee.

"Timmy," he said softly.

But Timmy ignored him. His attention was centered on Garcia, who was sitting on the couch like Jabba the Hut, staring at Timmy through slitted, piggy eyes. His fingers were still steepled under his chin as he shut out Jasper completely, every ounce of his concentration centered on Timmy.

When he spoke, he did so with careful deliberation. Emotionless and calm. But now there was a cruel edge to his voice. A dangerous edge. He ignored Timmy's final question.

"I tell you something, little one. If I find you are lying to me, I will be forced to do what I had hoped we might avoid. You and your lover will die, and you will not die easily. I'm a romantic, señor, and as you know, I am gay myself, so I understand your attraction for each other. I admit it would be a pity to break up your blossoming love affair, but I will do it in a heartbeat if I have to. It is a matter of business. A matter of respect. Do you understand?"

Still crouched on the floor at Jasper's feet, Timmy gripped Jasper's ankle, as if needing the sense of touch to give himself strength. "Yes. I understand."

"You will show me where you burned the truck. We will all go. It is not far, is that right?"

Timmy nodded. "Yes, that's right." Then he asked, "What about Pizza Face?"

Garcia smiled. "His name is Batista, although he prefers to be called Bateman. Ashamed of his Mexican heritage, I presume. We all have our little foibles. Anyway, we will take him with us. I will be interested to see what he has to say."

A moment later, he added, "Untie your lover, little one. He will accompany us." Garcia stood and, once again, ran his fingers through Timmy's hair, obviously admiring his beauty. Before Timmy could pull away and do what he was told, Garcia smiled down at him. "And remember, my friend. If you are lying to me you have just signed your death warrants. You will both be dead before the sun sets."

"I'm not lying," Timmy said.

And Jasper wondered if that was the last lie Timmy would ever utter.

Chapter FOURTEEN

JASPER winced at the pins and needles as the blood rushed into his hands and legs. Jesus, blood flowing into starving tissues felt wonderful and excruciating at the same time. But he had other things to worry about. After struggling to his feet and pulling Timmy awkwardly into his numb arms, he pulled his shirttail up and wiped the blood from Timmy's nose where El Poco had popped him one.

Jasper winced again, this time for Timmy. "Does it hurt?"

Timmy tried to smile. "Considering the circumstances, a minor difficulty."

"No shit." Jasper rolled his eyes and wondered how he could still make jokes. "I wonder if you know what you're doing," he whispered, barely loud enough for Timmy to hear.

Timmy gave him a nervous wink. He seemed to be wondering the same thing Jasper was, and when they both realized it, they grinned at each other. Then Garcia called out in his high-pitched voice for the men to come inside. Jasper and Timmy jumped at the sound of El Poco barking orders, and the sudden jarring motion knocked the smiles right off of their faces.

Jasper had another surprise coming—perhaps the biggest of the morning—when Garcia turned to him and said, "I knew your father, señor. You might not be aware of this since you were just a baby at the time, but we did a lot of business together back in the eighties, your father and me. He was a fair man and always delivered what was paid for."

Jasper was stunned. "You mean my father did business with *you*?"

Garcia gave him a searching look. "You are learning all sorts of unexpected truths today, I think. And yes. Your father and I did business for many years before his mind went south for the winter. I see by your face that this surprises you. You might be even more surprised to learn that we were friends. I miss him."

Jasper was not touched by the sentiment of friendship coming from the mouth of a criminal. Actually it was just another reason to be disappointed in his father. Jasper had not known his father dealt with the scum of the earth, but now he did know, he had to admit it didn't surprise him. The man had left his son with a long trail of disappointments throughout the course of his life. No, Jasper held no illusions of sentiment concerning his father. Nor any concerning Manuel Garcia.

"You mean you miss his guns."

Jasper's sarcasm was loftily ignored. "No. I miss the *man*, señor. I understand your bitterness. I heard he gave everything away to charity before he died. He did it to atone for his sins, I think. He did not do it to hurt you. A lot of human suffering was brought about by the guns he delivered to Mexico. That was his way of pleading forgiveness to a higher power, I suppose. I wonder if that higher power ever truly forgave him." El Poco crossed himself and touched a fingertip to his forehead in obeisance.

Jasper was speechless. Not only at Garcia's display of devotion, but by this news of his father as well. He had always thought it was the Alzheimer's disease that made his father liquidate his holdings and give the money away to strangers. But if what Garcia said was true—and Jasper could think of no reason for the man to lie—perhaps Jasper owed his father a bit more understanding than he had previously been willing to offer.

Still, Jasper could not resist mocking this man who pretended to be so pious and at the same time threatened to murder them in cold blood. "And I suppose you had nothing to do with all the human suffering brought about by the guns Pop sold you."

Garcia clucked his tongue. "I did not say that, señor. But that is between me and my own higher authority, is it not?" He impatiently turned to the door. "Where are those morons?"

At that precise moment the two goons walked through the front door. There was a smile on Blondie's face, and he had his hand on the butt of the gun in his shoulder holster. He was obviously expecting his services to finally be of use, and it was also obvious he was a man who loved his work. There was a cold glint in his ice-blue eyes as he stared past the boss to Jasper and Timmy. A cruel smile tipped the corner of his mouth into a satisfied sneer.

What an asshat, Jasper thought. *An asshat about to be sorely disappointed.* Or so he hoped.

And indeed, the light went out of Blondie's eyes when Garcia said to Surly, "Bateman, you will be driving myself and our two guests in the town car." Then he aimed a fat grin in Blondie's direction. "*Your* services are no longer needed. Take the other car back to the border. And do not look so disappointed. Maybe you'll get to kill someone *next* week."

Surly—*Bateman*—laughed as he stepped aside to let an obviously furious Blondie stalk back through the front door. A moment later, they heard the beige Toyota start up, and a moment after that, the car was trundling down the lane and splashing through the potholes until the sound of it vanished in the distance.

One down, Jasper thought. He and Timmy's odds had drastically improved. In fact, the odds were now even-steven. Two against two. His eyes skittered yet again to the closet door. Desperately, he wondered if he had time to make a move. Were his blood-starved appendages up to the task?

He had no sooner asked himself that question when the opportunity was snatched away.

"Outside, everyone," Garcia stated. "Let us see where our little car thief's story leads us, shall we?"

Hand in hand, Jasper and Timmy were led to the black town car. El Poco himself held the door open in mocking politeness and ushered them into the back seat, with some rough prodding provided by Surly, who looked like he had won the lottery. He was obviously as excited as Blondie had been at the prospect of putting a few bullet holes in them.

When Jasper and Timmy were inside, Garcia leaned in the door with a smile and said, "Buckle up, señores. It's a law, you know. We would not want to break any laws."

He laughed as he swung the door shut with a *thunk*, strode around the vehicle, and maneuvered his bulk into the passenger side of the front seat, his weight tilting the car about twenty degrees when he did.

At this point, there wasn't much Jasper could offer Timmy in the way of encouragement, but he did find a little comfort himself clasping Timmy's hand. Timmy accepted it with an iron grip of his own. Jasper noticed Timmy's hand was as sweaty as his. Jasper's underarms were soaked too. His antiperspirant obviously wasn't designed to cope with life and death situations propagated by the Mexican underworld. *Jeez*, Jasper thought, *they should put that kind of shit on the label.*

"Here we go," Bateman said, turning the key, and with a lurch, the town car headed off down the lane.

Jasper wished they had allowed him to release the dogs and feed the two pigs before they left the ranch, but hopefully, he and Timmy would be back, all in one piece, to do it later. Please God.

"Nice car," Timmy sighed beside him, and Garcia laughed a mirthless laugh.

Jasper couldn't help but notice the fat man was staring at Bateman all the while.

As the end of the lane approached, Surly asked, "Which way?"

Garcia shifted his bulk around to stare at Timmy in the back seat. "Well, car thief? Where to? Where did you set fire to my Caddy?"

Timmy pointed east, indicating they should turn left when they came to the gravel road.

To Jasper's surprise, Timmy then asked Garcia, "What was in the suitcase? Drugs?" Jasper was mostly surprised because he had not thought to ask the question himself.

Garcia gave Jasper an amused moue, quite effeminate actually, then riveted his attention back on Timmy. "So you wish to continue playing the game, I see. Fine. If you must know, little one, then I will tell you." And here Garcia turned his eyes to the man behind the wheel, coolly staring at him as he spoke. "The suitcase contained money, señor. A great deal of money. Clean, untraceable cash. Does that surprise you?"

"How much cash?" Timmy asked, as if commenting on the weather.

Again Garcia smiled. "More cash than you will ever see in your lifetime. You and your friend put together, undoubtedly. For me it is merely petty cash, you understand, but I do not tolerate being stolen from. My business would suffer if I did, you see." He again focused his attention on the man driving the car. "Don't you agree, Bateman?"

Surly jumped like someone had poked him with a needle. The last thing he had expected was to be included in the boss's conversation. He was a flunky and he knew it. Something about the boss centering his attention on him made Bateman nervous. More than nervous. He turned surprised eyes to the man beside him.

"Yeah," he said, considering his words very carefully. "You'd lose credibility. People would think you're losing control. You gotta protect your turf. If certain people thought you were weak, they'd probably try to relieve you of your business altogether. With a bullet. Is that what you are asking me? Sir?"

"Precisely what I am asking you, Bateman. And thank you for answering with such a crystal perception of the circumstances."

"Uh, sure. No problem."

Bateman turned his eyes back to the road. The pockmarks in his face were bright red.

Garcia apparently found it too uncomfortable to keep twisting his bulk around to peer at Timmy in the back seat. He shifted his shoulders around to the front and settled his eyes on the road ahead.

"So you see, little one. In my line of work, thievery is a very bad thing indeed. Almost as bad as betrayal." Again he turned to watch the man behind the wheel. "Although I must say, betrayers are even more loathsome than simple thieves. Wouldn't you agree, Bateman?"

"Uh… yeah."

"Very succinct. Thank you, Bateman."

Jasper saw a drop of sweat dribble an awkward path in and around the pockmarks on the side of Bateman's face, not unlike the town car dodging potholes in the lane. Before he could stop himself, Jasper made a mental note to use that simile in the novel he was working on back at the cabin, then he realized abruptly that might be putting the cart a little before the horse. Better see if he would survive the day first.

Jasper understood now Timmy had done a smart thing planting a seed of doubt in Garcia's mind about his flunky Bateman. But he still didn't see how it would get them out of the predicament they were in. And, Jasper quickly realized, Timmy still had a few more seeds of doubt to cast around. As far as Timmy was concerned, planting season wasn't over just yet.

"You still haven't told me *how much* money was in the suitcase," Timmy said. "It must be a lot to warrant two cold-blooded murders. And turn right up ahead. We have to go north from here."

Per Timmy's directions, Bateman turned at the intersection onto the old two-lane highway that ran abeam of the interstate and abutted the coastline. The Pacific, a hundred feet down the cliff to their left, was gray and as smooth as glass all the way to the horizon.

"Ah," Garcia said. "The scenic route. Lovely." He took a moment to stare past Bateman to the ocean below. Jasper followed where he was looking and saw splashes of color in the distance where sailboats skimmed across the water. He wished the hell he was on one of them. Him and Timmy both.

Jasper was brought back to reality by Garcia's laugh. "Oh, little one. Surely you know how much money we're talking about. Rather than wasting my time asking foolish questions, which you already know the answer to, you might try simply telling me where the money is. No? All right, I'll play your game a little longer, but I warn you it's beginning to weary me. The suitcase contained a hundred thousand dollars. Or more, conceivably. Possibly even a great deal more. I'm not exactly sure."

"How can you not be sure?" Timmy asked, as bright-eyed and curious as a kitten.

"It was drug money," Jasper said. "Wasn't it?"

"Yes, señor. Drug money. Taken from the feebleminded to feed their nasty habits. The users are cattle. Why should I not profit from cattle? Farmers do it year after year without repercussions. And please wipe that holier-than-thou look off your handsome face, Mr. Stone, before I have Bateman knock it off."

"It would be my pleasure," Bateman snarled, casting Jasper a nasty leer in the rearview mirror.

Figuring he didn't have much to lose anyway, Jasper stuck his tongue out at the man. Bateman didn't seem amused.

"I don't have it. And you know I don't have it," Timmy explained once again. "You also know who does. Why don't you ask *him*?"

This time it was Bateman who peeled his eyes from the road and turned to stare at Timmy. "What the hell does he mean by that?"

Garcia's fat hand patted Bateman's shoulder, not to comfort, but to draw his attention. "Watch the road. This conversation does not concern you."

Bateman's face burst into flower like a red, red rose. Timmy laughed at his discomfort, and the man's face grew even redder, but he kept his mouth shut, although it was obvious he didn't want to. Jasper knew if they were alone right now with the inimitable Mr. Bateman, he and Jasper would probably both be riddled with bullet holes.

Garcia seemed to know it too.

"Now look what you've done, car thief. You've upset my henchman." And Garcia burst out with a feminine laugh that could as easily have come from a nine-year-old schoolgirl.

Jasper was so damned confused by this point, he didn't know *what* the hell was going on. He didn't have long to fret about it, either, because Timmy suddenly pointed his finger up ahead and exclaimed, "There! See where the weeds are disturbed and the path leads off into the scrub? Go that way! We're almost there!"

What Timmy was pointing at wasn't really a path at all. It was merely two furrows in the roadside weeds leading toward the water. The weeds had been smashed flat beneath the wheels of an automobile. The ocean was perhaps an eighth of a mile away. A few yards down the path, a copse of pepper trees hid them from the highway.

Bateman eased the car off the road, aware that with Garcia sitting in the front seat they were damn near dragging bottom anyway. Even on the asphalt. But there was no asphalt where they were going now, just weeds and mud and scree. Still, it was smoother than Jasper's lane, a fact which wasn't lost on anyone in the car.

Unless he was dumber than a stump, Jasper thought there might be a cliff coming up shortly. Had Timmy really brought the man's Cadillac here and destroyed it as he'd said he did? Why would he do that?

Jasper gave Timmy a questioning look, but Timmy said nothing. He did sport an enigmatic smile, however, on that handsome face of his.

Jasper didn't have a clue as to what it meant. It sort of pissed him off, though. What the hell could the nitwit possibly be finding to smile about?

Up ahead, Jasper spotted what he knew he would be seeing all along. A vast expanse of blue sky, looming out across a distant sea. And the beginning of that sea was situated directly beneath the lip of the cliff, a hundred feet below.

Bateman tapped the brakes, and the town car slid to a stop a good two hundred yards from the edge of the line where the sky began and the land ended.

"Everybody out," Garcia commanded. "The moment of truth is at hand, car thief. What happens next will determine if you live to see another day." He cast a sympathetic glance at Jasper as they all scrambled out of the car. "And when I say 'you,' Mr. Stone. I mean both of you. I'm sorry, but that's just the way it is, your father's friendship notwithstanding."

Jasper could think of nothing to say. No words formed in his mind at all. There was fear there, though. Oh yes. Plenty of that.

He clambered out of the town car right behind Timmy. As soon as Garcia had closed the door behind them, Jasper was comforted to see Timmy's hand reaching out for his.

Hand in hand, they stared about them. It was a beautiful spot. The air was saturated with the smell of seawater. The sun lay hot on the back of their necks. Up ahead, somewhere over the lip of the hill, they could hear sea birds and the roar of the surf pounding the rocks below.

Jasper didn't suppose he could ask for a nicer place to die.

Still, all things considered, he'd rather skip the dying part and hop right back into bed with the man beside him.

"I love you," Jasper whispered as Bateman walked a few paces ahead and Garcia busied himself readjusting his gigantic guayabera until it hung properly over his bulging belly.

"I know," Timmy whispered back, squeezing Jasper's fingers. "I know."

Chapter FIFTEEN

BATEMAN called out from up ahead. "There's a burn place here in the weeds where the path rolls down toward the cliff! And car tracks!"

"Well, well, well," Garcia stated, sounding as if he had expected as much all along. "Maybe our little car thief isn't a complete liar after all."

The weeds stood waist high on either side of the wheel ruts. Garcia maneuvered his three hundred pounds daintily through them, looking a bit unnerved at being surrounded by this much nature. He herded Jasper and Timmy along in front of him—as much to stomp down the weeds and get them out of his path as anything.

Garcia's voice rang high and feminine in the sea air, sounding totally out of place, like a coloratura warbling in a treetop. "I still do not understand why you destroyed the Cadillac, little one. What did you hope to achieve by that?"

Timmy turned to face Garcia as they walked along. His eyes opened wide when he saw the small pistol in Garcia's hand. Aside from the knife with the ivory handle, it was the first time he had seen the man with a weapon. He had a feeling this was not a promising development.

"The CB came to life the minute I drove the Caddy away from downtown. Someone tried to contact me. The only way they could know the SUV had been moved was if there was a LoJack installed on the vehicle. I knew right away I was no longer on a joyride. When I heard your name mentioned, I figured I was in deep shit. The only way I could protect myself was to remove the LoJack. I stopped on side roads a couple of times, trying to find it, but never did. As a last resort, I decided to destroy the car. At least then you couldn't track me anymore."

Bateman had moved on ahead, but now he returned to the others to see what the holdup was. He stood listening to the conversation. His gun was in his hand as well.

Garcia ignored his flunky and focused all his attention on Timmy. "But why not just abandon the vehicle and be on your way? Something is not adding up, little one. And there are too many bugs and too many weeds and too much fucking sunlight out here for me to be in a good mood. I suggest you get to the truth, or you're going to find your brains seeping out into the dirt. So tell me. Why did you not simply walk away and abandon the Caddy?"

Jasper stood behind Timmy as they both faced Garcia with their backs to Bateman. The main threat was from the big man now, and they both knew it.

Timmy pushed his hair from his eyes. He still had dried blood smeared across his face. His eyes were red and weary. "When I heard them mention El Poco on the CB, I knew I couldn't just walk away. Nobody crosses El Poco and walks away, or so I've always heard. You do have a reputation, you know. You could still track me down if I abandoned the vehicle. My fingerprints were all over it. It was parked right across from my hotel room in the city when it was stolen. And for all I knew, I might have been seen taking it. I couldn't risk just leaving the Caddy behind and walking away. I had to get rid of it completely."

Garcia's shirt was soaked in sweat and sticking to his gut. He looked uncomfortable as hell. But he looked fascinated, too, like a scientist staring at a brand new strain of virus through a microscope. He was clearly enthralled by what Timmy was telling him.

He was also clearly skeptical. "You could have gone a long way with a hundred thousand dollars, señor. So far away that El Poco would probably never find you. My arms do not reach everywhere. I am only a small businessman, after all."

Weary of the conversation, he turned to Bateman. "Show me this burn mark you spoke of. Let me see it for myself."

Bateman headed back up the path of broken weeds and Garcia and his two prisoners followed.

Jasper had a horrible sensation things were getting out of hand. Why would both men be holding guns? It's not like he and Timmy could take off, run away. Were they going to be executed right here?

They had taken no more than three or four steps when Jasper clutched Timmy's hand and pulled him to a stop, forcing Garcia to stop as well. Jasper turned to Garcia, trying to ignore the sweat burning his eyes. And he was sweating from nerves as much as the heat. Before he centered all his attention on the fat man, he caught a glimpse of real fear on Timmy's face too. That, more than anything, told him things were *truly* spiraling out of control.

He pulled Timmy close in a protective hug, then squared off with Garcia and the nasty-looking gun he held in his hand. "Let us go. Please. You must know Timmy's telling the truth. If he had your fucking money, don't you think he would have handed it over by now? Please. Don't do this. It's taken me a lifetime to find a man I love. Don't take him away from me now."

Bateman chuckled behind him, but Jasper ignored the bastard. He was concerned with Garcia now. Perhaps he could play on the fact they were both gay men. It implied a *certain* camaraderie, after all, even if the man *was* pointing a gun at his fucking head. Jasper would deal with Bateman later, and he hoped the opportunity would present itself soon, he really did. Nothing would make Jasper happier than pounding the smirk off the bastard's potholed face.

Garcia did not look amused by the hold up, nor particularly swayed by Jasper's logic. If he was touched by Jasper's declaration of love for Timmy, he sure as hell didn't show it. What he did, in fact, was say nothing. He merely waved his gun around, indicating for Jasper and Timmy to keep walking.

But Jasper wasn't about to keep walking. Death was to be found in that direction, and he knew it. "If you kill us, you never will get your money back," he blurted out.

At this Garcia smiled. "But according to your boyfriend, the money is already destroyed. How could I possibly get it back?"

A thought Jasper had been considering since this whole fiasco started suddenly spilled out of his mouth. "I'll pay you the money if you'll set us free."

At this Garcia and Bateman both laughed. Bateman said, "Yeah, you look like you've got that kinda loot!"

Furious, Garcia whirled on Bateman. He spat his words like a fat cobra spitting venom. "Bateman, shut up!"

Bateman fell silent, but the hatred in his eyes intensified. He obviously didn't appreciate being spoken to like that, neither by prisoner *nor* employer, but he was smart enough not to mention it.

Jasper tried again, enjoying the sudden friction between Garcia and Bateman but knowing it wasn't enough to save them. Not by a long shot. "I *do* have the money. My father gave it to me a long time ago. It's been sitting in a bank ever since. Let me go to the bank and I'll show you. I can have a hundred thou before the day is over. Cash. And I'll give every penny of it to you if you'll let us go. I'd rather have Timmy than the money. I can... I can live without the money."

Timmy gazed up into Jasper's face, then tilted his head to Jasper's shoulder, snaking his arms around Jasper's waist to hold him tight.

"Very romantic," Garcia drawled. "The two of you should have your own television show." He glanced at his watch. "It's getting late. Keep walking."

Jasper couldn't believe it. "But the *money!*"

Garcia stared at Timmy, his piglike eyes narrowed in disgust. "You are perfectly willing to let this man who loves you pay the price for your lie, are you not, little one? Mr. Stone, I fear you are loving the wrong person. A thief cares only for himself. It is a universal truth, I'm afraid. As they say in America, you have barked up the wrong tree by trusting, and *loving*, this *thief*."

"No!" Timmy jerked himself out of Jasper's arms and whirled to face his accuser. "I may be a thief, but I didn't steal your money! I didn't even know it was there! How can I steal what I don't know exists? And do you really think I would have burnt up your car if I knew there was a hundred thousand bucks stuffed in the trunk well? Huh? Do you?"

Garcia actually laughed at Timmy's attempt at logic. "Señor, it makes very little difference to me whether you stole the money or set it ablaze. Either way, I'm out the money, no? Now it is you who are barking up the wrong tree. Ask forgiveness from your boyfriend if you wish, but do not ask it of me. He is perhaps more in need of it anyway."

"Let me kill them both," Bateman said quietly.

And all three of the men in front of Bateman screamed, "Shut up!"

Bateman fell silent but the smile did not leave his lips. Nor did the gun leave his hand. Jasper couldn't help but notice it was pointed directly at his heart.

Garcia's voice was cold and dangerous now. He was tired of playing games. "One more time, little one. Either you and your friend start walking or you will die right here. It is your choice."

Jasper saw they were beaten. He touched Timmy's arm and again they began walking down the path of beaten weeds toward that endless swath of blue sky up ahead.

In a spot where the weeds were thin, Jasper saw a tire tread in the drying mud. His eyes opened wide at the configuration of the tread. Holy crap! He glanced at Timmy but said nothing. More confused now than ever before, Jasper chewed the inside of his cheek and tried to figure things out. That tread was from his Jeep! He knew it like the back of his hand. What the fuck was it doing way the hell out here? Then Jasper thought of the two hours Timmy had been gone with the Jeep when he went to fetch his tools and clothes. Had Timmy used that time to set up this whole masquerade? And what would be the point of it if he did?

Had Timmy stolen Garcia's money or not? And if he had, was he truly willing to risk both their lives to keep it?

With a horrible pain in his gut brought about by the fear Garcia was right after all, about *everything*, Jasper quietly slid his hand away from Timmy's. At the same moment, Timmy stumbled. In that split second of time while he lost and regained his balance, Timmy didn't seem to notice he and Jasper were no longer touching. Or perhaps he simply didn't care.

His face solemn, Jasper turned to look ahead. He suddenly felt he was facing his fate alone. That, too, broke Jasper's heart. Love had been there only a moment ago. At least he thought it had. Maybe in reality it had never been there at all.

Never. Not with this man. Not with Timmy. And certainly not *from* Timmy. He swallowed hard. How could he so quickly be on the brink of losing everything? Timmy, his life, the love he thought he had found. Shit. He could be rotting in the underbrush in five minutes. Both of them could. It would be a little hard for love to survive that.

Jasper's face darkened. He had to do something. He couldn't just amble along to his death. *He had to do something.*

Up ahead, Bateman paused long enough to point into the bushes.

"Gas can," the man said, then continued on, walking toward the edge of land where the fabulous blue sky began.

"My bad," Timmy grinned, still sweating bullets but forcing a self-satisfied grin to his face. "Told you I set fire to your Caddy."

Jasper couldn't believe Timmy's cavalier attitude. What the fuck did he think he was doing?

"Tell me how you did it," Garcia said. "Tell me exactly. And keep walking while you speak."

Jasper watched the fat man's every move, still looking for an opportunity to save himself. But while he was watching and drawing ever closer to the edge of the cliff ahead, he also spotted Garcia casting wary glances in the direction of his evil fucking henchman. Unless Jasper was sorely mistaken, there didn't seem to be a lot of trust in the way he was looking at the man. And not much trust in the way Bateman was staring back at Garcia, either. In fact, Bateman seemed to be as nervous about the gun in Garcia's hand as Jasper did. The only one who didn't look nervous at the moment was Timmy. And Jasper didn't understand that either.

Timmy understood the emotions behind every face surrounding him. Being a thief, he had learned to read people fairly well. In Timmy's mind, Garcia was torn between believing Timmy and not believing Timmy. He was obviously leery of Bateman, especially after what Timmy had told him, but he had yet to make up his mind about what he was going to do. His main objective at the moment was to ascertain whether the Cadillac Escalade had truly been destroyed, and if the money was inside when it was. Garcia was a businessman. He was simply conducting business.

As for Bateman, Timmy could see the fury inside him building to a point where he quite possibly wouldn't be able to control it much longer. He hated Timmy and Jasper, and he feared Garcia. He didn't like the fact that Garcia was now holding a gun. Perhaps he had never seen the fat man stoop to arming himself before. Timmy imagined Bateman wondering what the little faggot had said to Garcia to make the man no longer trust the men who worked for him. Bateman could clearly see Garcia's mistrust of him now, and it worried him. It also pissed him off. That much was made evident by the stubborn tilt to his chin, the darting looks he cast in everyone's direction, especially Garcia's. And the pure unadulterated hatred he displayed every time he glanced at Timmy's face. That, more than anything, made Timmy think maybe he was doing something right.

Lastly, Timmy knew exactly what was going on inside Jasper's head. And that truth was the worst of all. For he saw Jasper pulling away from him now. He saw the hurt in Jasper's eyes, the conviction building that maybe everything he thought he had was now a bullet hole away from being lost. It was Jasper's doubts about Timmy that tore at Timmy the most. But in all honesty, how could Timmy blame him? All Timmy could hope for was a chance to try to explain himself when this was all over.

Because the one truth Timmy had told in all this was the most important truth of all.

He did love Jasper. And in that love, there was not the faintest glimmer of a lie.

Timmy steeled himself for what he was about to do. It was time to end this and try to reclaim Jasper. He hoped to God he had all the players pegged properly. Of course, there was really only one way to find out.

Bateman, still walking ahead, was the first to stop when the land ran out. He stood there at the edge of the cliff, staring down at the crashing surf far below. A covey of sea terns, perhaps nesting on the underside of the cliff's lip, burst out into the open air with a furious cry and scattered to the four winds.

They all four jumped at the surprise of it.

Without giving himself too much time to think about it, Timmy stared at the back of Bateman's head and asked point blank, "What did you do with the money?"

Bateman whirled, only inches from the cliff. His eyes, hot with hatred and surprise, centered on Timmy's face.

IN THE stunned silence that followed Timmy's question, it was the determined lack of interruption by Manuel Garcia, aka El Poco, that gave Timmy the most hope.

And it was the look of pure shock on the face of Bateman, aka Surly Pizza Face, that gave Timmy the most enjoyment.

Bateman's brow furrowed, and his mouth narrowed to a thin pale line slashing across his face. His pockmarks were suddenly infused with a deep rosy hue, like maybe he was about to have a stroke. The gun in his hand swung from Jasper to Timmy, and the man was so tense no one present could believe he hadn't started pulling the trigger yet.

Timmy wished to Christ the man would topple over backward off the cliff and disappear into the ether, but of course that wasn't about to happen. Timmy wasn't that lucky.

"What did you say?" Bateman snarled. The significance of Garcia's silence wasn't lost on Bateman, either, and that infuriated him even more.

Timmy dredged up every ounce of chutzpah he possessed, which was considerable, to stare right back at the man. "I asked what you did with the money. I saw you take it from the back of the SUV in the parking garage. I was across the street, looking through my hotel window. You took a suitcase, wiped your prints off the back of the Caddy, and split. You and I both know it's true. Might as well fess up. And while you're fessing up, you should probably tell your boss where you stashed his money. Then Jasper and I can go home."

Timmy struck a patient pose, at least on the surface. He cocked his head to the side for all the world like a schoolmarm waiting for an answer from a slowass pupil, but on the *inside*, his heart was hammering away like a blacksmith forging a fucking horseshoe. He was actually more afraid to look at Jasper than he was either of the other two. What he had said about he and Jasper going home made him realize maybe Jasper didn't even want him there anymore.

That fear overrode even the fear of Bateman's gun. Almost.

Jasper's eyes skittered from one to the other of the people surrounding him. Timmy, Garcia, Bateman. His eyes finally settled on Bateman's hand. The one holding the pistol. It was shaking, Jasper noticed. Shaking with fury. Jasper hoped the safety was on because Bateman seemed to be applying a whole lot of pressure to that fucking trigger.

Jasper watched, so fascinated by everything happening he had almost lost his fear for himself.

It was then Bateman finally found his voice. He didn't aim his words at Timmy. He aimed them directly at Garcia.

"You believe this lying little fuck, don't you? You think I stole your money."

Garcia let a tiny smile puff up his fat cheeks. He actually looked like a man having a good time. "I do not have to explain my feelings to you, señor. Just tell me what you see when you look over the edge of that cliff. Is there the remains of a very expensive Cadillac Escalade scattered across the rocks below, or did it sink into the ocean never to be seen again? After you tell me that, then I would be interested to hear you prove you did not steal my money. But only if you'd like, of course. It's entirely up to you."

For the briefest of moments, Jasper was sure Bateman was about to swing the gun in his hand in Garcia's direction completely. But at the last second, he seemed to understand that would not be the wisest thing for him to do. Mainly because Garcia also had a gun in his hand. And while Bateman enjoyed causing pain in others, he wasn't that fond of suffering pain himself. Bullet holes cause considerable pain. It's a simple medical fact. They also cause death. Bateman wasn't fond of that prospect either.

He peered down through the empty air beside him. He was so furious, it was not only his gun hand shaking now. He was shaking all over. Still, he forced himself to do as Garcia asked. Even Jasper could see him secretly weighing his options as he did it.

"The cliff undercuts here," Bateman said, his voice tight, his lips barely moving. "There is nothing directly beneath this cliff but water. It looks deep."

Garcia nodded as if he had expected as much. "I see. So if the car was driven over the cliff, it is lost forever. Is that correct?"

"Yes. That is correct. And it *was* driven over the cliff. The car tracks go right up to the edge. As you can see for yourself, the burn marks on the ground also go right to the edge. Your little faggot friend must have doused the car in gas while it was still running, then released the hand brake and let it slowly roll forward as it burned. I guess he really wanted to get rid of those fingerprints he was talking about." Bateman shifted the gun in his hand, edging it a little more in Garcia's direction. "See for yourself if you don't believe me."

Garcia accepted the invitation. If he noticed the movement of Bateman's gun, he didn't show it. He stepped to the edge of the cliff, holding his own gun down now, aimed at the ground. Remaining two feet back from the edge, he carefully leaned his bulk forward enough to peer downward. He could hear the surf so much louder here. It was deep water indeed down below. Deep, *rough* water. There was no beach to speak of.

The water came all the way up to the cliff. The incoming surf pounded the rocks with such fury, any sort of retrieval attempt would be doomed to disaster before it started. Even scuba divers could not survive in that surf. They'd be dashed against the rocks before they got underwater.

Garcia looked down at his feet and saw the car tracks disappear over the edge of the cliff.

He looked up at Bateman and gave the man a chilling smile. "My little faggot friend, as you so quaintly put it, seems to have done the job up good and proper, wouldn't you say?"

Bateman said nothing. A bead of sweat ran down the side of his face into his collar, but he ignored that too. He merely stood there, face-to-face with Garcia, waiting for what was coming next. His gun was now pointed directly at Garcia's gut.

Jasper was silently praying the gun had enough punch to actually penetrate all the fat and kill the fucker, if it came down to gunshots. And then Jasper thought, *wait*. That would leave him and Timmy alone with Bateman. And Jasper had no illusions as to how *that* scenario would play out. Bateman would kill them both in a heartbeat. And enjoy the fuck out of doing it.

Garcia gazed placidly down at the gun pointed at him. It was only now Jasper saw the courage in the man that must have propelled him into the dangerous business of drug running and kept him at the head of that game for as long as it had. He might be a fatass fruitcup, but he had guts when it came right down to it. Jasper supposed he should have known it all along.

"So robbing me is not enough, then? Now you also threaten me with your little gun."

There was no longer any reason for Bateman to think the circumstances were anything other than what he already knew them to be. He brought his gun arm forward and poked the tip of his pistol directly into Garcia's belly button.

"I didn't steal your money," he said.

Garcia gave him a wink. "No? Then why threaten me?"

"Throw your gun off the cliff," Bateman ordered. "Throw it in the water." He risked one brief glance at Jasper and Timmy. "You two stay back. I deal with you as soon as I take care of fat fuck here."

Jasper didn't like the sound of that. Neither did Timmy.

And neither did Garcia. "So now I'm 'fat fuck,' am I? Frankly, señor, I preferred 'sir.'"

"Throw the gun," Bateman said again.

"As you wish." Garcia smiled, and with one swift motion, he swept the gun in front of Bateman's face and flung it over the cliff.

In the split second Bateman flinched as the gun swept past his eyes, Garcia took the ivory handled knife, which he had been holding in his other hand, and which no one had seen, and swept it, too, across Bateman's face in the opposite direction. The keen blade sliced through both of Bateman's eyes, splitting the nose as it passed. Optic fluid spilled out. Then came the blood. It gushed over Bateman's cheeks and onto his shirt.

Bateman screamed. The gun in his hand went off, and Garcia looked down at himself with an expression of immense surprise as a red flower of blood blossomed across his stomach, staining the guayabera red, seeping down onto his perfectly creased trousers, and dribbling onto his shoes. Garcia clutched his gut, and immediately a fresh gout of blood spilled over his fat hand. Still screaming, Bateman raised his gun one more time and fired blindly into the darkness before his ruined eyes. This bullet caught Garcia squarely in the throat. His eyes, small and piglike before, now bulged out of his head as a gurgling scream erupted from his lips.

Garcia began to topple, and as he leaned toward the emptiness beyond the cliff, he reached out and snagged Bateman's shirt collar, dragging them both over the edge, where they instantly disappeared.

Moments later, the sound of terns filled the air. Terns and surf.

Jasper and Timmy stood alone among the weeds.

Then, slowly, they stepped toward the cliff and looked down. There they saw… nothing. Only water, and rocks, and a crashing surf pounding the shore.

Bateman and Garcia were gone. Swallowed by the sea.

Chapter SIXTEEN

"HOLY shit!" Timmy cried, when he finally found his voice. "I didn't see *that* coming!"

Jasper could not bear to look at Timmy's face. He could not bear the ache in his heart to become any stronger. And he could not bear to think of what he had just seen.

Turning away from the water, the *empty* water, simply because he had to, he stared up at the molten blue sky instead. "They're dead," he said, stunned to hear his own voice. Sounding normal. Sounding alive.

And Timmy nodded. "Yeah. It's over."

At that, Jasper did look at Timmy's face. The shock he saw there probably mirrored what was plain to see in his own eyes. There was relief on Timmy's face, too, but Jasper had yet to reach far enough inside himself to feel relief. He felt only a bone-numbing weariness. And disgust. Disgust at the bloodshed. Disgust at what he'd seen. Disgust at what he'd lost.

Timmy. He'd lost Timmy.

"So," Jasper finally said, stirring himself before settling in to decide exactly what the hell should be done here. "I still don't know if you stole the money or not."

Timmy smiled a sad little smile. "No, I don't suppose you do."

Standing on tiptoe, Timmy looked around 360 degrees to see what he could see, which turned out to be mostly weeds and pepper trees and ocean and nothing else. They could not be seen from the road, he decided, and there was no one to see them from the sea. That was good. Much to

Jasper's surprise, Timmy peeled off his T-shirt as he walked back down the path toward the town car.

"What are you doing?" Jasper asked, his voice flat. Wary.

"Prints," Timmy said, opening the car's back door and proceeding to wipe down every surface: windows, door handles, arm rests, leather back of the seat in front, everything.

"We have to call the police," Jasper said. "Or an ambulance. We don't really *know* they're dead."

Timmy looked at him like he had sprouted a second head. "You nuts? One was shot twice and one was stabbed through the eyeballs and they both fell off a hundred-foot cliff into a pounding surf. You really think they're still alive?"

He went back to wiping down the interior of the car and the outer door handles. When he was satisfied, he shook the dust off the shirt and slipped it back over his head. "Get in," he said. "Let's go home."

Jasper took a firm stance in the mud. "I'm not taking this car back to my place. Besides, *we have to call the police.* Two people just died out here. The police need to know."

Timmy laughed. "You must be delirious from the heat. What the police need to know they'll find out in their own good time. But you are right about one thing. We're *not* taking this car back to the mountain. We'll abandon it somewhere and then hop a cab to go the rest of the way home. We need to talk a few things over, you and I."

"About what just happened?" Jasper asked.

"No," Timmy said. "About us."

Reluctantly, Jasper climbed in the front seat while Timmy took the seat behind the wheel.

"Don't touch anything," Timmy ordered. "Keep your hands in your lap. We'll wipe it all down again before we dump the car."

"Yes, boss," Jasper said, feeling sad somehow. Sad that Timmy could be so cold in the face of such horrors. So focused on taking care of himself, even with two dead bodies sinking into the surf a hundred yards down the cliff.

Timmy cranked up the engine and adjusted the rearview mirror, all business. If he thought about the bodies they were leaving behind, he certainly didn't show it. "I've always wanted to drive one of these babies," he said.

And Jasper looked away.

BACK at the cabin, Timmy paid the cab with a hundred-dollar bill and told the driver to keep the change. Not such an extravagance when you figure the fare was seventy-three dollars.

They had dumped the town car on a secluded street in the poor part of town after wiping it down one more time, both inside and out. It would probably be stripped down to a pair of hubcaps and a gearshift knob before the police spotted it, which was fine with Timmy.

As much to get away from Timmy as anything else, since Jasper still didn't know how he was feeling about all this, he headed straight for the lean-to out back to release the dogs the minute the cabbie pulled away. As soon as he opened the door, the dogs were all over him. Jasper was on the ground before they were finished, howling with laughter, covered in dog spit. When the dogs figured they had reaped about as much enjoyment as they were going to get out of Jasper, they headed for Timmy.

By the time the dogs were worn out, Timmy and Jasper were both laughing and about as tired as they had ever been in their lives.

Jasper dumped a gallon of mash into Harry and Harriet's food bowl. After watching them eat for a minute, their little curly tails trembling with delight, Jasper left the gate open so they could follow him into the cabin if they wished, which was exactly what they did.

Inside the cabin, Fiji and Guatemala merely pried open sleepy eyes and stared at the two humans until they fell asleep again. It's hard to impress a cat. Near death experience? That's nice. Wake me when it's over with a can of tuna.

Absently watching the two pigs curl up in front of the cold fireplace like a couple of hunting dogs, Jasper's mind was troubled by the uneasy feeling he had just broken a goodly number of laws. He supposed a lot of people witness crimes they are too afraid to inform the cops about, either from dread of being dragged into court as a material witness, or from fear of retribution from one of the criminal's cronies. Still, to witness a double homicide and say nothing about it tore at every shred of honor and goodness Jasper carried within himself. His father might have skirted the law now and then, and according to the late and unlamented El Poco, the fat dead fuck, that's exactly what his father had done, but Jasper was cut from a different cloth than his old man. So much guilt rampaged through Jasper's system at the moment, one would have thought he was the one who wielded the weapons that did all the damage.

Judging by appearances, witnessing a crime did not bother Timmy in the least. He seemed to think he and Jasper would be best served by staying away from police scrutiny altogether, and to be perfectly honest, Jasper wasn't so sure he was wrong. These weren't two upstanding citizens who had killed each other. They were the worst of the worst. The crème de la scum. Maybe they simply got what they deserved, and it was a fair bet the police would be as glad to see them gone as Jasper was.

So against his better judgment, Jasper tried to put them from his mind. He had other things to worry about anyway.

Timmy mostly. And that was a worry indeed.

Jasper watched, amazed, as Timmy sat at the kitchen table after emptying out the refrigerator and began pounding down enough food to feed a rhino. He said he was starving, and he clearly meant it. Jasper sipped at a beer, watching him with awe, wondering how anybody could eat *anything* after what they had just witnessed.

Jasper soaked a washcloth under the faucet, and during those few moments when Timmy's fork was away from his mouth, he wiped the blood from Timmy's face, for all the world like a mother cleaning up her filthy kid. Timmy hissed as if it hurt, also like a kid, but he very sweetly said thank you when Jasper finished. He also gave Jasper a little smile of appreciation, which made Jasper's heart ache a little more.

Again Timmy tore into his food while Jasper watched, spellbound.

The only time Timmy stopped eating long enough to speak was when he spat up a nervous chuckle, and with shuddering wonder, said, "I've never seen a pair of human eyeballs explode before. Don't think I want to see it again either. No sir."

Jasper gave him a silent toast with his beer bottle to indicate total agreement, and once again silence reigned over the table while Timmy continued to pound down food. It took him a full twenty minutes to get his fill, while Jasper sipped at a second beer to calm his still-frazzled nerves.

By his fourth beer, Jasper's hands had stopped shaking, and he knew what he had to say. He was pretty sure he even had the nerve to say it.

As soon as Timmy looked like he might be in a mood to listen, Jasper decided to let him have it. All of it. Jasper was determined to hold nothing back.

But before Jasper could open his mouth to begin, Timmy reached across the table and took his hand. "Are you all right?" he asked. His beautiful dark eyes peered through the curtain of hair hanging over his face. He impatiently pushed his hair aside and asked again. "Jasper? Are you all right? You look a little shell-shocked."

Jasper tilted his beer back and drained the last drops. He tossed the empty bottle toward the wastebasket in the corner, but it missed, clattering across the floor and making the dogs jump in surprise. Jasper jumped a little too. He really was a bundle of nerves.

"You lied to me," he said. "You lied to me from the very beginning."

Timmy sighed. "I didn't lie to you. I just didn't tell you everything."

"Oh please."

"Okay. I lied."

Jasper stroked his thumb over the back of Timmy's hand, even now relishing the heat of the man in front of him. "I guess what I need to know is whether you were lying about everything. Were you just saying what you had to say to continue to stay here and hide out or—"

"No!" Timmy cried. "No! It wasn't like that at all." He clutched tighter at Jasper's hand. "The way I feel about you is all new to me, Jasper. I guess I did everything wrong. And I'm sorry I lied. I am. But I figured if you knew the truth about me then you'd never love me back. And I know I love you, Jasper. That wasn't a lie. My heart aches with happiness every time I look at you. That's love, isn't it? Or maybe I just don't know how to do it right. Maybe I don't… maybe I don't know *how* to love."

Jasper closed his eyes. When he did, he could feel his heart pumping blood through his body, almost hear the sound of the blood swooshing through his arteries. And in there, in the dark silence behind his closed eyes, in his listening mind, Jasper heard himself thank God for what Timmy had just told him.

He opened his eyes and saw fear on Timmy's face. The fear of being turned away. The fear of rejection. Jasper brought Timmy's hand to his lips and held it against his mouth while he spoke, savoring the heat of it, the texture. The taste.

"Nobody has to know *how* to love. It's not something you *learn*. It's something you *feel*. Something you just *do*. If you love someone, your heart will let you know it. There's no way to do it wrong, Timmy."

A tear welled up in Timmy's eye and gathered on his lower lash. Jasper watched, fascinated, as that crystal bead of moisture sparkled there for a moment before skittering down Timmy's cheek. "What does your heart tell you about me, Jasper? Huh? Does it tell you to run away, or does it tell you to hang on?"

Again, Jasper gave Timmy a weary smile. He rested their hands on the table, still clenched. On his lips, Jasper could still taste the sweet, salty flavor of Timmy's skin. Amid the emotional turmoil and the soul-searching, he was surprised to feel a tremor of sexual desire stir his cock. He had to shift around in his seat to make room for it.

"You already know what my heart tells me, Timmy. It tells me to hang on. It tells me—"

"But does it tell you to love me? Does it tell you that?"

And Jasper nodded. Quietly, he answered, "Yes. That's exactly what it tells me."

Hope shone in Timmy's eyes. He straightened his back, scooted the chair a little closer to the table, and took a firmer grip on Jasper's hands.

Timmy's face fell when Jasper added, "It also tells me to be careful. The big problem here isn't the mess you got us into, but the fact you also lied to me." The hurt Jasper saw materialize on Timmy's face made him want to weep, but he had to go on. He had to tell Timmy exactly how he felt. Otherwise, they would be lying to each other all over again. "How can I trust you not to do that again? Especially when you did it once with our very lives on the line. You must be a great poker player, Timmy. But sometimes you can't bluff your way out of reality. Sometimes it's just liable to get you killed. Today it almost got us *both* killed."

Jasper cast a look through the kitchen window. Evening would be upon them soon. Soon it would be another night. With him and Timmy alone in the cabin. But what kind of night would it be? Would it be the beginning or the end? The first night of their lives together, or the last? He supposed it was all up to him. He knew where Timmy stood. But what about himself? Where did he stand?

"I still don't know if you stole Garcia's fucking money. But if you did, it seems you were just a little too willing to expose us to a great deal of danger to keep it."

"I'm sorry," Timmy said.

"I know you are. But you were also just a little too willing to let me offer up my life savings to get us out of the mess you got us into in the first place. There were a lot of things you were willing to take from me today, Timmy. But there was very little you offered me back."

Timmy stood, pushing his chair out of the way. It screeched across the linoleum, causing the dogs to lift their heads to see what was going on.

"Come with me," Timmy said, reaching out yet again for Jasper's hand.

Jasper closed his eyes. "Timmy, I—"

"Please, Jasper. Come with me."

So Jasper hauled himself to his feet, and hand in hand, Timmy led them through the back door and across the compound. To Jasper's surprise, Timmy stooped and ducked through the doorway of the crooked hog house, pulling Jasper in behind him. When Timmy finally turned, he grinned at the confusion on Jasper's face.

Timmy pointed to the straw. "Have a seat."

Jasper was too weary to argue at this point. He simply dropped, Indian fashion, into the straw, his two strong legs folded in front of him.

Facing away, and still stooping because the ceiling was low, Timmy began running his hand inside the top of the wall where it met the eave of the roof. There, from the rafters, he began pulling out small plastic bags, one after the other. Sandwich bags, they looked like. Jasper watched, fascinated.

And when Timmy tossed a couple of the Baggies in his lap, Jasper was even more fascinated. Each one held a stack of bills. Hundred dollar bills. They were stuffed in the bags and neatly held together with rubber bands.

Timmy continued to toss Baggie after Baggie into Jasper's lap, and when he finally stopped, there were an even dozen of them. Each and every one containing a neat stack of hundred-dollar bills.

"The money," was all Jasper could think to say.

Timmy grinned. "The *clean, untraceable* money. I hid it here that night I borrowed your Jeep. I had hidden it in a rented garage the day I stole it, but I knew that garage wouldn't be safe much longer, so I brought it here. Harry and Harriet have been guarding it for us."

Jasper's mind seemed to have stopped working. "But—"

"If I had told Garcia I had his money, he would have tortured me until I told him where it was, and then he would have killed us anyway. Both of us. I admit I dragged you into danger, and I'm sorry, but I didn't think they'd find me here. I thought we were safe. After they did find us, I knew the only way to get free of them was to bide my time and see if an opportunity arose to make it happen. It's funny, Jasper, but if you give things time to work out, they almost always do. I found a way to drive a wedge between Garcia and old Pizza Face. I made them stop trusting each other. Although I have to admit, the way they resolved the issue was a complete shock. But it certainly solved *our* problem."

"Did it?" Jasper didn't sound convinced. He set the packets of money in the straw beside him, unsure if he wanted to touch them or not. Two people had died over this money. Two *assholes*, but still. This was also drug money. Jasper wasn't sure he wanted anything to do with *that* either.

"How much?"

Timmy laughed. "There's one hundred hundred-dollar bills in each bag."

"That's—"

"Ten thousand dollars. Twelve bags, a hundred and twenty grand. More than even El Poco thought there was. I counted it when I was lying out there in the bushes sick as a dog. That's before I broke into your cabin and dragged you down to hell with me. By the way, it's two hundred dollars short. I gave one to the cabbie and one to the old lady I rented the garage from. Business expenses."

Jasper had to smile at that. "Business expenses," he echoed. "Well, at least I know now. You really did steal the money."

"Yep. And let me remind you once again. It was the *clean, untraceable* money I stole."

Jasper felt disappointment well up in his heart again. "So you intend to keep it."

Timmy dropped into the straw in front of Jasper and reached out his hands to rest them on Jasper's knees. "No, baby. I intend for *both* of us to keep it. What good would it do to give the money back? I would have used it, you know, to bargain for your freedom if the shit had really hit the fan with El Poco, but happily, he got his own shit stuck in the fan first. Him and Pizza Face are the last two people who can trace this money back to us, and their tracing days are pretty much over, don't you think? They're fish food. And El Poco alone makes for a *lot* of fish food."

Jasper reached up to brush the hair out of Timmy's eyes. He knew the moment he did it how things were going to turn out. And he smiled a little at the knowing. "There's Blondie. You seem to have forgotten about him. You don't think he'll come looking for revenge?"

"You shitting me? He'll probably be thrilled to death to have those two nitwits dead. He might even try taking over the cartel. There's no honor among thieves, and no one knows that better than me, since I am one." Timmy saw the smile falter on Jasper's face so he did some fast backpedaling. "Sorry, Jasper. Bad joke. Still, I don't think we need to worry about Blondie. And after all, he doesn't really know about the money, does he? He certainly doesn't know I took it. Okay? Feel better?"

Jasper stared at Timmy's hands as they rested on his knees. He was afraid to touch them now. He still had things he needed cleared up.

"Where's the Cadillac?" he asked. "I know it isn't resting at the bottom of the ocean under that cliff. You might have driven my Jeep down to the edge of that cliff, but you didn't drive the Caddy over it."

Timmy laughed at that. "No, I certainly didn't. It's parked about five hundred yards down your lane. I drove it into the bushes and it's still sitting there, safe and sound."

"And you didn't think they could trace it here?"

"They *did* trace it here. That's how they found me. I didn't get the LoJack device removed and destroyed until I dumped the Caddy in the bushes by your lane. I should have kept running, gotten farther away from where I parked it, but by then I was too sick to go on. They didn't know exactly where the Caddy was, but they knew the general location where the last signal went out. And that led them here to us."

Timmy sorted things out in his head. Then he said, "It was when I took your Jeep into town that I bought gasoline and made the burn marks on the ground to make it look like the Caddy had burned, and that was also when I used the Jeep's wheels to make the car tracks leading up to the cliff, as you so cleverly figured out, so El Poco would believe I'd truly rolled his burning Cadillac out of this world forever. It's off the grid completely as it is. No one knows where it is but us. One of these days I'll wipe it down like we did the town car and dump it on a side street somewhere. If the cops trace it at all, they'll trace it back to the person it was originally stolen from, not to us."

"You've got it all figured out," was all Jasper could think to say.

Timmy simply nodded.

They sat in the silent hog house, feeling the straw crunch beneath their butts and watching the shadows deepen around them as another day dragged to an end. A day neither of them would ever forget. Now and then their eyes fell to the twelve bundles of cash lying in the straw between them.

Once again, Timmy asked the question foremost in his mind. "So what's it going to be, Jasper? You know everything now. Can you forgive me? Do you think you can still… love me?"

Jasper merely shook his head. The kid was so fucking innocent. He thought love could cure all manner of doubts. But could it really?

Jasper's voice was as soft and warm as flannel. He laid his hands over Timmy's and said, "I never *stopped* loving you. I lost faith for a while, but love was never the problem."

Like a child, Timmy asked the most important question of all. "Can I stay with you then? Can we be lovers? Real lovers?"

Jasper leaned forward and pressed his lips to Timmy's. They kissed for a long time, eyes closed, hearts thumping. And while they kissed, Jasper tried to ignore the explosion of desire thundering through him long enough to think things through. He only ended the kiss when he knew exactly what he wanted to say.

Cupping Timmy's face in his hands, he smiled. "My heart will be the last thing you ever steal. Got it?"

Timmy nodded. Again the tears welled up and slid down Timmy's cheeks. His pink tongue poked through the dawning smile on his lips, and he licked the tears away as they fell.

"Got it," Timmy said. "So you do still want me then."

Timmy's tears were still falling, so Jasper thumbed them away. "Yes, dipshit. I still want you. More than anything. But you have to get a job. A real job."

Timmy shrugged. "No problem. I'll be a mechanic. Been thinking about it anyway."

Jasper laughed. "You'll probably make more money than I do."

Timmy chucked him gently under the chin. "That's the idea. Don't want my lover to be ashamed of me."

"Never," Jasper said. "Never."

They gazed at each other, hearts pounding, one just as misty-eyed as the other.

Finally Timmy asked the one final question left to be answered. "And what about the money? Can we keep it?"

Jasper groaned his way to his feet and pulled Timmy up beside him. He wrapped his strong arms around Timmy's small waist and scooped him in like a kid with a teddy bear. Burying his face in Timmy's hair and breathing in his scent, Jasper said, "We'll talk about it."

Timmy's smile fell away as he kissed the hollow place at the base of Jasper's throat and felt a rush of hunger bloom for the man who held him. And a rush of fear.

"That isn't an answer," Timmy said. "You're disappointed. You're disappointed in me."

"Timmy, we can't keep the money. You do know that, don't you?"

Timmy burrowed his face into Jasper's broad, welcoming chest. Being lost in Jasper's arms was a comfort Timmy knew he would never grow tired of. The pounding of Jasper's heart was like a song beating its gentle rhythms just for him. Timmy couldn't allow that music to stop. Ever.

"If we call the police, they may arrest me for stealing the Caddy." He sounded calm when he said it. He also sounded resigned. As if he'd already made up his mind.

Jasper looked down into Timmy's face and hooked his thumb under Timmy's chin to make him look back. "They might," he said. "Then again they might not. We did help do away with the notorious El Poco. Surely that will count for something."

Timmy smiled. "Always the optimist." The fear of jail was a lump in Timmy's throat. But the fear of losing Jasper was a cold hard fist squeezing his heart like a vise.

Jasper stroked Timmy's back, comforting himself as much as Timmy. Wishing he didn't have to do it, but knowing there was no other way. "If we have to, we'll get you the best lawyer we can, Timmy. A simple car theft isn't going to put you in the big house. If you're gone, it won't be for long. Plus, when you return the money, they'll see you for who you really are. And they'll see you're trying to do what's right. They'll take that into consideration, Timmy, I know they will. And even the police will see that neither one of us had anything to do with those two morons killing each other. They did that all on their own."

Timmy reached up to bury his fingers in Jasper's thick, curly hair, as if anchoring himself to the planet through Jasper's strength. Jasper's love. Jasper tilted his head into Timmy's hand, obviously relishing the touch of Timmy's fingers in his hair, needing the contact as much as Timmy did. He kissed Timmy's forearm, inhaling the scent of the man, feeling the heat of his arm.

"If—if I do have to go to jail, will you wait for me?" Timmy asked, shivering with desire even now at the feel of Jasper's lips on his skin.

And it was then Jasper laid his lips over Timmy's mouth once again. This kiss was gentle and long and sweet. As it ended, Jasper pulled Timmy tighter into his arms and held Timmy's head close to his heart. When he spoke, Jasper's words were but a whisper, for they came from so deep within, they could barely get out.

"Yes," Jasper said, his breath rustling Timmy's hair. "I don't believe it will come to that, but if it does, I'll wait for you. I promise. And when you come home, you'll be home for good. We'll be together. Please tell me that's what you want, Timmy. Please. Say the words. Tell me you love me."

"You know I love you. I think you love me too. I don't know how you can, but you do. And you're right, Jasper. We can't start out with something like this hanging over our heads. I've got to fix it. And I will. I swear. I'll do it for us. I'll never let you be ashamed of me again."

Jasper closed his eyes, savoring Timmy's words. Still holding Timmy close with Timmy's head upon his chest, Jasper finally opened his eyes. He laid his hand to Timmy's cheek and looked out at the trees of Endor, darkening in the fall of evening around them. The clean scent of pine filled the growing shadows. Already, the doves were cooing a night song in the branches, unseen, only their voices giving away their presence.

"I love you so much," Jasper sighed, a tear slipping down to fall in Timmy's hair. Even while his heart broke a little bit inside, he felt contentment too. Contentment in knowing Timmy would make things right. And once he did, there would be nothing to stand in the way of their happiness. Nothing.

Timmy looked up and grinned as he wiped a tear from Jasper's cheek with his thumb, just as Jasper had done for him. He couldn't explain it, but he felt lighter inside. He felt freer. "Let's go inside, Jasper. I need to make a phone call."

Jasper nodded, and hand in hand, they headed for the cabin.

Only the dogs and the cats and the doves heard the click of the latch as the cabin door closed softly behind them.

JOHN INMAN has been writing fiction since he was old enough to hold a pencil. He and his partner live in beautiful San Diego, California. Together, they share a passion for theater, books, hiking and biking along the trails and canyons of San Diego, or, if the mood strikes, simply kicking back with a beer and a movie. John's advice for anyone who wishes to be a writer? "Set time aside to write every day and do it. Don't be afraid to share what you've written. Feedback is important. When a rejection slip comes in, just tear it up and try again. Keep mailing stuff out. Keep writing and rewriting and then rewrite one more time. Every minute of the struggle is worth it in the end, so don't give up. Ever. Remember that publishers are a lot like lovers. Sometimes you have to look a long time to find the one that's right for you."
You can contact John at john492@att.net
on Facebook: http://www.facebook.com/john.inman.79
or on his website: http://www.johninmanauthor.com/.

Also from JOHN INMAN

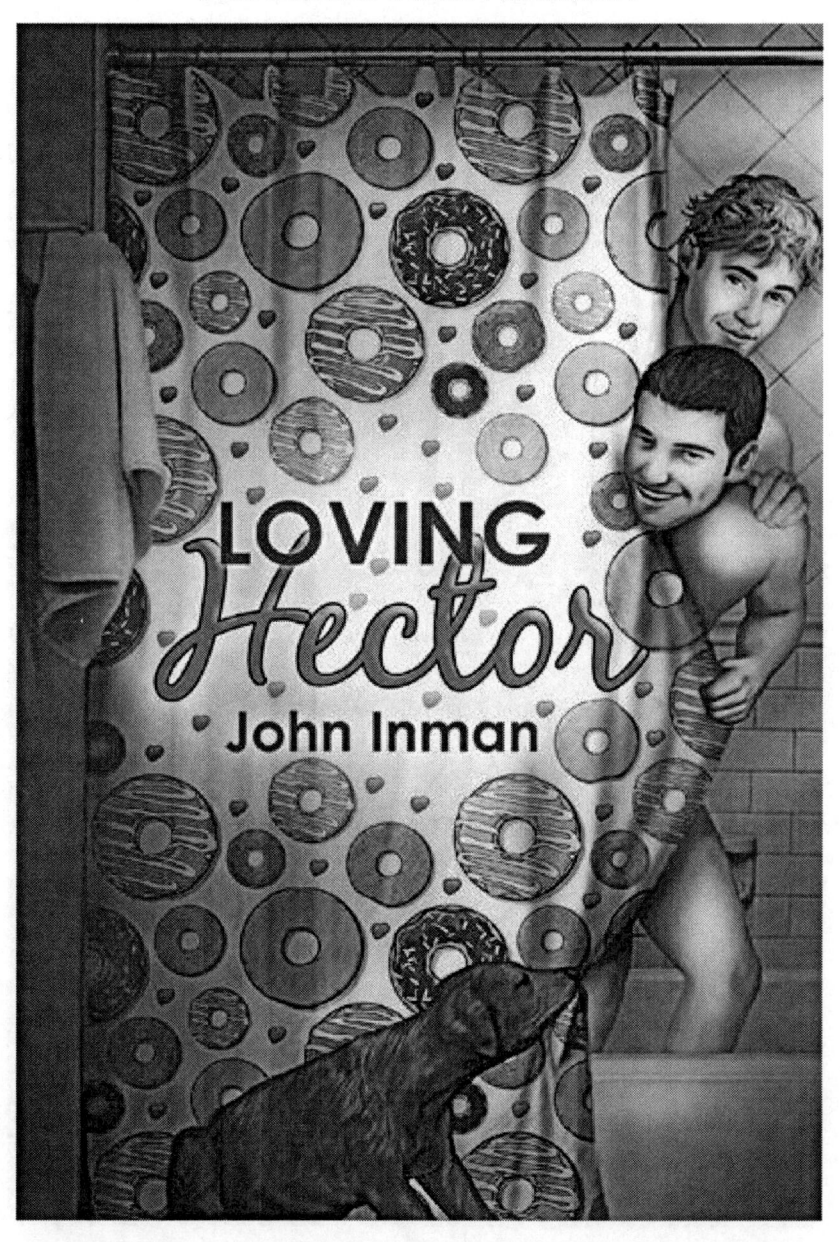

http://www.dreamspinnerpress.com

Also from JOHN INMAN

SHY

John Inman

http://www.dreamspinnerpress.com

Also from JOHN INMAN

http://www.dreamspinnerpress.com

Also from DREAMSPINNER PRESS

A LUCAS & ALEX ADVENTURE
In Which Lucas Would Rather Not (Have an Adventure)

THE QUEEN'S LIBRARIAN
Carole Cummings

http://www.dreamspinnerpress.com

Also from DREAMSPINNER PRESS

YOU'RE the ONE

Gene Taylor

http://www.dreamspinnerpress.com

Dreamspinner Press
For more of the
best M/M romance,
visit
Dreamspinner Press
www.dreamspinnerpress.com